**AS THEY TURNED THE CORNER,
TWO MEN SUDDENLY APPEARED.**

Both had the lower portion of their faces covered by a bandanna. From their build and the way they moved, Matt took them both to be young.

"Give us the bag," one of them said, his voice muffled by the bandanna covering it.

"What?" Kate said, stunned.

They each took a gun from their belts, pointed them at Kate.

"Give us the money!"

"N-n-now!" the other man said, and reached for the bag.

"Hey, wait!" Matt said, moving to get between the two men and Kate.

There were two shots, a bright light, a spark of pain, and then . . . nothing.

RALPH COMPTON

RIDE FOR JUSTICE

A Ralph Compton Western by
ROBERT J. RANDISI

BERKLEY

New York

BERKLEY
An imprint of Penguin Random House LLC
penguinrandomhouse.com

Copyright © 2020 by The Estate of Ralph Compton
Penguin Random House supports copyright. Copyright fuels creativity, encourages
diverse voices, promotes free speech, and creates a vibrant culture. Thank you for buying
an authorized edition of this book and for complying with copyright laws by not
reproducing, scanning, or distributing any part of it in any form without permission.
You are supporting writers and allowing Penguin Random House to continue to
publish books for every reader.

BERKLEY and the BERKLEY & B colophon are registered trademarks of
Penguin Random House LLC.

ISBN: 9780593102268

First Edition: October 2020

Printed in the United States of America
1   3   5   7   9   10   8   6   4   2

Cover art by Dennis Lyall
Book design by George Towne

THE IMMORTAL COWBOY

This is respectfully dedicated to the "American Cowboy." His was the saga sparked by the turmoil that followed the Civil War, and the passing of more than a century has by no means diminished the flame.

———◆———

True, the old days and the old ways are but treasured memories, and the old trails have grown dim with the ravages of time, but the spirit of the cowboy lives on.

———◆———

In my travels—to Texas, Oklahoma, Kansas, Nebraska, Colorado, Wyoming, New Mexico, and Arizona—I always find something that reminds me of the Old West. While I am walking these plains and mountains for the first time, there is this feeling that a part of me is eternal, that I have known these old trails before. I believe it is the undying spirit of the frontier calling me, through the mind's eye, to step back into time. What is the appeal of the Old West of the American frontier?

———◆———

It has been epitomized by some as the dark and bloody period in American history. Its heroes—Crockett, Bowie, Hickok, Earp—have been reviled and criticized. Yet the Old West lives on, larger than life.

———◆———

It has become a symbol of freedom, when there was always another mountain to climb and another river to cross; when a dispute between two men was settled not with expensive lawyers, but with fists, knives, or guns. Barbaric? Maybe. But some things never change. When the cowboy rode into the pages of American history, he left behind a legacy that lives within the hearts of us all.

—Ralph Compton

CHAPTER ONE

After prison, 1889 . . .

THE MAIN GATES of Yuma Territorial Prison opened. A man walked two steps forward, stopped, and took a deep breath. Just a few feet away from the prison, and the air smelled different.

His clothes were loose on him. When he had gone to prison seven and a half years ago to serve a twelve-year stretch, he'd been a bigger, healthier man. Now he was about thirty pounds lighter—even with the governor's pardon in his pocket.

He looked down at his shirtfront and could see the pinholes left from where he used to wear his badge. They had been hard on him when they sentenced him because he had been a lawman. But the new governor had given him his pardon because he was an ex-lawman. So the tin had gotten him in, and the tin had gotten him out.

He started walking. No one was there to greet him

or pick him up, but that was okay. He wanted to walk, because these were his first steps as a free man in seven and a half years, and he wanted to enjoy every one of them.

M ATTHEW WHEELER WAS released from Yuma with enough money for a meal and a hotel room. He'd had a shave and a quick bath before being released.

When he got to the center of town, he paused to take in the activity around him. People were going about the business of living. In prison, they went about the business of just existing, just trying to get by, to survive until they were released or died.

Here people walked around with smiles on their faces, without haunted looks in their eyes. Granted, some of them looked at him and could tell he'd just been released. But several women actually smiled at him, and those smiles lifted his spirits, even though he knew they stemmed from pity.

He stopped in the first restaurant he came to, a small café, and ordered a steak dinner. The waitress, a middle-aged, faded-looking woman, brought him a mug of beer while he waited for his meal.

"On the house, honey," she said, "'cause you just got out."

"Thank you."

His first sip of beer in seven and a half years went down as smooth as silk. His first bite of steak was a revelation. After that, he wolfed down both the meal and the brew, and the waitress brought him a second mug.

"No more after that, though, honey," she said. "You're gonna have to get used to drinkin' again."

"Thanks."

"You're also gonna need a job," she said. "We could use somebody here to wash dishes."

"Wash dishes?" he repeated.

"Look," she said, putting her hands on her hips. Other diners were watching the exchange. "We've had lots of ex-cons work here when they first got out. They saved their money and then moved on. You can do the same. And there's a rooming house near here that's cheap. Interested?"

"To tell you the truth," Matt said, "I ain't thought past this meal."

"Well, think it over while you finish," she suggested. "You can let me know when you're done." She started to turn away, then turned back and said, "Oh, yeah, if you take the job, this meal's on the house."

While Matt finished his meal, he wondered how many other places in Yuma offered the same extras—a job and a place to stay. And what did they get from it? Satisfaction, cheap labor, or both?

He really hadn't thought beyond his first meal now that he was out. What he was going to need was a place to do that, and a cheap rooming house might fit that bill. But taking a job washing dishes was quite a comedown from having been a lawman. He probably shouldn't have been thinking of it that way. Instead, the comparison should have been washing dishes here instead of breaking rocks in prison.

Dishes won.

THE WAITRESS TURNED out to be the owner. Her name was Kate Hardin. Once the lunch rush was over, she sat down across the table from Matt and introduced herself.

"What's your name?" she asked.

"Matt Wheeler."

"What did you do for a living before you went to prison, Matt?"

"I was a lawman."

"Oh? Sheriff? Marshal?"

"Yes."

"And what did a lawman do to get himself tossed into Yuma Prison?"

"I killed a man."

"Why?"

"Because he killed my wife," he said.

"So you're not a murderer."

"No, I'm not," he said. "But occasionally, in the course of my duties, I killed men."

"And you did kill the man who killed your wife?"

"Yes," he said, then added, "He was one of them."

"One of what?"

"One of the men who killed my wife," he explained.

"So there are others out there?"

"Oh, yeah."

"And are you gonna kill them?"

"I think my days of trackin' killers and killin' them are gone. Don't you?" he asked. He held out his right hand to show her the shakes.

"I suppose so. You can start in the mornin'," the woman said. "Go around the corner and tell Esther at the rooming house that Kate sent you."

"Thanks."

She stood up and asked, "You are gonna be able to wash dishes without dropping and breakin' any, aren't you?"

"Yeah," he said, "I will."

"If you want," she said, "come back later for supper."

"I could start tonight," he offered.

"That's okay," she said. "Tomorrow's good enough. Get yourself settled and do whatever thinkin' you need to do tonight. Come in here in the mornin' knowin' what you want to do."

As Matt stood up to leave, Kate started for the kitchen, then stopped and turned. "Oh, one more thing."

"Yes?" he asked.

"You didn't escape, did you?"

"No," he said, "the governor gave me a full pardon."

Kate nodded, said, "Good enough," and continued on to the kitchen.

MATT WALKED AROUND the corner to the boarding-house and found that Esther was an older, pleasant woman with a gentle smile, stooped shoulders, but strong-looking hands.

"Of course," she said at the door, "if Kate sent you, I have a room. Come this way."

He followed her through a hall and up a flight of stairs. She led him past several closed doors to an open one, and then she stepped aside.

"This will be your room," she said. "Breakfast is at eight. Supper's at five. You can eat with us or not. It's your choice."

"Thank you. Um, I can't really give you a lot of money now—"

"Give me a dollar."

He did.

"In the future you can pay me when Kate pays you. Is that fair?"

"Very fair," he said.

"I hope you enjoy staying with us, Mr. Wheeler."

"You can just call me Matt."

"I call all my tenants by their surnames," she said. "But you can call me Esther."

"All right, Esther."

She went down the hall, and he went into his room.

He was wearing the clothes he had been wearing when he entered to prison. He had been stripped and supplied with his prison trousers and shirt. His own clothes had been stored for him until such time as he was released. The only other things he had were the few dollars they'd given him.

The room had a chest of drawers, but it was unlikely he would ever fill it with clothes. He was, however, going to have to buy something new to wear when he went to work. But that couldn't happen until after he got paid for the first time.

He closed the door to his room, undressed, and cleaned his clothes off as well as he could with the brush he found on top of the chest. Then, clad only in his drawers, he went and sat on the bed. It was early, and for the first time in seven and a half years, there was no one to tell him what to do next.

He sat there for a very long time. . . .

T HE ONLY REASON he knew when five o'clock came was the dinner bell someone downstairs rang. He got dressed again and left the room. He didn't bother to lock or even close the door, as there was nothing inside just yet.

Rather than eat with the other tenants and suffer the inevitable questions that would be put to the new man, he decided to go back to the restaurant and take Kate up on her offer of supper.

CHAPTER TWO

6 weeks later...

Matt got to the café before the supper rush was set to start.

"Have a seat," Kate said to him. "Your supper's almost ready."

There was one table set up in the kitchen with four chairs for the employees to use when they had their meals, which were free.

Matt went and sat across from a waiter named Woody.

"Stew?" he asked.

Woody nodded. He always had stew for supper. After a few days, Matt became determined to take advantage of the gratis meal and usually ordered a steak.

Woody's stew came first, with a hunk of bread, and the younger man attacked his food with gusto.

Matt's steak came next, and then Kate herself sat

down with them to eat, preferring some baked chicken. She made sure her employees knew that once the supper rush began, there would be no eating on their part.

"Is that a new shirt, Matt?" Woody asked.

"I bought it last week," Matt said. "Wore it a couple of times then."

"Huh," Woody said. "Looks new. Is that what you're spendin' your pay on? New clothes?"

"Well," Matt said, "I sure need them."

"Don't they give ya some clothes when ya leave prison?" Woody asked.

"Woody," Kate scolded, "let the man eat."

"It's okay," Matt said. "No, they only gave me the clothes I came in with."

"All those years ago?" Woody said, shaking his head. "Man, you'd think they'd at least give ya some new duds."

"You'd think," Matt agreed.

"They treat everybody like that?"

"Every inmate," Matt said.

"So that's why yer buyin' new clothes," Woody said.

"Right," Matt said. "I don't have any."

Woody finished his stew and pushed the bowl away. "Hey, when you were inside—," he started, but Kate cut him off.

"That's enough, Woody," she said. "You've finished eating, so get to your tables."

"Yes, ma'am." He got up and hurried out of the kitchen.

"I'm sorry about that," Kate said.

"That's okay," Matt said. "He's a kid, and he's curious."

"That shirt does look good on you, though," she said. "In fact, you look a helluva lot healthier than you did when you walked in here six weeks ago."

"I've put some weight back on," he admitted.

"And tell me," she said, "what do you do when you're not here washing dishes?"

"Whataya mean?" he asked.

"I mean, in your off time," she said. "What do you do to pass the time?"

He didn't want to tell her that he still just sat in his room, staring, because he didn't know what else to do. In the old days, he had worn a badge and had plenty to do. And in prison, they had given him enough to do to pass the day. Now that he was out, he had no tin on his chest to justify. And he couldn't imagine going out and finding something to do that was . . . pleasant. Not without his Angie.

So he pretty much knew every crack in one wall of his room. He had them memorized. That was when he decided to switch sides of the bed and start staring at the other wall.

"I don't do much," he said. "I still don't have much money and what I have I spend on clothes, haircuts, shaves, things like that."

"What about a stake?" she asked.

"What about it?"

"Well, your second week here, you mentioned how when you got a stake, you'd pull out," she said. "Leave Yuma and the prison behind. How's your stake?"

"Nowhere near enough," he admitted.

"You haven't been gamblin', have you?" she asked.

"What? No . . . Why would you ask me that?"

"I don't know," she said. "I thought lots of ex-cons came out and gambled. You know, in the saloons."

"I don't have the money to go to saloons," he said.

She finished her food, grabbed her plate and Woody's, and took them to the sink for Matt to wash when he was ready.

"I wish I could give ya a raise, Matt," she said, "but I just can't do it."

"That's okay, Kate," he said. "Don't worry about it. I'm grateful you gave me a job the day I got out. I would've been . . . lost for a while."

"Well," she said, "Woody's gonna be comin' in with orders, so I gotta get cookin', and you gotta get washin'."

"Right." He ate the last bite of his steak, then carried his own plate to the sink.

B ECAUSE KATE HAD brought up the subject of his poke, when he went home to the rooming house that night, he went to his room to check on it. In the beginning, he hadn't been locking his door because there hadn't been anything in the room to steal. But once he started getting paid and building his fortune— such as it was—the door started getting locked.

He entered, locked the door behind him, sat on the bed, and fished the envelope holding his money from underneath the night table by the bed. He counted the money and saw that he had instinctively told Kate the truth. He did not have near enough money to leave Yuma. He was going to be washing dishes for the foreseeable future.

As he was shoving the envelope back under the table, there was a gentle knock on his door. He walked to it, unlocked it, and opened it.

"I hope I'm not disturbing you, Mr. Wheeler," Esther the landlady said.

"No, you're not," Matt said. "In fact, I just got in."

"I actually heard you," she said, "and I wanted a word before you turned in."

"Do you want to come in, Esther?" he asked.

"Uh, no," she said. "You know I don't go into my tenants' rooms. But if we keep our voices down, we can talk right here."

"Keep our voices down?"

"Yes," she whispered, "I don't want the others to hear what I'm about to say."

"All right."

"I've noticed that you never eat your meals with us in the evenings," she said.

"It has nothing to do with the food you serve, Esther," he said. "I really enjoy your breakfasts. But I *am* at the café almost every night at suppertime, and Kate *does* give her employees a free meal."

"I'm aware of that," she said. "That's why I wanted to propose that I charge you less money for your room."

"Less?"

"Well, since you never take part in the evening meal, why should you be paying the same rate as everyone else? And since you only recently got out of prison, I'm sure you must be trying to—you know—put some away?"

"Esther," he said, "that's real generous of you, but what would happen if Kate suddenly put me on a different schedule and I had to start taking my supper here?"

"In that case, we could go back to the original amount."

He smiled at her. "I think we should just leave things the way they are," he suggested. "But I'm really grateful for the offer."

"Well," she said, "you'll let me know if you suddenly have the need to take me up on it, and I'll just keep the offer open."

"Thank you," he said. "You're a very nice lady."

She almost blushed at the compliment. "I'll say good night, then."

"Good night, Esther."

She padded off quietly down the hall. Matt stepped back inside, closed the door, and locked it.

So far the two people who had been the nicest to him since he got out had been Kate and Esther, and he couldn't find it in himself to try to take advantage of their generosity. So he would keep washing dishes for one and keep paying the regular rate for the other while trying his best to build himself a stake.

Kate had asked if he'd been gambling, and he had answered honestly that he had not. But now he was wondering if that might not be the answer. He had been a pretty good poker player years ago, and playing for matchsticks in prison shouldn't have lessened his skill any.

Maybe it was time to find out.

CHAPTER THREE

O VER THE NEXT few weeks, Matt managed to find himself some penny-ante poker games in three different saloons. He played conservatively, losing at first, but then began to increase his small stake.

Matt stayed with penny ante, as his job at the café in the evenings meant he had to play during the day. Most of the bigger-money games took place at night.

He kept it from Kate that he was playing cards, but on occasion somebody he played with would come into the café. As long as he stayed in the kitchen, he was safe from being found out. However, Kate had increased his responsibilities, sending him out to the dining area to clear tables. By doing that, she was able to increase his salary a small measure.

His stake grew and grew, and before long he figured another month at the café, or a big run at the tables, and he would be able to leave town. At night, in his room, he began to make a list of what he would need for the trip:

A horse
a saddle
saddlebags
a coffeepot
a skillet
a knife, spoon, and fork
a bedroll

He already had two shirts, a pair of jeans, his boots, a bandanna, and a hat. He thought he would also need a new knife. Once he had all those things, he would quit his job and move on.

But for now, he was still collecting dishes from the tables and washing them.

As he was picking up the plates from one table, a man at a nearby table said, "Oh, hey, Matt."

Matt turned and saw Clell Taylor, a man he had been playing poker with at a saloon called the Abilene House. They were nowhere near Abilene, but apparently the owner had come from there. Clell owned a mercantile store in town.

"Oh, hey, Clell," Matt said.

"Didn't see you at the game today—"

"Shhh," Matt said, moving closer to him. "Not so loud. I don't want the people I work with to know that I'm playing."

"Oh, sorry," Clell said, putting a piece of bread in his mouth.

"I've never seen you here before," Matt said.

"Well, you talked about it," Clell said, "so I thought I'd try it. The food's pretty good."

"Yeah, it is," Matt said. "Listen, I've got to get back to the kitchen."

"Sure, sure," Clell said, then lowered his voice. "Are you gonna play tomorrow?"

"I am," Matt said. "See you then."

"See ya," Clell said, and stuffed a chicken leg into his mouth.

As Matt carried the plates to the sink and began putting them in the water, Kate asked, "Friend of yours?"

"Huh?"

"That man at the table," she said. "Friend of yours?"

"I've seen him in the saloons in town," Matt said, "and I think I bought a shirt in his mercantile store."

"Ah," she said, "one of your two shirts."

"How many shirts does a man need?" he asked. "Two's plenty."

"If you say so." She took two steaks off the stove, put them on plates, added vegetables, and then picked both the plates up. "Gotta go."

"Yeah, right," Matt said.

He wasn't sure if Kate actually had anything against poker, but even if she did, she probably wouldn't fire him if she found out he was playing.

But his business was his business, and he wanted to keep it that way.

MATT HIT A bad streak at the poker tables and started to lose. Even in penny-ante poker, losing could be a disaster. It went on for weeks. Little by little, his stake began to decrease. That meant that his time in Yuma as a dishwasher was starting to look as if it was going to last longer.

He had two options: He could stop playing poker, or he could get a job that paid more.

YOU WANT A second job?" Kate asked. She stared at him from across the table in the café's kitchen. He had asked her to sit for a minute so they could talk.

"No," he said, "I need a new job, one that will pay

me more. A second job would just take up too much of my time."

"Well," she said, "I didn't expect you to stay here and wash dishes forever. If you feel you have to leave, I can't stop you. And I can't pay you more."

"I wouldn't ask you to," he said.

"When do you want to leave?" she asked.

"Well, not until I have another job."

"When will you start looking?"

"Uh, tomorrow, I guess."

"Okay, then," Kate said, standing up, "I'll get you your supper, and then you can start workin'."

She made him a steak and set the platter down in front of him, then went back to the stove to fill the orders Eddie, the other waiter, had brought in. Woody had worked earlier in the day. Eddie was a good waiter; he just stammered a bit when he talked.

As the evening went on, Kate bumped into Matt from time to time, each time harder than before. Once she slammed into him so hard, he dropped a plate, and it shattered on the floor.

"That's comin' outta your pay!" she snapped.

At the end of the night, after Eddie left, Matt turned and said, "You're mad at me."

She turned away from her sweeping and stared at him. "I am," she said, "and I shouldn't be. I knew you weren't going to wash dishes forever, but I have to admit, I like havin' you around."

That baffled him. "Because I'm a good dishwasher?" he asked.

"No."

"Then why? We don't even talk all that much during the day. Kate, we're not really even friends."

"And that's why I like havin' you around," she said. "You do what I pay you to do. You don't try to be friends. I'm not an attractive woman, Matt, but you'd be surprised how some fellas who have worked for me still try something after a while. With you, I don't have to worry."

"Thanks," he said. "I think."

"Look," she said, "this has nothing to do with you havin' been in prison or how you look—which, as I've told you, is better and better each day. It just has to do with . . . comfort."

"I'm not very comfortable washing dishes, Kate," he admitted, "or clearing tables."

"What would you be comfortable doin', Matt?" she asked. "Wearin' a badge?"

"No," he said immediately. "Those days are gone. But there are other things a man could do comfortably. A lot of things."

"Then you have to find one, Matt," Kate said. "And I understand."

"Kate," he said, "I really appreciate that I walked in here my first day on the street and you gave me a job. I'll always be grateful."

"Okay," Kate said. "I'll finish up sweeping here, and then we can walk together."

"You want to walk me home," he asked, "or you want me to walk you home?"

She smiled.

"Whatever makes you the most comfortable."

WHAT'S IN THE bag?" Matt asked as they left.

"The day's receipts," she said.

"Do you carry them with you every night when you go home?" he asked as they walked.

"Pretty much."

"Why haven't you ever asked me to walk you before?"

"I'm usually fine by myself," she said.

"Then what's different about tonight?"

"I don't know," she said. "I just felt like doin' some-thin' different."

"How far do you live?" he asked.

"Blocks," she said, "just blocks. Right around this corner."

As they turned the corner, two men suddenly appeared. Both had the lower portion of their faces covered by a bandanna. From their build and the way they moved, Matt took them both to be young.

"Give us the bag," one of them said, his voice muffled by the bandanna covering it.

"What?" Kate said, stunned.

They each took a gun from their belts, pointed them at Kate.

"Give us the money!"

"N-n-now!" the other man said, and reached for the bag.

"Hey, wait!" Matt said, moving to get between the two men and Kate.

There were two shots, a bright light, a spark of pain, and then . . . nothing.

CHAPTER FOUR

M ATT AWOKE, LOOKING up at three men.
"He's awake," one said.

"Then sit 'im up," someone ordered.

Two men helped Matt to a seated position. From there he saw that the man who had issued the order to sit him up was wearing a badge.

"What happened?" Matt asked.

"You tell us." He wore a suit with a vest that had a watch chain hanging from it; a badge was pinned to his suit. His hair at the temples was gray, as was his mustache.

"Who are you?"

"Fred Holding," the man said, "Yuma territorial marshal. And you're Matt Wheeler."

"I—How do you know that?"

"I recognize you," Holding said. "You used to be a lawman before you went to Yuma Prison. When did you get out?"

"I don't know—a couple of months ago." Matt suddenly realized he was sitting on the ground. "Where's Kate?"

"There was a woman lying next to you when we got here," the marshal said.

"Lying?"

"You'd both been shot," Holding said. "She died. You didn't."

"Shot?" Matt looked down at himself. "Where?"

"The bullet creased your scalp," one of the other men said. "I'm Dr. Smith. I was called here to examine you."

"And Kate?"

"She was shot through the heart," the doctor said. "I'm sorry, but there was nothing we could do."

"Can you stand?" Marshal Holding asked.

"I think so," Matt said.

The doctor and another man—a helpful passerby apparently—assisted Matt to his feet.

"Good?" Holding asked him.

"I'm a little dizzy, but I think I'll be all right."

"Fine," Holding said. "Then we can go to the nearest police station."

"Police—"

"Yes," Holding said. "Yuma has a sheriff and a police station. The sheriff's out of town, so the police it is."

"Why there?" Matt asked.

"So we can talk," Marshal Holding said, "and I can decide whether or not to arrest you."

W AIT!" MATT SAID. "Things are still fuzzy. What are you saying?"

They were sitting in a room in the closest police station to the incident. Matt, who was more used to Western sheriffs' offices, realized how much law enforcement had progressed while he was in prison. He knew a new century was coming, but he didn't like it.

"I said," Marshal Holding repeated, "your partners probably tried to kill you, as well."

"My partners?"

"I bet they were supposed to wound you to make it look good," Holding said. "Only they tried to kill you and made off with . . . what? Money? Was the woman carrying money?"

"The woman's name was Kate Hardin, and she was carrying her day's receipts from her café, where I work."

"You work?" Holding asked. "As what?"

"A dishwasher."

"Ha!"

"What's that mean?"

"You expect me to believe that a man like you, an experienced lawman, could only get a job as a dishwasher when you got out?"

"I'm not a lawman anymore, Marshal," Matt said. "I'm an ex-con."

"And did she know that when she hired you?"

"Of course. It was what she did. She gave ex-cons jobs."

"Not knowing that one day one would try to rob her?"

"I—What? You mean . . . me?"

"Why else were you walkin' with her?" Holding asked. He'd removed his hat, which revealed a full head of gray hair beneath it.

"I was just walking her home."

"And did you usually do that?"

"Well, no—"

"Just on this night, when she was robbed," Holding said.

"Now, hold on," Matt said. "I'm still trying to get my bearings." He touched the bandage the doctor had put over his scalp wound. "Two men approached us, demanded the money, pointed guns at us, and then . . . that's it. I woke up, and you were there."

"How much money?"

"I don't know," Matt said. "She didn't tell me. She had it wrapped in brown paper."

"Did you know the two men?" Holding asked.

"No," Matt said.

"Didn't recognize them?"

"No, they had bandannas over the lower part of their faces."

Marshal Holding was about to ask Matt something else when the door opened and another man wearing a suit stuck his head in.

"We need to talk."

Holding looked annoyed but stood up. "I'll be right back," he said, and stepped outside.

Matt heard raised voices from the other side of the door. Apparently, the two men were arguing about whose jurisdiction the shooting had taken place in. When the door opened again, it was the other man who stepped in. He was in his thirties, about ten years younger than Holding. He removed his jacket, hung it over a chair, and sat across from Matt in his shirtsleeves.

"What happened to the marshal?"

"He's no longer involved," the man said. "He just happened to be in the area."

"And who are you?"

"My name's Detective Evers," the man said, "and suppose you start from the beginning, Mr. Wheeler?"

M ATT STARTED AGAIN from the beginning, going back to when he walked out of Yuma Prison, and ended with the shooting.

"Marshal Holding is crazy if he thinks I had anything to do with it," he finished.

"I told you," the detective said, "he's not involved anymore."

"Well, what do you think?" Matt asked.

"I think just because you're an ex-con doesn't mean you're involved," Evers said. "After all, you're also an ex-lawman."

"How do you know that?"

"The marshal told me he recognized you."

"Look, Detective," Matt said, "all I am now is a dishwasher. I was walking my boss home when this happened."

"Okay," Evers said, "tell me what you can about the two gunmen."

"They were young, tall," Matt said, "and they were both yelling—" He stopped short.

"What is it?"

"Who would know she was carrying money home with her?" Matt asked.

"Well," Evers said, "you and anybody else who works for her."

"I only knew because she told me just before we left," Matt said, "But the waiters, they might've known sooner."

"The waiters?"

"Yeah, Woody and Eddie," Matt said.

"Are they ex-cons?"

"Eddie is," Matt said. "Not Woody. But, Detective, Eddie also stammers."

"And?"

"One of the gunmen stammered."

"Okay," Evers said after a moment. "Do you know where Eddie lives?"

"No," Matt said, "but they'll both have to come to work tomorrow, either because they don't know Kate's dead or because they won't want to look suspicious."

"Good point," Evers said. "I'll be there in the morning with a couple of men. Are you gonna make it?"

"I may be a little off-balance," Matt said, "but I'll be there."

"Okay," Evers said. "Then you'd better go home and get some rest. Or see another doctor if you want."

As they both stood up, Matt asked, "Do you know the doctor who treated me?"

"Doc Smith, yeah, I know him. He's pretty good."

"I'll take your word for it, then," Matt said, "and head back to my hotel."

Detective Evers walked Matt to the front door, where the two men shook hands.

As Matt stepped outside, somebody snapped, "Hold it, Wheeler!"

He turned and saw Marshal Holding coming toward him. He had apparently been waiting just outside.

"Can I help you, Marshal?" he asked.

Holding stuck his forefinger in Matt's face.

"You may have that young detective fooled, but you and me, we're too old to play games."

"You're right about one thing, Marshal," Matt said. "I'm not playing games. Just what do you have against me? We never met before today."

"I hate lawmen gone bad, Wheeler," Marshal Holding said. "You had yourself quite a reputation in your day, but your day is done. I'm gonna have my eye on you while you're in Yuma, Wheeler."

"Then maybe I won't be here much longer."

"Oh? Plannin' on leavin' town now that you've got some money?"

"I'm not the one with Kate's money, Marshal," Matt said. "Maybe you'll find that out tomorrow. Now, if you'll excuse me, I have to go to my hotel and get some rest." He started down the steps, then turned and added, "Doctor's orders."

CHAPTER FIVE

MATT COULDN'T SLEEP.
It had been a lot of years since he'd faced a gun, and he was finding out he wasn't quite up to it after all that time. Initially, when he had entered his room, he sat down on the bed and couldn't stop shaking.

Later, when he'd undressed and slipped under the sheets, he still couldn't stop trembling. He'd had fights in prison, faced makeshift blades and clubs, but no gun for seven and a half years. Did this experience mean he would never be able to hold a gun again?

Washing dishes had just been a way to make some money. He hadn't given up on ever carrying a gun again. But now . . . he rolled himself up into a ball and closed his eyes, but sleep just didn't come.

WHEN THE SUN came up Matt rose, washed, and dressed. The trembling had stopped, but he didn't know if the calm would last the rest of the day.

Normally, he would have simply gone down to the boardinghouse dining room for breakfast, since he wasn't due at work till the supper rush. But since Detective Evers was going to be at Kate's café, he decided to head there himself. If Eddie *had* been involved in shooting and robbing Kate, Matt wanted to be present to hear it.

So he made his way to the café and let himself in with the extra key Kate had given him. Moments later there was a knock at the door.

"Detective," Matt said, opening it.

"The waiters here yet?" Evers asked.

"No."

"I'll leave my men outside, but I'll come and stay in the kitchen." He saw the look on Matt's face. "Is that a problem?"

"The waiters usually eat in the kitchen before we open for business."

"Okay, then," Evers said, "I'll be outside the back door, listening."

"Good."

"You gonna start cookin'?" Evers asked.

"I don't cook," Matt said. "I just wash dishes."

"You were a pretty decent lawman in your day, weren't you?" Detective Evers asked.

"I guess."

"And now you're doin' this?"

"I'm a pretty decent dishwasher," Matt said.

IT WAS A good half hour before Eddie showed up. Matt had started to worry that maybe Eddie—or both Eddie and Woody—had taken the money and lit out. But here was Eddie, coming through the front door like nothing had happened.

"I d-don't smell anythin' c-cookin'," he said to Matt. "Where's Kate?"

"She's dead, Eddie," Matt said, "but then you know that already."

Eddie looked confused. "H-how would I kn-know that?"

"Because you killed her," Matt said.

"Yer crazy!"

"I was there, remember?" Matt asked. "You shot me, too, or your accomplice did. Who was it, Woody? Or somebody else?"

"W-why would I k-kill Kate?" Eddie demanded.

Matt wondered how long the waiter was going to drag this out? And he wondered if the detective could hear them from outside the kitchen door. He decided to take the conversation into the kitchen. As he had hoped, Eddie followed him.

"You killed her for yesterday's receipts," Matt said. "Somehow, you knew she'd be carrying that money on her last night. But you probably didn't know I'd be with her."

"Yer crazy, Wheeler," Eddie said. "You c-can't prove a thing."

"You stammered last night, Eddie," Matt told him, "just before you shot us."

Matt studied the younger man's face, saw several things pass there before Eddie suddenly pulled a gun from his belt.

"It w-was your fault, damn it!" he swore. "If you hadn't been there, she woulda gave us the money."

"Who was the other man? Was it Woody?"

"Woody?" Eddie laughed. "He wouldn't have any part of it, even though he's the one who told me she'd be carryin' the money."

"Why'd you even come to work today, Eddie? Why not just take the money and run?"

"You'd've liked that, wouldn't ya?" Eddie asked. "Then the police would know I'm the one who killed Kate and took her money."

"I'm afraid they already know, Eddie," Matt said, pointing at the kitchen door.

The door opened, and Detective Evers entered, holding his gun.

"I heard it all, Eddie," he said. "All I need is your partner's name. And, oh, yeah, the money."

Eddie's eyes began bouncing around in his head. He was either going to shoot or run.

"Eddie, if you try to shoot, the detective will kill you," Matt said. "And if you try to turn and run, he has two more men outside waiting."

Eddie stared at Matt, who was acutely aware that the gun was still pointing at him—probably the same gun that had shot him and Kate last night.

"Eddie . . ."

"Come on, Eddie," Detective Evers said.

"I didn't mean it," Eddie said. "I didn't mean to shoot her." He handed the gun to Matt. "It was an accident."

Matt turned and handed the gun to Detective Evers.

"You can tell your story in court, Eddie," the detective said. "Right now you're under arrest."

The detective walked Eddie through the dining room at gunpoint. His two uniformed men met them at the door.

"Eddie," Matt said, "it would mean a lot if you told the detective who your partner was."

Eddie nodded as he was led away.

Detective Evers put his gun away and turned to face Matt. "Thanks for your help, Mr. Wheeler," he said. "What will you do now?"

"What can I do?" Matt asked. "I'll close up the café and look for work somewhere else."

"Did she have any family to take the place over?" the detective asked.

"I don't know."

"What about you?"

"I'm a dishwasher," Matt said. "I told you that. I wouldn't know the first thing about cookin' or running this place."

"Too bad. I heard the food was good here."

"It was."

"I'll let you know if Eddie gives up his partner," Evers said.

"Oh, one more thing," Matt said.

"Yeah?"

"It seems Marshal Holding is after me for some reason," Matt said.

"Yes, apparently he thinks you've sullied the reputation of all lawmen."

"And you don't?"

"We're all individuals," Evers said. "But if I was you, I'd get out of Yuma as soon as possible, Mr. Wheeler."

"That's my plan," Matt said, "as soon as I have a big enough stake."

CHAPTER SIX

W ELL," ESTHER SAID when Matt entered the dining room, "joinin' us for supper tonight?"

"I thought I might," Matt said, "if it's all right."

"Of course," she said, "just sit over there next to Mr. Meyer. That's your chair whenever you want to eat here."

Matt sat and the fat man next to him smiled and said, "Fred Holly."

"Matt Wheeler!"

They shook hands.

One of the men seated across from him said, "I'm Stan Wallace." He jerked his thumb at the small man on his left and said, "This is Ken Davis. We're all drummers."

Matt nodded. At the moment, there were only the four of them seated at the table, which had six chairs.

"Esther's told us you usually work at this time," Stan said. "Not tonight, huh?"

"No," Matt said, "not tonight."

It had only been that morning when Eddie had been

arrested and Matt had locked the door of the café. He hadn't told Esther yet that Kate was dead. He figured he'd do that after supper.

She came into the dining room, carrying platters of food that she set down in the center of the table.

"Now, just help yourself, Mr. Wheeler," she said. "Everyone here eats family style." She went back to the kitchen.

"Esther doesn't eat with us?" Matt asked.

"Never with the guests," Fred said. "She always eats alone in the kitchen."

They all covered their plates with chicken and vegetables, then dug in.

The other four guests usually ate together, so they had things to talk about, comparing the experiences they'd had since breakfast. Matt simply ate quietly.

"So, Matt," Fred said finally, "how's it goin' with your job, the one that usually keeps you away from supper?"

"Well, it was good for a while, but I'm looking for a change."

"To what?" Stan asked.

"I'm not sure yet," Matt said. "I have to think about it."

"You should become a salesman," Stan said. "There's good money in it."

"If you're good at it," Fred pointed out.

The small man, Ken, concentrated on his food.

"What do you fellas sell?" Matt asked.

"Ladies' delicates," Fred said.

"Men's ties," Stan said. "Ken here sells guns."

"Guns?" Matt asked.

"Pistols," Ken said, speaking for the first time. "Colts."

"Interesting," Matt said.

"You can sell anythin' you want," Fred said.

"Somehow," Matt said, "I don't think selling is for me."

"Well," Fred said, "I hope you figure out what is for you."

"Yeah," Matt said, "so do I."

A FTER SUPPER MATT remained at the table as the four drummers left.

Esther went in and out, clearing off the table. As she did, she asked, "You want some more coffee, Mr. Wheeler? Or another piece of pie?"

"No, Esther," Matt said. "I was waiting for you to finish so we could talk. Can you sit for a minute?"

"About a minute is all I have," she said, sitting across from him. "What's on your mind?"

"Kate."

"What about her?"

"She's dead."

A look of shock came over Esther's face. "What? How? When?"

"Last night," he said. "She was shot for her day's proceeds."

"She was killed for money?"

"The best reason for it," Matt said.

"And that bandage on your head?"

"Yeah," he said, touching it, "I was shot, too. Luckily, I have a thick skull."

"Who did it?" she asked.

"Her waiter Eddie."

"I don't know him," she said. "What about Woody?"

"You know him?"

"He's my nephew," Esther said. "Is he all right?"

"Well . . . I haven't seen him since the shooting. The detective is probably going to want to talk to him, though."

"Why?"

"Well, uh, Eddie said it was Woody who told him Kate would be carrying money when she went home."

"Wait," she said. "They don't think Woody was involved, do they?"

"With the actual shooting? Eddie said no, but . . . they'll still want to talk with him."

"Oh, my," Esther said, "this is terrible. What will happen to the café?"

"It'll go to Kate's next of kin," Matt said.

"As far as I know," Esther said.

"Well," Matt said, "the café is locked up for now, and I have a key."

"She must've thought a lot of you to give you a key," Esther said.

"It's a spare," Matt said with a shrug. "I was just a dishwasher."

"No, no," she insisted, "she wouldn't give a key to just anyone."

"You have one, don't you?"

"Yes, but that's different."

"Why?"

"She was my cousin."

"Oh," Matt said, "I didn't know. Wait. So was Woody her son?"

"No," she said, "to her he was a second cousin."

"Then who's her next of kin?"

"Me and then Woody. But there are no others."

"So the café is going to be yours, Esther."

She looked startled. "I wouldn't know how to run it."

"You can get somebody to run it for you."

She seemed to think about that for a few moments; then her eyes brightened. "What about you?"

"Me?" Matt asked. "I'm a dishwasher, Esther. You need somebody who knows how to run a business."

"You've been working there for many weeks now," she said. "You must've seen how she ran it."

"That doesn't mean I could do it," he said. "I think you'd be better off letting Woody run it." *If,* he thought, *Woody doesn't turn out to be partially responsible for her death*.

"I don't think I could trust Woody to do it," she said. "He's not smart enough."

"There must be somebody else. I'm going to be leaving town soon."

"How soon?"

"As soon as my stake is big enough."

Esther thought a moment, then said, "If you don't do it, I'll have to close it. You'll have to find work elsewhere. That may take a while, and that'll keep you here longer. On the other hand, run it for me, and I'll pay you a lot more than a kitchen worker."

Matt thought it over for a moment, then asked, "How much more?"

CHAPTER SEVEN

Three months later . . .

M ATT LOOKED AROUND his room, but there was
nothing else to pack. He didn't have that much to
begin with. Since he would be riding out of Yuma on
his own horse, all he needed was his bedroll and saddlebags. He went down to breakfast carrying those.

"So you're really goin'?" Esther asked when she
saw him.

"I really am," he said. "I've already been here too
long."

"And you're sure Woody is gonna be able to run the
café?" she asked.

"Between him and the cook, they've pretty much
got things figured out. They really don't even need me
anymore."

"Well, sit down, then," she said. "You might as well
have a hearty breakfast before you leave."

Matt agreed and sat in his usual spot. The other tenants changed on a regular basis and sometimes—like now—the house wasn't full. There were only two other boarders at breakfast.

Sitting to his right was another in an endless line of drummers, this one called Lee Beckett. And across from him was a new young man in town named Nick Sykes, who was looking for work. Matt was thinking about telling him to go to the café to talk to Woody, but it was no longer his business who worked there. Not since he had walked out last night for the final time.

He could have remained in town, stayed at his post running the café, but for one thing: the shadow of Yuma Territorial Prison. It lay over everything he did in Yuma, and he had to get away from it.

He had been guilty of what they charged him with, killing one of the men who killed his wife, but he had not believed he deserved to be sent to prison. After all, what would any other man have done in his place?

Today was the day he had been waiting for since his release more than five months before. His stake was large enough for him to outfit himself and hit the trail.

"Where will you be goin', Mr. Wheeler?" Lee Beckett asked.

"I can't say I know, Mr. Beckett," Matt said, "but the point really is just to get away from here. Where I go after that is really not important."

"But what will you do for a livin'?" Nick Sykes asked. "You sound like an educated man, but I understand you used to be a lawman?"

"A long time ago," Matt said. "Yes, I was educated back East, but I came west when I was about your age, discovered I could use a gun, got a job as a deputy, and just went from there."

"So you were a lawman for a long time?" Sykes asked.

"Over twenty-five years, Nick," Matt said.

"So will you go back to that?"

"I doubt it," Matt said.

"Why not?"

"I'm not sure anyone would want to hire an ex-con as a lawman," Matt said. "Besides, I'm not quite the man I was before I went inside."

"You must have suffered terribly in there," Sykes said.

Next to him, Beckett snorted. Both Matt and Sykes looked at him.

"Oh, sorry," Beckett said, "but I thought that's what criminals are put in prison to do, suffer and pay for their crimes?"

"Mr. Beckett!" Esther snapped. She had come from the kitchen just in time to hear his remark. "That is so rude! Some of those men don't deserve to be in there at all, like Mr. Wheeler here."

"Oh," Beckett said, "so you didn't do what they said you did, Wheeler?"

"I did, Mr. Beckett," Matt said. "I killed a man."

"And why did you do that?"

Matt turned his head and looked the other man in the eye. "He was rude to me."

Beckett's mouth snapped shut.

M ATT REINED IN his horse in front of the café, dismounted, and tied it off. As he went inside, he saw that the breakfast rush was once again in full swing, as it had been each morning for the past two months since he'd hired the new cook.

"Matt!"

He turned, saw Woody rushing toward him with a big smile on his face. The young man was smarter than his aunt Esther had given him credit for, and Matt was convinced Woody would be able to run the café as well as he himself had been. And that was a surprise to him, as well. After Kate's death, he had gone from dish-washer to proprietor with amazing ease, hiring not only a new dishwasher, but a new cook, and business had picked up considerably.

"Want breakfast?" Woody asked.

"No," Matt said, "I ate at.the boardinghouse. I just came to say goodbye, Woody, and good luck."

The two men shook hands.

"I can't thank you enough, Matt. After what Eddie did, I felt so bad about tellin' him about the money—"

"You're not to blame, Woody," Matt said. "It was all done by Eddie and his partner. But now they're back where they belong, in prison."

Yes, Matt Wheeler might not have belonged in Yuma Prison, but he knew that there were plenty of men incarcerated there who deserved it. Eddie would be there until he was executed.

"So where are ya goin'?" Woody asked. "When will you be back?"

"I don't know," Matt said, "and probably never."

"Never?"

"Well," Matt said, "maybe if they tear that prison down."

"So never."

"Right."

They shook hands again.

"I gotta get back to work," Woody said. "Take care of yerself."

"Yeah, you, too."

Matt turned and walked out, saw a man standing by his horse, and cursed under his breath.

"Matt Wheeler," Marshal Fred Holding said, "what a coincidence."

"Coincidence?" Matt asked. "Does that mean you came here to eat, Marshal?"

"Why else would I be here?"

"Because you heard I was leaving town, and you wanted to threaten me one last time."

"Threaten you?" Holding asked. "I don't threaten, Wheeler."

"Every time I look over my shoulder, you're there, Marshal," Matt said. "What do you call that?"

Holding smiled and said, "Haunting."

"Well," Matt said, "I'm leaving town. You're going to need a horse to keep haunting me."

"Do you have a gun?"

"What?"

"A gun," Holding said. "Do you have a gun?"

"There's a Winchester on my saddle."

"Everybody's got a rifle, Wheeler. Do you have a pistol?"

Matt was wearing a jacket. He opened it and said, "Not on me."

"Do I have to look in your saddlebags?"

Matt walked to his horse, dug his hand into one of his saddlebags, and came out with a used Peacemaker he had picked up in a gun shop cheap. He turned and handed it to Holding, butt first.

"Seriously?" Holding said. "This is the gun of an ex–famous lawman?"

"I was never famous," Matt said.

"This thing will explode in your hand if you ever try to fire it."

"I'm going to retool it," Matt said. "I just haven't had the time."

"And then what?" Holding asked.

"What do you mean?"

"I mean, what're you gonna do with this once it can be fired?" the lawman asked.

"Protection," Matt said. "What do you think?"

"I think there are still two men out there who you hold responsible for killing your wife."

"You got the wrong idea," Matt said. "I'm not that man anymore, Marshal. Even if I wanted to kill those two men, I'd probably end up getting killed, which probably wouldn't upset you at all."

"What upsets me is lawmen who don't respect the badge," Holding said.

"Well, don't worry," Matt told him. "I doubt I'll be wearing a badge again anytime soon."

"You wore it long enough to dishonor it," Holding snapped.

"Luckily, we have lawmen like you to make up the difference, then, Marshal," Matt said.

Holding seemed to take offense at that remark and stepped closer to Matt, growing red-faced. He shoved the Peacemaker back into Matt's hand.

"I hope this thing blows your fool head off, Wheeler!" he snapped. "And you may be leaving town, but you take one wrong step, and I'll be right there!"

I T WASN'T NECESSARY for Matt to ride past the prison on his way out of town, but he did it, anyway. He felt it was necessary in order to truly put the place behind him. He reined his horse in for a moment to just sit there and stare at the walls. He had spent many years looking at them from the inside, so now he wanted a last, long look from the outside.

While he stared, he thought about Marshal Fred Holding. He hoped the man would forget about him, but his visit that morning showed that he hadn't. Though it could hardly have been called a "visit." It had been more of an attack. The lawman obviously hated Matt for some reason, and he had no idea if it was more than just hatred for a lawman with "no respect for the badge." He couldn't remember having ever met the marshal before, let alone having crossed swords with him on some personal matter.

Matt noticed an armed guard up on the wall looking out at him, so he dug his heels into his horse to get it moving to leave Yuma Territorial Prison behind for good.

CHAPTER EIGHT

Eight years ago

Before prison, 1881 . . .

S HERIFF MATT WHEELER walked from his office to the house the town of Fairview, Montana, supplied its duly appointed lawman. It was a small one-story house on the north edge of town, with no other structures around it. Matt didn't mind not having neighbors. He dealt with enough people during the course of his day. When he went home, he wanted only to speak to his wife, not to any noisy or nosy neighbors.

At forty-two he had been married only a little over two years and sheriff of Fairview roughly the same amount of time. Prior to that, he had been a federal marshal working under Judge Parker out of Fort Smith, Arkansas. But after he met his wife, Angie, and realized he wanted to marry her, he'd had to abide by her wishes and get a more permanent job, one that wouldn't have him riding all over Indian Territory for days or weeks at a time.

So he gave in, and when he heard that the town of Fairview was looking for a sheriff, he applied for the job. It was to be an appointed position, not an elected one, and with his impressive background, the town fathers jumped at the opportunity.

He had now been wearing their sheriff's badge for two years and doing whatever he could not to die of boredom.

When he got home, the usual heady aromas were coming from the kitchen. The house was small, but all the rooms—a sitting area, the bedroom, and a kitchen—were separate, so he could smell what Angie was doing, but not see her from inside the front door.

"I'm home!" Matt called out.

Angie came to the kitchen doorway, an attractive woman of medium height, in her late thirties. She had her honey-colored hair pinned back, but there were tendrils that had come loose and were hanging down on either side of her face.

"Supper in ten minutes," she said. "Get washed up."

"Yes, ma'am."

He stepped back outside, removed his gun belt, hung it on a peg on the side of the house, and used the water in a barrel there to wash his hands and face. His wife not only kept him well-fed but clean, as well. He dried off, hung the gun belt over his shoulder, and stepped back into the house.

Once inside, he hung the gun belt on another wall peg and walked to the kitchen, where supper was on the table.

"Have a seat," she said, her back to him. "You look hungry."

"You're not even looking at me," he pointed out.

She glanced over her shoulder and, smiling, said, "You always look hungry."

He walked to her, put his arms around her waist from behind, and said, "Hungry for you."

"Go and sit, Sheriff," she commanded, "or your supper will get cold."

"Yes, ma'am."

He sat at the table, where there were already bowls of steaming vegetables. She came over and dropped a thick steak onto his plate and then a smaller one onto hers. She added a cup of coffee for him and a glass of water for each of them, and then she sat across from him.

She said a quiet grace before eating. He had been glad from the beginning of their marriage that she hadn't tried to force her religious beliefs onto him. And they were both too old to think about children, so there would be no question about how to raise them.

"And how was your day?" she asked.

"Quiet, as usual."

"Isn't that good?" she asked.

"When I took this job, I didn't realize how dull this town would actually be," he said.

"And isn't that because you're so good at your job?" she asked.

"Well," he said, "that's what we want people to think."

"You have the occasional drunk on Saturday night," she pointed out.

"Yes," he said, reaching his hand out to take hers. "Yes, I do." He took his hand back to cut his meat and put a piece in his mouth. "This is great."

A NGIE WHEELER KNEW that she had taken Matt away from an exciting life of chasing outlaws through Indian Territory. She also knew life in Fairview was boring for him, but for her "boring" meant "safe." She simply could not have married him if he had continued to wear a deputy marshal's badge.

So she tried to keep him happy with the two things she could give him an abundance of—love and food.

L ATER, MATT WAS sitting on the porch with a cup of coffee when Angie came out and joined him.

"The kitchen's clean," she said, sitting in the chair next to him. She put her hand on his. "I'm sorry."

"For what?"

"For making you live this life of sitting on the porch each night with me."

He grabbed her hand and squeezed it. "I love you," he said, "and I love sitting here with you."

"Yes, but wouldn't you love it more if you'd been out chasing outlaws today?"

"There'll be time for that, Angie," he said. "It won't be quiet around here forever."

They didn't realize how quickly Matt's words would come true. . . .

I T HAPPENED THREE weeks later.

There was a large ranch outside of town, the Double-K, owned and run by Karl Kaufman. On that day, a large payroll had been delivered to the Bank of Fairview, which had only one guard on duty.

"Where are you off to this morning?" Angie asked Matt.

"The bank. Kaufman's coming into town today for his payroll money. That fool bank manager's cut back on security again."

"If he thinks he only needs one man, why do you have to go?" she asked.

"Because he's wrong," Matt said.

"Are you taking Peter?"

Peter Brown was a young man who fancied himself a hand with a gun. Matt used him when he needed a deputy, because he knew he could trust him.

"No, Pete's out of town for some reason."

"But what about breakfast?"

As he went out the door, he called back, "I'll have a big lunch!"

W HEN MATT ENTERED the bank, Evan Horner, the bank manager, turned and looked at him. Standing next to him was his security guard, Jason Pardee.

"I was expecting you, Sheriff," the manager said.

"Oh? Who's that?" Matt asked.

"You've made it quite clear that this bank needs more than one security man," Horner said.

"And you've made it clear you don't agree with me."

"Mr. Pardee assures me he can handle anything that comes along," Horner said. "Besides, this is a nice, peaceful town."

"Yes, it is," Matt said, "and I aim to see it stays that way."

"Well," Pardee said, "that's your job, Sheriff, and this is mine."

"I'll just be here to give you a hand," Matt said, "if you need it."

"Much obliged, Sheriff," Pardee said, "much obliged."

"Mr. Horner," a young teller called from the front of the bank, "here comes Mr. Kaufman."

"Let's get the man's payroll ready for him, Roy."

"Yes, sir." The teller left the window and hurried behind his cage.

"I'll step outside and meet him and his men," Pardee said to Horner.

"Fine, fine," the bank manager said. "See them in."

Pardee nodded, opened the door, and started out. Before he crossed the threshold, he looked at Matt and said, "Comin'?"

"I think I'll just wait in here," the sheriff said.

"Suit yourself."

Matt watched through the window as Karl Kaufman drove a buckboard up to the front of the bank, accompanied by his foreman and one other man. They exchanged some words with Pardee, and then Kaufman stepped down and walked to the bank door with Pardee. His two men were behind them.

Pardee opened the door and said, "After you, Mr. Kaufman."

"Thank you."

The rancher was a big man in his sixties, with white sideburns that matched the hair beneath his hat.

"Mr. Kaufman," Horner said, rushing forward, "good morning, sir."

"You got my payroll, Horner?" the rancher asked.

"Right this way, sir," Horner said, and led the man to the teller's cage.

Kaufman's foreman and the other man stood on either side of the bank door. Pardee stood in the center of the room, watching everything. There were no other customers in the bank, just employees who watched from their desks.

Behind the teller's cage, the manager, Horner, was taking the money from the safe and putting it into a bag for the rancher. When Kaufman came around carrying it, Pardee, the foreman—named Chester—and the third man fell into step with him. Matt noticed Pardee taking a quick look at him as if to check where he was.

"Hold on—," Matt said, but they didn't pause. Instead, Pardee opened the bank door and literally pushed Kaufman out, followed by the other two.

"Hey, what the—," Kaufman snapped as he stumbled. He was cut off by Pardee's pistol as it clipped him on the head. While the rancher fell, Pardee grabbed the bag of money.

"Stop him—," Matt started, but the other two—supposedly working for Kaufman—drew their guns and pointed them at the sheriff.

"Don't, Sheriff," Chester said. "Just don't. Cover 'im, Ed."

They backed out the door, keeping their guns trained on Matt.

"Well," Horner shouted at the sheriff, "do something!"

The bank door closed, and Matt ran to it, looked out the window. The rancher Kaufman was on the ground. Pardee was climbing up onto the buckboard seat with the bag of money. The foreman, Chester, and the other man were running to their horses.

And when Matt saw who was crossing the street, his blood went cold.

He opened the door and ran out, drawing his gun.

"Angie! No!" he shouted to his wife.

But she had no idea what was going on. She was carrying a small wicker basket topped with a napkin.

"I brought you breakfast, Sheriff!" she called with a smile and a wave.

Matt looked at the three men who were robbing the bank. The foreman and the other man turned on him with their guns and fired. But even as the bullets struck him, he saw Pardee turn and fire two shots at Angie. Why, he didn't know. She was no danger to Pardee, unless he was only reacting to her movements. She staggered and fell in the middle of the street.

"No!" Matt screamed.

He raised his gun and fired at the three men, but

Pardee had the buckboard team moving, and the others had mounted their horses.

Matt fell onto his knees. Crawling into the street amid the dirt and dust the buckboard and horses had kicked up, and the biscuit and bacon that had fallen from the overturned basket, he desperately tried to get to Angie before blacking out. . . .

CHAPTER NINE

After prison, 1889 . . .

THREE MONTHS AFTER riding out of Yuma, leaving
the prison behind, Matt Wheeler rode into the
town of Mud City, Wyoming. He had made several
stops along the way to replenish his poke with an odd
job here and there. He had worked as a clerk in a mercantile and an assistant in a livery stable; he had even
done some time as a bartender. Each time he made
enough money to outfit himself again, he moved on.
But it was not until he reached Mud City that he realized what he was doing. All this time, he had been
working his way back north, to Montana Territory.

In Mud City, he dismounted, tied his horse off, and
entered the Big Muddy Saloon. Over a beer at a corner
table with little going on around him at that hour of
the afternoon, he realized that he was heading for Angie's grave.

He hadn't seen her grave since his arrest, and what

good would it do him to see it now? Well, maybe it would give him some peace to have gone full circle. Or maybe he could apologize for having lost control and killing the first man he found, thus leaving the other two at large—including Pardee, the man who had actually shot her.

And how would the people of Fairview, Montana, welcome him? He had run out on them to track down the men responsible for his wife's death and his own near death. And he had never been back. Would they accept him now eight years later, or would they run him right back out of town?

But he didn't need acceptance. He needed only to visit Angie's grave. Afterward, he could decide what to do with the rest of his life.

After seven and a half years in prison, he was a little behind on what was going on in the country. He'd heard about the OK Corral while inside, but he wondered what was happening with Judge Parker. Was he still in Fort Smith? Would he consider giving a deputy marshal's badge to an ex-con? Probably not. And he probably shouldn't. Matt Wheeler, almost fifty and fresh from Yuma Prison, was in no condition to wear a badge and do the job again.

He finished his beer, went to the bar, and bought a bottle of whiskey.

T HINK HE'S GOT any money?" a voice asked.

"Well," another voice said, "he bought a bottle of whiskey. All we gotta do is check his pockets."

Matt felt hands on him and sat up straight. The two men who were going to search him jumped back.

"What—," he started.

"Aw, he's drunk," one said. "Nothin' to be afraid of."

They were young. Combined they wouldn't be his

age. Before they could put their hands on him again, he pulled the Peacemaker from his belt. Marshal Holding had been wrong, it hadn't exploded in his hands the first time he used it. And it was serviceable enough to take care of these two.

"Whoa," one of them said, and they stepped back again. "Take it easy, old-timer."

"Go find yourself another drunk to roll," Matt said. "Move!"

Neither of them had a gun, so they put their hands out and said, "Yeah, yeah, sure, take it easy. We're goin'."

They backed away, then turned and went out the batwing doors.

The bartender came walking over. "Sorry about that, friend," he said. "You want another bottle?"

"No," Matt said. "Water, a glass of water."

"I can do that," the barman said. "Comin' up."

The bartender left and came back with a mug of water. Matt drained it and banged the mug on the table as he set it down.

"You need some coffee," the bartender said.

"Can you do that?" Matt asked.

"This place look busy to you?" the man asked. "I'll make a pot."

"Thanks."

"Hey, you almost got rolled in my place," the man said. "Least I can do."

Matt fought to stay awake until the man returned with a mug of strong coffee.

"Thanks," Matt said. "Do you know a cheap hotel?"

"We got three," the barman said. "They're all a dollar a day. Try the one down the street, the Pine House. It's probably the cleanest one."

"Thanks for your help."

"I just don't like folks havin' a bad time in my place,"

the man said. "You don't get no repeat customers that way."

"No, I guess you wouldn't." Matt put the coffee cup down. "The Pine House, you say?"

"Just down the street," the bartender said. "You can't miss it. Get yerself some rest and come on back tonight when we're a little more lively."

"I'll do that," Matt said, standing. "I'll just do that."

MATT GOT HIMSELF a room at the Pine Hose, then boarded his horse at a nearby livery. The steeldust was the second horse he'd had since leaving Yuma. He had very nearly ridden the first one into the ground, but succeeded in replacing it before it could expire. Now he rested the steeldust whenever he could.

"Take good care of him," he told the hostler.

"Yes, sir," the man said. "That's my job."

Matt went back to his room and sat on the bed with the Peacemaker in his hands. He wondered if Mud City would be a fitting end for him, or if he should actually just continue on to Angie's grave site, pay his respects, make his apology, and then go on from there.

He held the gun in both hands tightly, caressed the barrel a bit, then set the gun aside on the night table next to the bed. He wasn't in the mood for the liveliness of the saloon the bartender promised him he'd find if he went back, plus he was afraid he'd just drink more. Maybe this time he'd get so drunk, he would be rolled for what little money he had left.

He decided to turn in for the night, have breakfast in the morning in the hotel, and then get an early start. There were still many miles, days, and nights to go between Mud City and Fairview, Montana. Plenty of time to decide what his final decision was going to be.

* * *

S ITTING ON THE bed with his gun in his hand the night
  before had not been the first time Matt Wheeler
had considered suicide.

When he had woken up in the doctor's office in Fairview and they told him that Angie was dead, he had
wanted to die.

When he had arrived at Yuma Prison, he had considered different ways of ending his life, from hanging
himself in his cell to picking a fight with the biggest,
most violent con in there.

When he had been released and walked out the
gate, he had considered having a good meal and then
blowing his brains out.

Since he had left Yuma, he had woken each morning and gone to sleep at night with the thought in his
head that it would not be a bad thing to die.

And yet here he was, rising the next morning and
going down to have breakfast because, in the end, every
time, he couldn't take his own life without first standing
at Angie's grave site and talking to her. Of course, he
wouldn't be expecting her to respond, but some sort of
revelation while he was standing there would be helpful.

O VER BREAKFAST, AS he usually did, Matt reviewed
  his funds. He knew it would be some time before
he reached Fairview, and he was going to need to take
another job or two—or three—before he arrived there.

Despite the fact that Marshal Holding had referred
to him as an "ex–famous lawman," he did not consider
himself to be that. But his name *was* recognizable in
certain circles, specifically law enforcement. He had
already been in several towns where he had run into
the local law who knew not only who he was but what

had happened to him. It was an end many lawmen feared would come: not only losing their badge but going to prison.

So when he tried to get a job, he usually made it something transient, like in a mercantile or a livery. And he would give his last name as something other than Wheeler, especially if he was going to be in town for a while. Always afraid he'd come across the local lawman, whose job it was to be aware of strangers whether they were there for the day or longer. Matt wondered what there was in Mud City he could do for a few weeks or months to reinforce his purse and enable him to go back on the trail for an extended period of time.

The only thing he wouldn't ever do, though, was wash dishes.

CHAPTER TEN

A FTER BREAKFAST MATT decided to take a walk around town, see if he could scare up a job. After a couple of hours, it was obvious there wasn't much to Mud City. It was a small town with no jobs available. Everything that needed to be done was already being done by someone.

The problem was, Matt didn't have enough money to continue on. He might be able to get a job in the next town he came to, but the merchants he spoke to assured him that it would be many, many miles before he came to a town of any considerable size.

Late that afternoon he found his way back to the Big Muddy Saloon.

"You didn't make it back last night," the bartender said.

"I was worn out," Matt said.

"You still look worn out," the barman said. "Beer?"

"Thanks. Yeah, I've been job hunting in your little town."

"You wanna settle here?"

"No," Matt said, "I just need to earn a few bucks to keep on moving."

"Yer outta luck, friend," the bartender said. "Ain't no work available here."

"That's what I'm finding out."

"I'd tell ya to take a loan from the bank," the bartender said, "but we ain't got one."

"You don't need any help around here?" Matt asked. "A relief bartender, maybe?"

"Remember I told you to come back last night when it was lively?"

"Yes."

The man shook his head. "It ain't ever lively," he said.

"So I'm stuck in this town until I can make some money, only there's no money to be made."

"The sheriff gets paid for every stray dog he shoots," the bartender laughed.

"You have a sheriff?" Matt asked, surprised.

"No," the bartender said, "but it never gets lively around here, and we don't have a bank. Why would we need one? Why, would you be interested in that job?"

"No," Matt said right away. "I'm no lawman."

"Well . . . ," the bartender started.

Matt waited, but the man didn't go on. "What's your name?" he asked the barman.

"Robbie," the man said. "Robbie Gentry."

"What are you thinking, Robbie?" Matt asked. "Something just occurred to you."

"Well . . . ," Gentry said again. "Yeah, I did have a thought."

"Let's hear it, then."

"There's a ranch just outside of town, run by a fella named Andy Mannix. He lives there with his wife, Joan."

"And?"

"Well, they need help," Gentry said. "Andy got hurt a while back, and he can't do a lot of heavy liftin'. He needs somebody to mend fences, dig postholes, that sorta thing."

"And he can pay?"

"Not a lot, but then you don't need a lot, right?"

"No," Matt said, "just enough to get me to the next place. But what's the catch?"

Gentry hesitated.

"Come on, you didn't exactly come right out with this," Matt said. "Do they have any other hands out there?"

"No, it's just the two of them."

"And why's that?"

"Well . . . it's Joan."

"The wife."

Gentry nodded.

"Is there something wrong with her?"

"Let's just say, she's not exactly right," Gentry said.

"Robbie, you're making this real hard," Matt said. "Is there some reason I shouldn't go out there and get work?"

"Just one," Gentry said.

"And that is?"

"If you go to work there," Gentry said, "she'll try to hire you to kill her husband."

M ATT RODE OUT to the Mannix ranch.
Riding up to the one-story wooden house, he could already see a corral fence that needed mending, a porch step that needed to be fixed, a barn door that was hanging by one hinge.

During the fifteen minutes it had taken to ride there from town, Matt thought about what Robbie Gentry had told him.

"Several men who were hired out there, just to help out, came back to town and said that crazy woman tried to hire them to kill her husband."

"And everybody believed them?" Matt asked.

"Why would they lie about somethin' like that?"

But Matt decided to go out and take a chance, anyway. Even if the woman did try to hire him to kill her husband, he could just say no, do the other jobs, get paid, and ride out of there.

As he rode up to the front of the house, the door opened, and a woman stepped out. She was tall, angular, in her forties, with long dark hair that hung past her shoulders. She was also holding a rifle, which, at the moment, was pointing down.

"Stop right there," she said.

"Are you Mrs. Mannix?" Matt asked.

"That's right," she said. "What can I do for you?"

"I was told in town you could use some help around here," Matt said. "Riding in I could see some obvious problems."

"Are you any good?" she asked.

"Do you have any other offers?" he asked.

"You'll have to come inside and meet my husband," she said. "Put your horse in the barn, and I'll put on a pot of coffee. Just come on in when you're ready."

"Right."

As he started to turn his horse, she asked, "What's your name?"

"It's Matt," he said, and headed for the barn before she could ask for his last name.

M ATT WALKED IN and smelled the coffee. Joan Mannix was at the stove, and there was a man sitting at a large wooden table.

"This him?" he asked.

Joan turned, looked at Matt, and said, "Yeah, that's him."

"I'm Andy Mannix," the man said, standing and extending his hand. He was tall, thin, in his sixties. His handshake was firm.

"Have a seat," Mannix said. "My wife makes strong coffee."

"That's the best kind," Matt said.

"She says you're lookin' for work?"

"Nothing permanent," Matt said. "I need to put some money together, and I can see there are some repairs you need done."

"Oh, yeah," Mannix said. "I usually handle that all myself, but I recently hurt my back—"

"He can't bend or lift," Joan said, bringing coffee to the table, "so any help you can give us would be appreciated." She turned and went back to the stove.

"She's right," Andy Mannix said. "I can't pay you much—"

"Whatever you pay me will also be appreciated," Matt told him.

"And when can you start?" Andy asked.

"Right away."

"Drink your coffee first," Joan said. "Then we'll walk the place and decide where you can begin."

"All right," Matt said. He tasted the coffee and looked across the table at Andy. "Just like you said, strong."

"Wait till you taste her cookin'," Andy said. "It'll be part of the deal."

"Suits me," Matt said.

I T TOOK A week.

He was able to sleep in the barn, so he didn't need to pay for a hotel room in town, and he took all his meals with Andy and Joan Mannix. In between he fixed the porch, the corral, and the barn door.

At the beginning of the second week, he was digging a posthole behind the house when Joan came out, carrying a pitcher of lemonade and a glass.

"I thought you could use this," she said. "It's kind of hot."

"Yeah, it is," he said, accepting the icy glass. "Thanks."

"You've gotten a lot of work done in a week," she commented.

Matt noticed she was dressed in a more feminine manner than she had been all week, and her hair had been brushed. However, she still wasn't a very attractive woman, with the sharp edges her facial features had.

"Have we paid you enough yet for you to move on?" she asked while he sipped.

"No, not yet," he said. "I should be around for a few more days, doing an odd job or two."

"That's good," she said, "because I may have a very important job for you."

He hesitated while bringing the glass to his lips once again. "Is that right?"

"And it'll pay a bit more, too."

"But Andy said you really couldn't pay me more."

"Well," she said, "this would come from some funds he doesn't know about. My own money."

"I see."

"Are you interested?" she asked.

"I might be," he said, handing her back the glass, "but now I've got to get this done."

"That's okay," she said. "We'll talk later after supper."

He leaned on his shovel and watched her walk back to the house. Was this going to be it, the offer to kill her husband? And what had he done to give her the impression he might be ripe for the offer?

He went back to his fence hole, with some loose boards waiting for him on the roof of the house.

As usual, Joan was quiet at dinner, with Andy carrying most of the conversation. But Matt noticed he was getting more looks from Joan while Andy talked.

After supper Andy usually asked Matt to join him on the porch for a cigar. Most of the time Matt said no; he had to turn in early so he could get up and start work. But on this night he said yes.

Outside, while Joan cleaned up after supper, they lit their cigars and sat.

"You did a good job here," Andy said, banging his foot down on the formerly loose board.

"Thanks."

They smoked a bit longer while Matt tried to figure out how to bring up the question. Finally, Andy solved the problem for him.

"So," he said, "has she made you the offer yet?"

"What?"

"Has Joan offered to pay you to kill me yet?"

Matt stared at the man a few moments before saying, "You know about that?"

"Of course I do," Andy said. "I mean, jeez, everybody in town knows, right?"

"Well, apparently—"

"It's sort of a town joke," Andy added.

"A joke? To have your wife try to hire somebody to kill you?"

"Has she asked you?"

"No, not yet," Matt said. "But I think it's going to be tonight."

"Then she'll probably come to you in the barn with the offer," Andy said.

"The barn."

"Well, yeah," Andy said, "the offer is gonna include a roll in the hay."

"What?"

"Her charms," Andy said. "Her not-so-lily-white body."

"Oh," Matt said, "I, uh, I couldn't do that."

"It's okay," Andy said with a wave. "Nobody ever does. Everybody she's ever made the offer to turns her down and then leaves the next day."

"Well, I don't want to leave," Matt said. "I don't have enough money yet."

"And the roof still needs some work," Andy said. "What I suggest is you tell her you'll think about it. Then take a few more days to get some more chores done. See how much you've got in your poke the next time she brings it up."

"How can you stay with a woman who's trying to have you killed?" Matt asked.

"Oh, she's not really," Andy said. "It's just her way of blowing off some steam. She gets pretty frustrated out here with me, especially now that I can't do any work."

"That may be, but what if somebody takes her serious?"

"So far nobody has," Mannix said. "Unless you are?"

"Not even close," Matt said.

"Well, just do me a favor and let her down gently when you tell her that," Andy Mannix said.

"I will."

The situation still didn't seem right to Matt. In fact, it seemed crazy, but the man must have really loved his wife to be so understanding.

And one thing Matt Wheeler *did* understand was loving a woman that much.

CHAPTER ELEVEN

LATER, WHILE MATT was preparing his bedding in the barn, Joan Mannix came out, glancing behind her.

"I can't stay long," she said.

"You shouldn't be here at all, Joan," Matt told her.

"I just want to know if you gave any thought to what we talked about?" she said.

"The extra job you talked about?" he asked. "I'd have to know what it is."

"Matt," she said, "I need you to kill my husband."

"Why? What's he done?"

"I'm not happy," she said, "and he won't let me go."

"Well," Matt said, "I can't see myself doing that, Joan."

"It wouldn't be hard, Matt," she said. "Nobody ever comes out here. No one would even know he was dead for days."

"Joan," he said, "you two have been married a long time. Why would you want to do this?"

"We've been married too long," she said. "I need a change desperately, and like I said, he won't let me go. I don't know if this will sweeten the pot any, Matt, but once it's done, you could also have me and the ranch."

"Joan—"

"Shh," she said, "not now. I have to go. Take a few days to think it over."

She turned and rushed out of the barn.

Matt reclined on his bed of hay and thought about the couple. Joan seemed determined to hire somebody to kill her husband, and Andy seemed confident that she didn't really mean it. Could he stay another week, pad his poke, and then walk away, confident that she wouldn't ultimately find somebody to do what she wanted?

With no law in town, what else could he do?

M ATT WORKED AND slept on the Mannix ranch for another week without either of them mentioning the offer. After supper that night, he sat with Andy on the porch.

"I think I've got enough to get myself on the trail again, Andy," he said.

"Well, we'll miss ya around here, Matt," Andy said. "You're a helluva worker. I don't know what you did before in your life, or what you're runnin' from or to, but you can always come back here." Andy lowered his voice. "That is, unless you kill me before you go."

"Andy—"

"I'm just kiddin', Matt."

"Yeah, I know, but I'm not sure Joan is."

"Did she come to you again?"

"Well, no . . ."

"Then don't worry about it. She's not serious. Look, you gonna head out tomorrow?"

"I thought I'd give it another day or two," Matt said.

"Good," Andy said, "we can help you get outfitted, send you off with some extra for the trail."

"You've done enough for me, Andy—"

"By underpayin' you for all the work you did?" Andy asked. "I don't think so. We'll put somethin' together for ya."

"Okay," Matt said, "I'll take it. And I'll spend the next day or so cleaning up, trying to make sure this place is in shape."

"Good," Andy said. "It's already in better shape than it's been in a long time."

Matt stood.

"I'll say good night, then."

"Finish your cigar in the barn," Andy said.

"Not a chance," Matt said. "Too much hay in there. The last thing I want to do is burn down the barn I worked so hard on."

"Good point," Andy said. "Night."

Matt started to walk away, then turned back.

"Oh, you'll tell Joan I'm leaving in a couple of days?"

"I'll tell 'er," Andy said, and waved.

Matt walked to the barn. He spent a little time checking over his horse, making sure the animal was sound and ready to go. That done, he reclined on his hay bed, gave some thought to the continuation of his trek back to Fairview. Wise or not, it was something he had to get done before he could move on. Or before he could decide whether he even wanted to move on.

H E WORKED THE next full day and decided to leave the following morning. After supper, instead of sitting on the porch with Andy, he went back to the barn to start packing his gear. Not that he had all that much to pack. While he was doing that, Joan appeared at the barn door.

"So you're done?" she asked.

"Yup," Matt said. "It's time for me to get moving."

"And what about my offer?"

He stopped what he was doing and turned to face her. "I can't do it, Joan," he said. "In fact, I don't even think you really want me to do it."

She looked down at the floor and said, "You may be right about that, Matt. Will you have breakfast with us in the morning?"

"No, I think I'll just get an early start."

"I'll make up a package for you," she said. "Some food you can eat along the way. Maybe an extra shirt or two that Andy doesn't need."

"That'd be great," Matt said. "I'd appreciate it."

"And we appreciate everything you've done."

She looked as if she wanted to say more, but finally just turned and walked away. He went to the door and watched as she walked back to the house.

I N THE MORNING both Andy and Joan saw him off, with Joan handing him a bundle wrapped in a blanket and tied off.

"Just some food and, like I told you, a shirt or two that Andy can spare."

"I've never even worn them," Andy said. "Joan's always buyin' me new shirts."

"Thanks very much." Matt tied the bundle onto the back of his saddle, with his bedroll, then mounted up.

"I wish I had a horse to give you," Andy said, "but that steeldust you're on is better than anythin' we have here."

"What you've given me is good enough," Matt assured them.

"Good luck, then," Andy said. "Stop by here again if you're back this way."

"I will," Matt promised.

He waved again and headed north.

H E WAS CAMPING his first night out, after having gone at a leisurely pace for most of the day, just letting the steeldust stretch its legs while he did the same. He had opened the package Joan had given him, found the shirts and some cold chicken and another item he didn't understand.

He had finished the chicken and was drinking coffee when he heard horses approaching. From the sound of it, there were half a dozen or so. Something must have been wrong for them to be riding so determinedly at night.

He was standing when they reached him, with his Peacemaker tucked into his belt.

"Hello the camp!" someone shouted. "Can we come in?"

"Come ahead," Matt said.

He watched while six men rode in from the darkness to the light of his fire. One of the riders he recognized right away. It was Robbie Gentry, the bartender from the Big Muddy Saloon in Mud City.

"What brings you out here at night, Gentry?" Matt asked.

"Before we start," an older man said, "could we ask you to drop your gun to the ground, please?"

"Why?"

"Better just drop it, friend," Gentry said. "You're not gonna try to use it on the six of us."

Gentry was right. Even on his best day as a lawman, Matt wouldn't have tried that. He took the gun from his waistband and dropped it to the ground.

"Thank you," the older man said.

"What's this about?" Matt asked.

"Andy Mannix was shot and killed this mornin'," Gentry said.

"Ah, Jesus . . . who did it?"

"Well," Gentry said, "Joan says you did."

"What?"

"We don't have a lawman in Mud City," the older man said, "but I'm the mayor, and these men are a sort of vigilante committee."

"So you decided to come after me," Matt said. "Look, Andy was alive when I left. And, Gentry, like you told me, Joan did ask me to kill him."

"You told him that?" the mayor asked Gentry.

"I told him there might be some work out there for him, but to watch out for Joan. Yeah, I told him she might try to pay him to kill Andy."

"She made the offer," Matt said, "but Andy himself said he knew about these offers and that she never really meant it."

"Mr. Wheeler, we're gonna dismount," the mayor said.

"Come ahead," Matt said. "I've got a pot of coffee on. Don't know if I've got enough for everybody, but I can make another."

The vigilante committee dismounted and tied off their horses. The four men who hadn't spoken simply stood by and watched as the mayor and Robbie Gentry accepted coffee from Matt.

"My name's Hollis," the mayor said.

"Well, Mayor Hollis," Matt asked, "what proof has Joan offered that I killed her husband?"

"She says she saw you shoot 'im," the mayor said.

"Well, that's a lie. Anything else?"

The mayor and Gentry exchanged a glance.

"Well," Gentry said, "she says you stole his watch."

"I killed him and stole his watch?" Matt asked. "Did she say I stole his shirts, too?"

"Shirts?" the mayor asked.

"She made a package for me, wrapped in a blanket," Matt said, "some shirts and some food."

"Where is that package?" the mayor asked.

"Right there."

The mayor and Gentry both looked at the blanket off to the side tied with rope.

"Do you mind?" the mayor asked.

"Go ahead."

The mayor stood and walked to the wrapped blanket, started to untie it.

"You mind if I search you, Wheeler?" Gentry asked.

"Go ahead," Matt said, "and have your other men look in my saddlebags. You're not going to find a watch."

The mayor found the shirts and a few pieces of chicken.

"No watch," he said.

Gentry patted Matt down and said, "Not here, either."

They looked over at the other men, who had checked the saddlebags, as they shook their heads.

"So what do you want to do now?" Matt asked.

Mayor Hollis looked at him. "We've still got her word that she saw you shoot 'im," he said.

"Her word against mine," Matt said. "Mr. Mayor, was Gentry here right about Joan offering other men money to kill her husband?"

"Unfortunately, yes," Hollis said.

"It's a big joke in town," one of the other men said with a laugh. He subsided when the mayor gave him a stern look.

"Look," Matt said, "I figure you came all this way and figured to take me in if you found that watch."

"That's what we figured, yeah," Mayor Hollis said.

"You've got no other proof to take me in except for the word of a woman who is well-known for trying to hire somebody to kill her husband. You know what I think?"

"She finally decided to do it herself," Gentry said.

"And then blame me," Matt said, "the last man who turned her down. As a former lawman, I can tell you, you've got nothing to haul me in on."

As a lawman in the same situation, Matt would have taken himself in, anyway. He hoped that these men wouldn't be able to make that decision.

He saw with some satisfaction that the mayor and Gentry exchanged sheepish looks.

"We've got no authority to take you in without proof," the mayor said. "We've got no lawman, and the circuit judge comes to town once a year, and he was here last month."

"So we rode out here at night for nothin'?" one of the other men said.

"You fellas are welcome to bed down for the night and get a start back in the morning. Whenever your circuit judge shows up, you might want him to take a look at the situation with Joan."

Hollis and Gentry exchanged a look again.

"You might even want to appoint a lawman before then," Matt added.

"You said you used to be a lawman?" Hollis asked.

"Sheriff of Fairview, Montana," Matt said. "That was a while back."

"I don't suppose you'd be interested—"

"From chief suspect to lawman?" Matt asked. "Now, how would that look?"

"I think he's right," Gentry said. "We'd better just find our own candidate."

"I tell you what," Matt said. "I'm heading back to

Fairview after a few years away. I don't know when I'll be getting there, but that's your best bet to find me if you want me to come back to testify."

Hollis looked unhappy. "We'd better mount up and start back," he said.

"In the dark?" one of the other men complained.

"Let's make a few miles and then camp for the night," Gentry suggested.

Matt felt that at least Hollis and Gentry were too embarrassed to bed down in his camp after their "capture" and "interrogation" of him came to nothing.

The six men retrieved their horses, mounted up, then looked down at Matt.

"Sorry about this, Wheeler," Robbie Gentry said. "And I guess I'm sorry I sent you out there to find work."

"I'm not," Matt said. "I got what I needed, a few dollars to continue my journey with."

"Well," Gentry said, "good luck to you."

The six men rode off, leaving Matt alone to make himself another pot of coffee. While it was boiling, he walked into the bushes and retrieved the pocket watch he had secreted there. Obviously, Joan had put it in with the shirts for the vigilantes to find and use to take Matt into custody. Matt had no doubt that Joan had decided to kill her husband herself. Poor Andy. He had liked the man. It must have been a great shock to be killed by his own wife after he was convinced she never really wanted him dead.

Angrily, Matt turned and threw the pocket watch out into the darkness.

CHAPTER TWELVE

M ATT GOT A very early start the next morning, because he wasn't sure Hollis and Gentry wouldn't wake up and decide they had made a mistake. He didn't want to be there if they came back to get him. It was only after he had ridden a few days that he felt sure they wouldn't be coming up behind him.

The money he had made working at the Mannix ranch kept him in the saddle for two weeks. It was only when he crossed out of Wyoming Territory into Montana Territory that he needed to stop and replenish his poke.

He had to stop in Bozeman, which was okay with him, since it was a large enough town to find some work in. First, he found a livery stable for his horse, then a cheap hotel. It had been a long time since he had stayed in a decent hotel, but even a cheap one was better than a Yuma Prison cell.

That done he found a small café where he was able to afford a bowl of beef stew. The weather was starting to get nippy. One of the things he was going to need to get while in Bozeman was a jacket. He needed to ride at least four or five more days north to get to Fairview, and it was just going to get colder.

"A piece of pie?" the middle-aged waitress asked when he was done with his stew.

"No, thanks," he said. "Just some more coffee."

But when she returned, she had the coffee and a piece of pie.

"Don't worry," she said as she set it down. "It's fine. We had an extra piece back there."

"Thanks."

He didn't understand it, but ever since he had gotten out of prison, waitresses seemed to want to feed him— starting with Kate in Yuma. He figured he just looked hungry after all those years of eating prison slop.

While he ate the pie, he thought about Kate in Yuma and felt bad all over again that he hadn't been able to do anything to save her. He touched his scalp where the bullet had creased him. There was a small scar that would always be a reminder. Just like the scars on his body would remind him of when he couldn't save Angie . . .

Eight years ago

Before prison, 1881 . . .

Matt Wheeler walked out of the hotel two weeks after he and Angie had been shot. She had died on the spot, while he had been shot in the shoulder and the leg. The doctor wanted him to stay off his feet for another week, but he couldn't do it. He had to get out there and find the three men who had caused his wife's death. He had seen Jason Pardee shoot her, but as far as he was concerned, all three of them were to blame—Pardee, the foreman Chester, and the third man.

Once he left the hotel, he walked directly to the livery to saddle his horse. He was going to start his search for the three men at the Double-K, see if any of the men there—including Karl Kaufman, the owner—could offer a suggestion as to where Chester might have gone after the robbery.

Kaufman himself was still in a foul mood, not only from being robbed by his own foreman, but from being hit over the head.

"How the hell would I know where Chester and the others went?" he demanded of Matt. "That's your job."

"Yes, it is," Matt said, "and I'm trying to do it. I want those three men worse than you do."

Kaufman suddenly realized what Matt meant, and he instantly turned contrite.

"Aw hell, Sheriff, I'm sorry," he said. "Of course you want them for killin' your wife. I'm so sorry—"

"I'm going to need to talk to all your hands, Mr. Kaufman," Matt said, cutting off the man's sympathies.

"Of course," Kaufman said. "I still haven't replaced my foreman, but Bill Coleman is top hand. I'll have him show you around."

"That's fine."

"Here," Kaufman said, suddenly handing Matt a glass of amber liquid, "have a drink, and I'll fetch him."

The drink was whiskey, and Matt tossed it back. Following his wife's death and his own shooting, he considered taking solace in one bottle of whiskey after another, but that would have allowed the three men to get away with everything they had done. He couldn't allow that. He put the empty glass down and just waited.

Moments later Kaufman returned with a tall man in his thirties who had his hat in his hand.

"This is Bill Coleman, Sheriff," Kaufman said.

"Sheriff," Coleman said, "I'm real sorry about—"

"Forget that," Matt said. "I appreciate everybody's

sympathies, but I need to find these men. Tell me, where do you think Chester would go when he had a pocket full of money?"

"Well," Coleman said, "you can talk to a lot of the other boys if you want, but Al Chester used to always talk about Sacramento."

"California?" Kaufman asked. "That's a helluva long way to go to spend money."

"He said they had the best women there," Coleman said.

"What about the other man who worked for you?" Matt asked. "What was his name?"

"I don't know," Kaufman said. "I told Chester to pick someone to take with us to the bank."

"That was Ed Corbin," Coleman said. "He hung around with Chester a lot. I'd say if Al went to Sacramento, Ed went with him."

"And Pardee?" Matt asked.

Coleman shrugged. "I didn't know him," he said. "Never heard of him until he robbed the bank."

"All right," Matt said, "if I find the other two in Sacramento, maybe they'll tell me where Pardee is."

"You've got no authority in California," Kaufman pointed out. "In fact, Sheriff, you've got none outside of the county."

"I'm not worried about that," Matt said. "I'll be leaving the badge here for another man to wear. I'm not concerned with the law, Kaufman. I want justice."

But what he truly wanted was vengeance, pure and simple.

M ATT HAD NEVER been to Sacramento before. He had been to San Francisco once, years ago, and that was what Sacramento reminded him of. There was a lot of foot traffic going back and forth, in and out of three- and four-story buildings. It was starkly evident that the nineteenth century was coming to its end. The days of the trail drives, the Indian wars, and the law of the gun would soon be gone.

But the law of the gun was what Matt Wheeler had in mind. He had a gun tucked into his belt; he was wearing a jacket to cover it up. He didn't want one of these new uniformed police officers stopping him to ask why he thought he needed a gun in Sacramento.

The word he'd gotten from the Double-K top hand, Bill Coleman, was that Al Chester would come to Sacramento for the women. Matt could have started prowling saloons and dance halls, but he figured a man like Chester, with his pockets full of money, would have been haunting the whorehouses. And as civilized a city as Sacramento might have been, it was still going to have whorehouses.

Once Matt had checked into a hotel, he slipped one of the red-uniformed bellboys a dollar and asked about whores.

"Well, sir," the wizened old bellboy said, "I could have someone come to your room—"

"No," Matt said, "I need a whorehouse, the kind a man with money in his pockets would go to."

"Ah, you want the Ginseng Palace?"

"Where's that?"

"In Chinatown," the bellboy said.

"Aren't there others?"

"You said you're lookin' for a man with money in his pockets, right?"

"That's right."

"The Ginseng Palace," the bellboy said. "It's expensive, and the girls are beautiful."

"All right, then," Matt said. "I'll try the Ginseng Palace. But if my man's not there, I'll be back for more suggestions."

"If he's in Sacramento," the bellboy said, "your man'll be there, sir."

C HINATOWN WAS EASY to find. The Ginseng Palace was a little harder. Matt started by asking men on the street, but in the end, he had to go into a few different saloons before he found someone who would tell him where it was located. It was a bartender who called a small Chinese man over.

"This is Li," the bartender said. "He can take you to the Ginseng."

"It is a special place," the Chinese man told him. "Cost much money, but is worth it."

"I'm sure it is," Matt said.

"I take you there."

"If you can just give me directions, that would be fine," Matt said.

"No, no," the Chinese man said, "I take you there."

He turned and began to trot away, his long braid—the Chinese man's queue—bouncing as he went. Matt had to walk quickly to keep up.

Matt was very aware that this could have been a trap, the bartender and the Chinese man working together to perhaps rob him. He kept his hand on the handle of the gun in his belt as they went. At the first sign of trouble, the gun was coming out.

He followed the little man through many dim Chinatown backstreets and alleys until Li stopped and turned.

"That Ginseng Palace," he said, pointing.

There was a red door at the end of a dark alley.

"You're sure?" Matt asked.

"I very sure," Li said, pointing again. "Ginseng Palace."

It certainly didn't look like the entrance to an expensive whorehouse.

Matt looked at Li, saw that the little man had his hand out. He didn't know what the custom was, but he gave Li a dollar.

"You have good time," Li said, and ran off back up the alley.

Matt turned and looked behind him. There was no one. Nor was there anything between him and the red door—no stairs, no windows, no cartons or crates for anyone to hide behind. All he had to do was walk to the door and knock. If there was going to be trouble, it was probably going to be inside.

He walked down the alley to the red door and knocked. It was opened right away, and a small Chinese girl wrapped in red looked out at him.

"Is this the Ginseng Palace?" he asked.

"Yes."

She had a lovely face, a Cupid's bow mouth, and dark almond-shaped eyes.

"I'm looking for a man."

The girl giggled. "No man here," she said, "only girl. So sorry."

She started to close the door, but Matt stopped it with his left hand, keeping his right hand down by his gun.

"I'm sorry. I didn't mean . . . like that," he said. "I'm trying to find a man who might be a customer of yours. I have some business with him."

"You want come in?" she asked. "But you don't want girl?"

"Now you've got it."

"You must pay," she said.

"I'll pay."

She smiled broadly at that, swung the door open, and said, "You come in!"

"Thank you."

He stepped through the door, and it was like stepping into another world of vivid colors. Lots of reds and blues and yellows and girls of all colors—white, black, yellow—in various stages of undress. At one point Matt didn't know quite where to look, which some of the girls found quite funny.

The girl who let him in was still walking just in front of him.

"If I tell you the man's name—," he started, but she turned on him, cutting him off.

"No names!" she said. "You want find man, you look. But you pay first."

She stuck her hand out, and he put some money in it. The trip had put quite a dent in the savings he and Angie had built up.

The girl frowned when she saw how much money he had given her and said, "You pay more!"

"How much more?" he asked.

"You pay more," she said again, "or you see Ming."

The largest Chinese man he had ever seen suddenly appeared behind her and scowled at him. He was not only over six feet tall, but seemed to be at least that wide, as well.

"And you'd be Ming," he said.

"You pay more!" Ming growled.

Matt paid more.

CHAPTER THIRTEEN

THE FIRST FLOOR of the whorehouse was like a Chinese New Year party. There were girls climbing all over men, wanting to be chosen to go upstairs. Several girls also tried to influence Matt, but quickly got the message that he was not there for sex.

Matt didn't see any of the three men he was looking for after a good forty minutes of searching. In addition, the big Chinese man Ming was watching *him* very closely. Matt finally decided he had no choice but to take a look upstairs, and for that, he was going to need a girl.

He looked around, saw a small blond girl standing in a corner with her arms wrapped around herself. She seemed to want to be in that whorehouse about as much as he did, so he walked over to her.

"Hello," he said.

"Hi." She looked at him nervously, tightened her arms and a flimsy blue robe around herself.

"I get the feeling you and me, we're in the same situation," he said.

"W-what do you mean?"

"I don't really want to be here," he said. "You don't, either, do you?"

"No," she said. "It's my first night." She seemed to relax a bit. "What's your name?"

"I'm Matt," he said. "What's yours?"

"I'll Ellie. Why are you here if you don't want to be?" she asked.

"I'm looking for a fella, and I was told he might be here. But I don't see him."

"Maybe he's upstairs with one of the girls," she offered.

"That's what I was thinking," he said, "but can I get up there on my own?"

"No," she said. "You have to go up with a girl. Oh, I see. . . ."

"If you take me up there," he said, "I'll pay you, but I won't touch you."

"Really?"

"I promise," he said. "I'm just looking for someone."

"Why?" she asked. "What did he do?"

He decided to be honest. "He robbed a bank and killed my wife."

"Omigod!"

"Will you take me upstairs?"

She looked around at the debauched celebration that was going on around them. "Yes," she said. "Come on."

She led him through the crowd to a staircase, and apparently, since he was going up with a girl, there was no reason for the big man to stop him. But he stood at the bottom of the stairs and watched until they had gone all the way up.

Matt looked down an empty hall with doors on both sides.

"If he's up here," the girl said, "he'll be in one of these rooms."

"I assume we can't just burst in," Matt said, "although I would like to surprise my man, if he's here."

"If you describe him," she offered, "I could stick my head into each room and have a look."

"That'd be okay?"

"Sure," she said. "Somebody usually does check to make sure everything's okay. And sometimes the people in the room don't even notice." She looked embarrassed. "They're, uh, too busy."

"Well," Matt said, "I'm looking for three men actually, but the one that might be here is in his thirties, very tall and thin. . . ."

"That should be enough," she said. "If I see a tall, thin man, I'll let you know."

"All right," he said, "but I'll move down the hall with you, just in case."

They started, and Ellie began opening doors and sticking her head in. Three times she withdrew, looked at Matt, and shook her head. But as she started to open the fourth door, one opened farther down the hall and a tall man in his thirties stepped out.

It was Al Chester.

The former foreman of the Double-K ranch recognized Matt immediately.

"Hey, no, wait—," he shouted, holding one hand out to ward off any movement from Matt. His other hand seemed to go behind him.

Matt felt he had no choice, but later, while sitting in his prison cell and playing it over in his head, he thought that perhaps he acted too quickly. Rage overtook him, so he drew his gun from his belt and fired once. The bullet struck the man in the chest and knocked him flat onto his back, and the screaming started. . . .

People began to pour from the rooms, in various stages of semi- to full nudity, and as Matt turned toward the staircase, Ming appeared, and that was the last thing he remembered before everything went black. . . .

WHEN MATT WOKE, he was in jail. As it turned out, Al Chester had been unarmed, so Matt had immediately been arrested and charged with murder. He explained his situation several times to the police, to a lawyer, to a judge in court, to a jury, and in the end, he was sentenced to serve time in Yuma Prison.

His lawyer had managed to argue some sort of diminished capacity, saying that Matt was still suffering from having watched his wife be killed before his very eyes. A jury had taken that into account, found him guilty but pleaded leniency. The judge, however, felt he had to make an example of a lawman who had apparently gone rogue for whatever reason.

Twelve years . . .

After prison, 1889 . . .

Work was not hard to find in Bozeman. He did some carpentry for a few days, a few days in a mercantile, a day or two in a livery stable, anything that didn't require a gun. No badge toting, no security jobs in a saloon or a bank, nothing that harkened back to his previous career as a lawman. At fifty years of age, he just didn't feel he had the stomach or stamina for those jobs.

But the ones he took enabled him to replenish his cash enough to continue his journey north. This time he felt sure he could make it the rest of the way to Fairview, Montana.

His goal was finally in sight.

CHAPTER FOURTEEN

R IDING DOWN FAIRVIEW, Montana's Front Street
started his heart pounding. This was the street
Angie had been killed on. As Matt reached the bank,
he reined in and stared at the ground, swearing he
could still see her blood. Of course, that wasn't the
case. It had long since been absorbed by the earth or
washed away by rain.

There were some people watching him ride into
town, but he thought it was normal curiosity surrounding a stranger rather than the fact that they recognized
him. He didn't look the way he had eight years ago. He
was gaunt, had more hair and a full beard—something
he had been working on since leaving Bozeman. He
didn't want to be immediately recognized. He needed
some time to himself before reacquainting himself
with the citizenry of Fairview.

He hadn't done the job he was hired to do. When he
had left town to look for the bank robbers, he'd had no
intention of returning with the money. He hadn't been

concerned about the bank, at all. He had only wanted vengeance for Angie. That was the reason he had left the badge behind—that and the fact that it would have done him no good once he rode out of the county.

So he wasn't in a hurry to renew old acquaintances again—not yet, anyway. Not until he stopped to see Angie's grave.

He rode through town all the way to the north end, where the town's boot hill was. Reining his horse in, he dismounted, tied it off, and took two steps before stopping. He couldn't continue. One more step would have taken him through the iron gateway and onto the cemetery grounds. Then he'd have to walk up the slope to find Angie's grave, since he didn't know exactly where it was.

But he couldn't.

He hadn't gone to her grave before leaving Fairview to find her killers, because he'd wanted to be able to come back and tell her that he'd caught them. But he hadn't. He had killed only one of them and then been tossed into prison. There was still two parts of the job left to be done.

But was he the man to do it?

"Matt?"

He turned, saw a man standing there, wearing a badge and staring at him. He wore a six-gun in a hip holster. "Pete?"

Peter Brown nodded and approached him. "I wasn't sure it was you," he said. "You're . . . thinner."

"And older," Matt said. "And look at you. You've filled out." His sometime deputy had always been a very thin young man, but now he had shoulders, a mustache, and a few miles on him. He was also wearing a sheriff's badge—the very badge Matt had left behind.

"I'm older, too," Pete said.

"Yeah, like what . . . thirty?"

"Are you goin' up to Angie's grave?" he asked Matt.

"I was," Matt said, "but I don't think I can now."

"Then how about a drink at the saloon?" Peter asked.

"That I can do," Matt agreed.

THE SALOON PETE Brown took Matt to was new to him. There were also other new buildings he saw as they walked his horse over to the saloon. The town had grown while he was away.

The saloon was called the Cactus House Saloon. Matt tied his horse in front and they went inside. It was early, so there were only a few customers. Peter got two beers from the bartender, and they walked to a back table.

"How long have you been sheriff?" Matt asked.

"Right from the time they realized you really weren't comin' back."

"I'll bet you're good at it," Matt said.

"I learned from you."

"The town looks like it's growing," Matt said, ignoring the compliment.

"You don't know the half of it," Pete said. "After you didn't come back with the money, the bank manager was fired, and the bank closed. Then the Double-K changed hands."

"Kaufman sold it?"

"He lost it," Pete said. "He never recovered from that lost payroll. He had to sell out, and he did for a song. A little bit after that, a new bank opened. In fact, a lot of people have come and gone since you left, Matt. There might not even be anyone here who remembers you, except for me."

He recalled that Pete had never called him Matt back then. Maybe now he was trying to establish their new boundaries.

"You're not by any chance here to get your job back, are you?" Pete asked.

"What? Hell, no, Pete. The badge is all yours."

"Then you really came back just to see Angie's grave?"

"I did," Matt said. "But now I realize I can't do it."

"Why not?"

"Because I haven't kept my promise to her yet."

"What promise?"

"To catch the men who killed her."

"You got one, right?" Pete asked.

"Yeah, and then I got thrown into Yuma Prison," Matt reminded him. "There are still two more out there, including Jason Pardee."

"Pardee," Pete said. "He was the bank guard, right?"

"Right. And he's the one who shot Angie."

"Oh," Peter said, "I didn't know which one did it. Do you have any idea where he is?"

"None."

"Then how do you expect to find him?"

"Maybe I won't ever find him," Matt said. "I'm still not sure I'm going to keep looking now that I'm out."

"Why not?"

"Well, for one thing, I'm not the same man I was back then," Matt said.

"You still have a gun in your belt."

"And my hand shakes when I take it out," Matt added.

"It looks pretty steady on that mug of beer," Pete observed.

"Yeah, well, I'm in a little better condition than I was when I first got out," Matt said, "but still nothing like I was eight years ago."

"I can see you look older," Peter said, "but maybe a shave and a haircut would take care of that."

Matt ran his hand over his beard. "No," he said,

"believe me. I'd still look older. There's nothing I can do about that."

"Matt . . . I've got to ask," Peter said. "How long do you intend to be in town?"

"I honestly don't know, Pete," Matt said. "I thought I was going to ride in, talk to Angie, and leave. But now . . ."

"Well . . ."

"Is it a problem, me being here?"

"Not for me."

"Then for who?"

"Well . . . maybe the mayor."

Back when Matt was sheriff the mayor's name was Walt Hoffman. "Is it still Hoffman?"

"No," Pete said, "he's been gone a long time. The mayor's name is Ben Pickett, and let's say he's very involved in everything that goes on in town."

"Does he know I'm here?"

"Not yet."

"But you're going to tell him."

"I have to, Matt," Pete said almost apologetically.

"Is he really going to care?" Matt asked.

"I guess that'll depend on what he knows about you," Pete said.

"He's going to know what you tell him, Pete," Matt said. "Tell him I'm harmless."

"Are you?"

When Matt had first walked out of Yuma Prison, he would have said yes, that he was a broken, harmless man. At the prospect of facing Angie's grave site, he still felt "broken," but perhaps "harmless" didn't quite describe him anymore. What would he have done if he were face-to-face with Jason Pardee? He wasn't sure, but it certainly wouldn't be something "harmless."

"I didn't think so," Pete said before Matt could answer.

"Well," Matt said, "I'm not here to harm anybody."

"And if you saw Pardee or the other man walkin' down the street?"

"His name is Ed Corbin. I'd know him if I saw him," Matt said with certainty. "After all, he shot me."

Matt picked up his beer. Pete had noticed that his hand was steady. He had no idea how effective Matt would be with a gun, but he certainly looked deadly with a beer mug.

CHAPTER FIFTEEN

M ATT AND PETE left the saloon together.

"Are there any people still here who I knew eight years ago?" Matt asked.

"Matt," Pete said, "did you even have any friends here back then?"

"Not really," Matt said. "It's not a lawman's job to make friends. Not when he might have to throw them in a cell some night."

"Exactly," Pete said. "I'm still here. There are still some storekeepers, but a lot of people left before the town started to grow, and a lot more have come in since. It's pretty much a new place. In fact, the mayor is considering a name change."

"I hate to think Angie was buried in Fairview, but will be lying in some other town for eternity."

"You haven't seen the grave yet, Matt," Pete said. "Is she really there?"

"Good point."

"There's a priest in town," Pete said, "since we built a church. Maybe you should talk to him."

"I've never been a very religious man, Pete," Matt said.

"Like you said, you ain't the same man you once were." Pete put his hand on Matt's shoulder. "Let's get a steak together while you're here."

"Sure," Matt said, "let's do that."

Neither of them suggested a time to do it, though, and they went their separate ways.

S INCE HE HADN'T yet had the nerve to go to Angie's grave, it was necessary to board his horse at the livery and then get a hotel room. He didn't know the hostler, and he didn't know the clerk who checked him in at the Longview Hotel. (When he had last been in town, it had been called the Fairview.)

He got a room overlooking Front Street, stared down at the street after dropping his saddlebags and rifle onto the bed. Coming back to Fairview did not feel like coming home, but to be fair, it had never felt that way. He had taken the job because Angie wanted him to put down roots, and they had lived there less than two years when she was killed. So there was nothing about this town he had missed and nothing he was sorry to see had changed.

As for friends, what he told Peter was true. He had never felt it was part of a lawman's job to make friends—not a deputy marshal in Judge Parker's court, and certainly not a town sheriff. So while there might have still been people in town he knew, there were certainly no old friends.

With nothing to do, he decided to take a walk around town and see if he could work up the gumption to go back to boot hill.

He left the room and went downstairs.

* * *

A FTER A SHORT walk he found himself outside the house he had shared with Angie. Apparently, no one was living there now and hadn't been for some time. The fence had fallen flat a long time ago, and a tree had been knocked down, probably by a storm, and landed on the roof. Windows were shattered, and the front door was hanging by one hinge. He went inside and looked up at the gaping hole in the roof caused by the tree.

There was some furniture in the house, and he recognized it as the sofa and chairs he and Angie had bought. They had since been soaked by rain and infested with vermin. If he needed another indication that Fairview was not home, this was it. He turned and walked out and away, leaving the house behind for good.

His next stop was boot hill, but once again he stopped at the gate.

"Angie, if you can hear me," he said, "I'm sorry for what happened. They stuck me in prison. I wasn't able to keep my promise, and now I don't know if I'm the man to do it. If it's okay with you, my love, it'll take me a little while to find out. But I promise, the time will come when I'll be up there to visit you. Another promise, I know, but one I swear I'll keep."

He turned and walked away from boot hill with his shoulders slumped.

M ATT DIDN'T SEE Pete Brown again that day, so when he got hungry he went to get his own steak. There were a couple of places where he used to eat when he was sheriff, one alone and one usually with Angie. The second one, the Majestic Café, was still there, but he couldn't bring himself to go inside.

The first one had changed hands and names, which suited him, so he went inside and was shown to a table. The new owners had improved the furnishings. He only hoped they had improved the food. He had eaten at the previous incarnation only out of convenience and because they fed prisoners when he had them.

It had been called the Hot Stove Café, but was now called the Brick Oven Café. He didn't find much imagination present in either name, but it remained to be seen about the food.

Half the tables were empty, and there were two waiters, so he got attention pretty quickly.

"What can I get for you, sir?" the waiter asked. "A menu?"

"No," Matt said, "I'll just have a steak dinner and a beer."

"Good choice," the gray-haired man said. "It's what I usually have. I'll be right back with your beer."

Matt looked around the room while he waited, didn't see anyone he knew. There were a couple of families, two couples, one table with two men seated together. He was the only person dining alone.

The waiter returned with the beer and a basket of bread and said, "Your steak will be out shortly."

"Thank you."

Matt sipped the beer while he continued to wait, buttered a piece of bread. Since Fairview had been his destination for months, he wasn't at all sure how much money he had now that he was there. He decided to wait until he got back to his room to count it. Then he would have to decide what his next move was going to be. He knew he couldn't stay in Fairview, but neither could he leave until he was able to walk up boot hill to Angie's grave.

When the steak came, he decided to give it all his

attention and forget about everything else, at least for the time it took to finish his meal.

W HEN HE PUSHED the plate away and washed the last bite down with the last of the beer, he took a deep breath and sat back. For that short time, his mind had been blank, and it had been a blessed reprieve. He had also done that in his cell when he could, just put his head back and allowed his mind to go blank. But as always, it all came flooding back, and he had to deal with the memories.

But there was another way, something he hadn't tried yet, and he was now considering it. That was to buy a bottle of whiskey, take it to his room, drink it, and see what happened. Would it drive him into a dreamless oblivion, or would it open his mind up to all possibilities and allow him to come to the right decision?

Or would it simply turn him into the town drunk?

He decided to give it a try.

"Another beer, sir?" the waiter asked.

"No, thanks."

"And the steak?"

"It was fine." It had actually been kind of tough, but it had gotten rid of his hunger.

"What about some pie?"

"No, thanks." Matt actually wasn't sure he would have been able to afford a slice of pie. "I'll just pay my check."

When the waiter gave him his bill, he saw that—as he had feared—he wouldn't have been able to pay for the pie. In fact, he had just enough money for that bottle of whiskey.

He paid the bill and left.

* * *

HE WOKE THE following morning bleary-eyed, dry-mouthed, lying on his hotel bed still dressed, including boots. His gun wasn't in his belt. He looked around for it and found it under the bed, where he had to leave it for the time being. He could see it, but he couldn't reach it, and bending over would have been a very bad idea.

After a series of dry heaves, he sat up, grateful that he hadn't retched all over himself and the room. He staggered out of bed and to the window. Looking down at the street, he realized where he was. He frowned as he tried to remember the previous night.

He walked back to the bed and looked at the empty whiskey bottle lying on the floor. That was when he recalled the point of bringing that bottle to his room.

He sat on the bed, rubbed his hands over his face, trying to clear his head. When he got out of prison, it had been the start of winter. Now it was summer, and the heat was doing nothing to improve his physical condition. One glance at the pitcher and basin on the chest of drawers told him that wouldn't be enough for the task that needed to be done. He left the room and went down to the front desk.

"Yes, sir?" the clerk asked.

"Do you have bath facilities, or do I need to go elsewhere?" Matt asked.

"Oh, sir, we have fine facilities on the premises. Can I arrange for a tub?"

"Yes," Matt said. "A hot one."

"And a shave, sir?"

"Did I ask for a shave?" Matt replied.

"Oh, uh, no, sir," the young clerk said. "Sorry, sir. I didn't mean—"

"How long?" Matt asked.

"Fifteen minutes, sir?"

"I'll be down," Matt said. "Do you have towels, or do I need to bring one with me?"

"We have plenty of towels, sir," the clerk said, "and soap."

Matt nodded, went back up to his room, wondering how the hell he was going to pay for a bath and another night in the hotel.

CHAPTER SIXTEEN

M ATT LOUNGED IN the hot bath, allowing the water to seep into his pores, hopefully sucking the liquor out along with the despair. He knew that he needed to change his outlook and that it would take more than a hot bath to do it.

He dried off, dressed in the last fairly clean shirt he owned. He was going to need a job, and it would be to his advantage if no one in town remembered him from eight years ago. After all, he had only been sheriff there less than two years, and apparently anyone connected to the bank robbery was gone. That was going to work in his favor.

He went to the front desk and told the clerk he was finished.

"We'll add it to your bill, sir."

"You do that."

Matt left the hotel and walked to the sheriff's office, hoping to find Pete Brown in. Instead, he found a deputy, a young man about the age Pete had been eight years ago.

"The sheriff'll be in soon," the deputy said. "Is there somethin' I can do for you?"

"No," Matt said, "thanks. Pete and I are old friends."

"You're Matt Wheeler," the deputy said. "Used to be sheriff here before Sheriff Brown."

"That was a long time ago," Matt said. "But you remember?"

"I remember the day of the robbery," the young deputy said, "but don't worry, Sheriff. Nobody else does. This town has changed a lot since then."

"I'm not a sheriff anymore, Deputy," Matt said.

"Yes, sir," the deputy said. "Should I tell Sheriff Brown you stopped by?"

"Yeah, that'd be good. Thank you, Deputy."

T HE JOBS THAT had been the easiest for Matt to get over the past few months had been in livery stables. There were always chores to be done there, and he knew how to do everything from baling hay to shoeing horses.

There were two liveries in town. The hostler at the first one he went to said he didn't have any work. The man at the second one—the one where he had boarded his horse—said he had a few things that needed doing.

"But it won't take more than a day or two," Dwight Bennett finished.

"That's fine," Matt said.

"And I can't pay you much."

"Anything's better than what I have in my pockets now," Matt said.

He started right away, feeding stock, shoeing a couple of animals, and sweeping out some stalls. At the end of the afternoon, the hostler gave him a couple of dollars. If Matt got the same thing the following day, he'd be able to pay for a couple of meals and his hotel bill.

As he was walking back to his hotel, wondering how cheap a meal he could subsist on, he heard his name.

"Matt!"

He turned, saw Sheriff Pete Brown crossing the street toward him.

"My deputy said you were lookin' for me," Pete said.

"I just wanted to talk some more," Matt said.

"Well, let's do it over that steak," Pete said. "My treat—which means the town's treat, right?"

"Sounds good to me," Matt said. "You lead the way."

S HERIFF BROWN TOOK Matt to what he called "the best restaurant in town." It was called the Ponderosa Steak House.

"I eat here all the time," Pete said, which was obvious, because they were taken to an empty table, even though the place was crowded.

"Ah, Sheriff, good to see you," the waiter said to Pete.

"Harry," Pete said, "we'll have two steak suppers with all the trimmings and a couple of beers."

"Comin' up, Sheriff," the man said, and hurried away.

"What was it you wanted from me, Matt?" Pete asked.

"Just some advice. I was going to look for work today, something simple to make a few dollars."

"Did you find anythin'?"

"I swept out some stalls at the livery," Matt said, "changed some shoes. Got the few dollars I was looking for. Probably do that tomorrow, too."

"That's a little beneath you, ain't it?" Pete asked. "I mean, considerin' who you, uh, well—"

"Used to be?" Matt asked.

"Well, yeah."

"Those days are gone, Pete," Matt commented. "Like I said, I'm a different man. Honest work is honest work."

"I guess so."

"Did you talk to the mayor about me?"

"No, not yet," Peter said. "I had some things to do today. I'll talk to him tomorrow."

The waiter came with their plates and beers, quick service for the sheriff. To Matt, the waiter looked nervous as he set the food down.

"Everything okay, Sheriff?" he asked. "The way you like it?"

"It's fine, Eddie," Pete said. "That'll be all."

"Yes, sir," Eddie said, and scurried away.

"He seems shaky," Matt said.

"He's just not a very good waiter," Pete said. "Go ahead, Matt. Dig in."

As they ate, Matt noticed many of the other diners sneaking looks over their way, but never openly doing so. He didn't think any of them recognized him, so he assumed the looks were meant for Pete Brown. In some cases he would even have said they were frightened looks.

"How many deputies have you got, Pete?" Matt asked.

"Just the one you met," Pete said. "I've taken him under my wing, the way you kinda did with me."

"He was very respectful," Matt said.

"Well," Pete said, "I have to admit I did tell him you were in town, and he remembers you from when he was a kid."

"One of the few," Matt observed.

"Right," Pete said. "Look, Matt, if you want to get a better job I can probably help ya with that."

"I'm good, Pete. I don't need anything permanent, you know. I'm not going to be putting roots down here."

"You never did, did ya?" Pete asked. "You always seemed to be a little restless to me when you lived here."

"You're probably right," Matt said. "I'd spent a lot of time on the trail before coming here. It just didn't feel right."

"But you did it for Angie."

"I did," Matt admitted. "You know, I never thought I was the marrying kind, Pete, but she changed that."

Pete leaned closer. "What was it like for you in Yuma? I mean, a lawman in prison. That couldn't've been easy."

"It wasn't. Believe me. I had to make the right kind of connections to survive."

"Who could you've found inside to connect with?" Pete wondered.

"Believe me," Matt said, "there were others inside who didn't really belong there."

"Really?" Pete asked. "I just tend to think everybody in prison belongs there. Oh, except you, of course."

"Not a lot of people thought I was an exception, Pete," Matt said, thinking back. . . .

Yuma Prison

No time was wasted during Matt's first day in Yuma Prison. The inmates let him know they were aware he was an ex-lawman. Even as he was marched to his cell, they called out their thoughts, telling him he wasn't going to last very long in there.

When the two guards stopped outside a cell, he breathed a momentary sigh of relief. At least they weren't in on the plan.

"Here's your new cellmate, Cates," one guard said to the man in the cell. "Step back."

The man called Cates took several steps back, and they opened the cell door.

"In you go, Wheeler," one guard said.

Matt stepped through the open doorway, only to have it slammed closed tightly behind him.

His cellmate, Cates, sat on the bottom bunk and stared at him.

"Matt Wheeler," Matt said.

Cates stared a little longer, then stood up and stuck out his hand. He was lucky if he was five and a half feet tall.

"Harley Cates," he said. "Gladda meet ya. You're in here for murder?"

"That's right," Matt said.

"Top bunk's yours," Cates said. "We got a lot ta talk about."

"We do?"

"Well," Cates said, "you don't think they stuck you in with me by accident, do ya?"

"What do you mean?"

"You're an ex-lawman, Wheeler," Cates said. "Chances are, you'll never walk outta this place alive if you don't know how to survive. That's what I'm here for."

"So this was planned?" Matt asked. "You and me as bunkmates?"

"Why'd ya think they sent you to Yuma Prison from Sacramento?"

Matt had wondered that himself. He had been the sheriff of a Montana town and killed a man in California. Why the hell send him to Yuma?

"I figured they were overcrowded there."

"Not a chance," Cates said. "Somebody got ya put in here with me, and don't ask me who. All I know is I'm supposed to make sure you survive, so siddown and listen up. We don't know when they'll catch on and split us up."

Matt sat and listened.

CHAPTER SEVENTEEN

EVEN AFTER THE lessons he'd learned from Harley Cates, survival wasn't easy. Cates told him that every ounce of attitude he ever exhibited as a lawman had to be tossed aside.

"If you even try to act like you still got a badge on, you won't last a day," Cates said.

"Then what am I supposed to act like?" Matt asked.

"What you are," Cates said. "A con. I'm gonna teach you how to walk like one, talk like one, and eat like one."

"Eat?"

"They're gonna feed you slop in here, and you gotta eat it like you're afraid somebody's gonna take it from you. Wrap your arms around your plate and lean over it. Protect it. And if somebody does try ta take it from you, you fight for it."

"For slop?"

"Believe me, when slop's all they give ya, you'll fight for it," Cates said.

"How long have you been inside, Cates?" Matt asked.

"I been here a coupla days, waitin' for ya," Cates said. "But I been in one prison or another most of my life."

"And what do you get for helping me?"

"They're gonna put me in the prison of my choice."

"They're not going to let you go?"

"Let me go?" Cates said. "I don't wanna be out there. I wanna be in a nice warm prison where they feed me, dress me, and lemme sleep. I tol' ya, I been inside more than I been out. I like it better here."

"Where do you want to end up?"

"I ain't decided yet," Cates said. "Now, stop talkin' and listen up!"

L IFE INSIDE WAS hard, unless you were a lifer like Cates. Matt could see what the man liked about it, though. He didn't have to worry about making a living or feeding himself. It was all done for him. But Matt wasn't ready to live that way.

They took Cates out of his cell after a week.

"I'm bein' transferred," the little man said. "That means I've taught you all I can. The rest is up ta you."

"I'll do my best, Cates," Matt said as the two men shook hands. "Thanks."

"Good luck," Cates said as they led him from the cell.

Matt never found out who had put Cates in Yuma to be his mentor. He also never found out what happened to the little man.

The other cons tested him, tried to see how much they could get away with. Matt had several fights, got cut a couple of times, though not seriously. For the most part, the guards would stand around and bet on which con would come out on top. Of course, if the top guard was there or the warden was walking by, they would break it up.

Cates had been right about the slop. It took only a few weeks, but finally the hunger pains took over and Matt ate every bite.

His cellmate right after Cates was put there to test his fortitude. They had two fights, and once Matt broke the man's arm, they moved him. The next cellmate was a reader. All he did was sit on his bunk and read until he and Matt were taken out to eat, work, or just get exercise.

After the first year, Matt was accepted as just another con. Of course, every so often a new prisoner would come in and recognize him, and it would start again. But after the first few years, he had bonded with some of the other cons, and when a new man came in, he was read the riot act.

By the fourth year, with no more fighting to be done, Matt started to eat less, exercise less, and lose weight. It was all a product of depression. Having a cellmate who didn't talk left him alone with his thoughts, and they always strayed to Angie.

By year five, he was a shell of the man he was. The few fights he still had he lost and didn't much care. He would either lick his wounds in his cell or in the infirmary. By year six, he didn't care if somebody killed him. At least he'd be with Angie.

Then year seven began, and somebody came in from the governor's office and started to talk about a possible pardon. His name was Arthur Selwin, a tall, tweed-clad man in his late forties whom Matt had never heard of.

"Who's talking about a pardon?" Matt asked.

"The governor himself," Selwin said.

"Why?"

"Does it matter why, Mr. Wheeler?" Selwin asked. "Don't you want a pardon?"

"I'll have to think about that."

"I don't understand."

"I've sort of come to the decision that I'm going to die in here."

"Even without a pardon, you only have five more years."

"And during that time, I figured I'd probably either die or get killed."

"Is that what you want?"

"I told you, Mr. Selwin," Matt said, "I'll have to think about it."

"Well," Selwin said, "I'll come back in a few days and see how you feel. Meanwhile, the governor will move forward on this. It might take a while."

Matt nodded as Selwin left. It was only a few minutes later that he thought a pardon wouldn't be the worst thing to happen.

B Y THE TIME Selwin returned, Matt had come to terms with the idea of a pardon. Now if he didn't get one, he'd probably just hang himself in his cell rather than wait for somebody else to kill him. But once he told Selwin he was on board, it went through, and he walked out of Yuma seven and a half years into a twelve-year stretch.

A new man, all right, but not the man he had ever wanted to be . . .

After prison, 1889 . . .

Now back in Fairfield, Matt certainly couldn't return to being the man he had been before prison, and he didn't want to be the man he had become while *in* prison. And he definitely didn't like the man he had been since getting out of prison. So he had to come to a decision.

Just who the hell would he be now?

A S THEY FINISHED their supper and Matt finished telling Pete about the pardon, the sheriff asked, "How did that come about, anyway?"

"The pardon? I'm not sure, to tell you the truth. Apparently, the governor decided the sentence was too harsh for an ex-lawman who had lost his wife."

"I thought so when I heard about it," Pete admitted.

Matt looked around again as the waiter came back to their table.

"Pete," Matt said, "is it my imagination, or are these folks afraid of you?"

"I'm the law, Matt," Pete said. "It's like you said, the law don't make friends."

Matt *had* said that, but having the townsfolk fear you was going too far the other way.

"Dessert, Sheriff?" the waiter asked.

"I don't think so, Eddie," Pete replied. "I think we're done."

"Yes, sir," the waiter said. "I guess we'll see you for breakfast, then."

Matt noticed that they walked out of the place without paying. That was something he had never done when he had been the law. He didn't accept free meals. And come to think of it, while he didn't make friends, he also didn't have people afraid of him.

He wondered what it was about Peter Brown that scared them? He knew Peter had always fancied himself a hand with a gun. Had that attitude worsened with age?

"I've got rounds to do, Matt," Pete said when they got outside.

"That's okay. I think I'll get a drink at the saloon and then head to my room. Tomorrow I'll be back working in the livery stable."

"Make sure you tell Dwight you're a friend of mine and he'd better treat you right."

"I'll tell him," Matt said. "Thanks."

He watched as Pete walked off, noticed a couple of women sort of cringe as he went by. Pete ignored them. As they reached Matt, he tipped his hat to them, and they actually smiled, even though he knew his bath hadn't kept him from looking unkempt.

Maybe a shave and a haircut wouldn't be a bad idea.

CHAPTER EIGHTEEN

MATT HAD GOTTEN the word from the bartender in the Cactus House Saloon the night before. Pete Brown was quick to employ his gun when it came to keeping the peace.

"A drunk or a gunhand, he don't care," the man said. "He uses that gun of his. And he's quick with it."

At that point the bartender seemed to decide that he had said enough. He moved on down the bar, leaving Matt to finish his beer alone.

The next morning when Matt got to the livery, he decided to see what Dwight had to say about the sheriff.

"Does the sheriff keep his horse here?" he asked.

"Yeah, he does," Dwight said, "not that he pays for the privilege."

"The sheriff takes handouts?" Matt asked.

"And we ain't got much choice about it," Dwight

said. "The café, the saloon, me, it don't matter. You gotta give it to him free or else."

"Or else what?"

With a sour look, Dwight said, "Nobody wants ta find out. Can you check that bay for me? I think she's got a loose shoe."

"Got it."

Matt didn't question Dwight about the sheriff anymore, and he certainly didn't tell him that they were friends. He just kept quiet the rest of the day and did his work.

At the end of the day, Dwight gave Matt three dollars and said, "I'm sorry. I can't use ya after today."

"That's okay, Dwight. I appreciate the two days."

"But a friend of mine's got a warehouse at the far end of town. I talked to him, and he said he could use some help. His name's Jeff Bond. Go and see him in the mornin'. But don't let him underpay you the way I did. He's got more money than me."

"Hey, thanks, Dwight," Matt said. "I'll do that. And if you come over to the saloon later, I'll buy you a beer."

"You ain't spendin' that money I just gave ya buyin' me a beer," Dwight said. "I'll do the buyin'. I'll see ya later at the Cactus."

"It's a deal," Matt said, and left.

Well, the word he had gotten on Sheriff Peter Brown was not what he had hoped. Apparently, his young deputy had grown into a full-blown bully, using his ability with a gun—and his badge—to get his way.

It was disappointing, but there was nothing Matt could do about it, even if he wanted to. It wasn't his responsibility to save the town of Fairfield from being under Pete Brown's thumb.

He had his own problems to deal with.

He decided to start with a haircut and a shave.

* * *

T HE BARBERSHOP WAS still open, so Matt wasted no time spending fifteen cents of his money. When he got out of the chair and looked in the mirror, he was shocked.

"No good?" the Italian barber asked.

Matt stared at his face. He was amazed that it was the same face he'd had eight years ago. A little older maybe, but he had been afraid to shave off all the hair for fear of what he would see underneath. And what he saw was . . . Matt Wheeler.

"No," he said, "it's fine. Good job."

He touched his face, which, while in prison, had acquired an angular shape, sharp points and edges because of the weight loss. But now that he had shaved, he could see that, during the months he had been outside, he had put the weight back on.

"Here," he said, giving the barber money, and then added a nickel tip.

"Thank you, sir," the barber said. *"Buona sera."*

"Yeah, right," Matt said.

He left the barbershop, his hat pulled down over his eyes, in case somebody might recognize him now that he was clean-shaven. But he needn't have worried. Now that he wasn't shaggy, nobody was even looking at him.

He went to his hotel, and as he walked through the lobby to the stairs, the clerk called out, "Sir? Can I help you?"

Matt walked to the desk. "Matt Wheeler, room five," he said. "I've had a shave."

"Oh, yeah," the clerk said. "Now I recognize you. Okay, go ahead, Mr. Wheeler."

Matt went up to his room, took his gun from his belt,

and set it on the table next to the bed, then sat. He put his hands out in front of him and stared at them. They still trembled, but not as much as they had when he had walked out of prison. He picked up the gun and held it out, watched it tremble slightly. He hadn't used this weapon since his release, didn't even know if it would fire or just blow up in his hand. But he never really expected to fire it, because he didn't want to be that kind of man again.

Now he was having second thoughts.

He couldn't walk up boot hill to Angie's grave until he fulfilled his promise to her to see that the men responsible for her death came to justice one way or another. But in order to get that done, he was going to need two things.

A gun he could rely on.

And a badge.

THE NEXT DAY Matt could easily see why Jeff Bond had more money than Dwight. His warehouse was the largest building in town.

"Dwight's right," Bond said. "I could use some help. I might even need you for a week."

"That suits me," Matt said.

"You got any objection to usin' a broom?"

"Just point me to it," Matt said.

Bond, a big, barrel-chested man, slapped Matt on the back with a big hand and said, "This might work!"

THEY AGREED ON a price, and Bond agreed to pay Matt at the end of each day. In a week's time, Matt would have enough money to outfit himself. All he had to figure out was where he was going.

It was hard work, involving a lot more than using a

broom. Bond had Matt lifting and moving things, sometimes crates that took the two of them to shift around.
And Bond had him working till late in the day, so some
days he paid Matt more than others.

At the end of the week, Bond even asked Matt to
stay on for three more days, so in all Matt was paid for
ten days' work. Matt no longer had to worry about how
he was going to pay for his hotel.

During the ten days, he had eaten cheaply, stayed
away from the saloons, and kept away from poker for
fear he would lose what he had. And because Bond
kept him late most days, he didn't have much time to
spend talking to Pete Brown.

A T BREAKFAST THE morning after his last day, he
continued the soul-searching he had been doing
most nights. He knew now he was going to have to continue the search he had started eight years ago, which
had ended so abruptly in Sacramento. But to do that, he
also knew he was going to need more authority than
he'd had back then, which had been none.

He was eating the last of his flapjacks in a café near
his hotel when Sheriff Pete Brown walked in.

"You mind if I sit?" Pete asked.

"No, go ahead," Matt said. "Have some coffee."

"That's okay," Peter said. "This ain't a social call."

"Oh? What's on your mind, Pete? Or should I call
you Sheriff?"

"We ain't talked in a while, Matt," Pete said. "You
remember I was gonna tell the mayor about you?"

"I remember."

"Well," Pete said, "he's kinda worried that you've
been in town for so long."

"Yes, I know. I've been here longer than I figured,
but I needed to build up a stake before I could leave."

"And have you?"

"Enough to get me back on the trail, yeah," Matt said.

"Well, that's good," Pete said, "because he told me to run you out of town today."

"Did he?"

"And he's my boss, Matt."

"So that's why you came here this morning?"

"That's it," Pete said. "You've got to go."

"Tell me something, Pete," Matt said. "Is the mayor the only person in town who's not afraid of you?"

"Like I said, he's my boss," Pete said. "Everyone else is beneath me, but not him."

"Beneath you," Matt repeated. "That's really how you feel about the citizens you serve?"

"I don't serve them," Peter said. "I serve the town and the mayor."

"Does that mean—"

"I don't have to explain myself to you, Matt," Peter said, cutting him off. "You ruined your life, so I ain't gonna be takin' any advice from you about mine." Pete stood up. "You gotta go. You got a horse?"

"I do."

"Then get it saddled and be out of town before dark," Pete said.

"I've got a few provisions to pick up," Matt said, "but I think I can do that, Sheriff."

"Good," Pete said, "because I don't wanna have to force you out, Matt."

"With your gun, you mean?"

"With my badge," Pete said. "*My* badge, Matt."

"I'm not here for your badge."

"That's what you say, but look at you. You cut your hair and shaved. You're doing jobs, tryin' to get known around town. Do you think you're gonna run against me?"

"Pete," Matt said, "I'm leaving town."

"Yeah, you are."

"Pete!" Matt called as the sheriff started to leave.

The young lawman turned around.

"I'll be coming back," Matt said. "When I'm finished, I'll be back, but only to see Angie's grave."

Pete walked back to the table. "You decided to go lookin' for them?"

"Yes," Matt said, "it's what I told Angie I'd do."

"It's what got you tossed into prison, Matt."

"Yes, and that's slowed me down some. But I'm going to get back on track."

"And it's got nothin' to do with wantin' this badge back, huh?"

The badge on Pete's chest would have been no good to Matt at all. He had other plans.

"Not a thing," he said.

Pete gave him a hard look, turned, and walked out.

If Matt had any doubts about getting started that day, they had been cleared away.

CHAPTER NINETEEN

Fort Smith, Arkansas

Approximately six weeks later . . .

B Y THE TIME Matt Wheeler rode into Fort Smith, he
thought he had his future figured out. Of course,
it was all going to depend on Judge Isaac Parker. Matt
had ridden for the judge for almost six years before
resigning to be the sheriff of Fairview, Montana. He
hadn't had any contact with the man since then, and
he had no way of knowing what Parker's reaction might
have been to Matt's incarceration. Known as "the Hanging Judge," Parker was an outspoken law-and-order fa-
natic. Matt wondered how his presence in Fort Smith
would be treated.

He had taken some odd jobs along the way, so when
he arrived, he had enough money to board his horse
and get a hotel room for a few days. Hopefully, his plan

was going to work, and after Fort Smith, he would no longer have to worry about money.

After he left his gear in his room, he went down to the street to see how Fort Smith had changed since he had last been there. Ever since his release from Yuma, he had been noticing how modernized the West had become in just the seven and a half years he was inside. As the year eighteen ninety approached, he realized men like him—the man he had been before prison— were fading away. The law of the gun, which had existed in the West for years, was considered a thing of the past. But his concern now was how much Judge Parker had changed since he had last seen him.

He knew of a steak house the judge had frequented for his suppers, and he hoped this was still the case. He had no intention of presenting himself to Parker in his chambers. Rather, he was going to simply let himself be seen and hope for the best outcome.

The Bighorn Steak House was still there, still doing a brisk business, probably even more successful now that the town was growing. Matt hoped it was still where Judge Parker took his supper.

Matt had a steak dinner, but Judge Parker never showed up. The second night he had a bowl of beef stew—it was cheaper—but the judge still didn't appear. There was, however, an empty table in the corner, even though the dining room was full. Matt had never had a meal there with the judge, so he didn't know if the table was reserved for him.

When the waiter brought the bill, Matt said casually, "How come that table's empty when this place is so busy?"

"Oh, that's reserved every night for Judge Parker, sir."

"Even when he doesn't come in?"

"Well, we never know what nights he'll be here, so we just hold it for him. After all, he's a very important man."

"Still?" Matt asked. "I thought with things changing—"

"Ain't changed so much," the waiter said, "that the judge's court ain't still busy."

"I see. Well, thanks."

Matt left the Bighorn, knowing he couldn't afford to eat there every night, hoping the judge would show up. He needed a new plan.

THE JUDGE HAD himself a huge building, with jail cells on the first floor and his office and chambers on the second. When his sentences were carried out and men were scheduled to hang on the gallows, a permanent fixture out front, he would watch from the window of his office. When the trapdoor tripped and necks snapped, he'd close the window.

But it didn't look like anyone was going to die soon. Matt decided to take up a position across the street and just wait for the evening the judge would come out and head for the steak house. Luckily for him and his dwindling purse, it happened within the next two days.

The front doors opened, and Judge Isaac Parker came out. He looked the same from across the street, tall and straight, clad in a black suit and a black hat. Matt knew that he and the judge were about the same age, but Parker didn't seem to have changed.

Matt gave him a head start and then followed. Even if Parker wasn't going to the steak house, Matt might be able to contrive a chance meeting. But he didn't have to worry about that. The judge went directly to the Bighorn Steak House and entered.

Matt gave the judge time to sit down and order,

maybe even get served, before he entered the restaurant.

"I'm sorry, sir," he was told by the man who greeted him at the door, "but there are no tables at the moment."

"That's okay," Matt said. "I can wait."

"Very well, sir," the older man said. "I'm your host, and I'll let you know when a table is empty."

"Thanks."

Matt stole a glance over at the judge's table, where the man was intent on cutting into his steak. He stared at the judge, hoping Parker would feel his eyes and look up. He didn't. He was very preoccupied by the food on his plate.

"Sir?"

Matt realized the host was trying to get his attention.

"Sorry. What?"

"A table has become available. This way, please."

Matt started to follow the man when he heard his name, this time from across the room.

"Matt Wheeler?"

He turned, saw Judge Parker looking at him.

"Judge?"

"Come over here," Parker said, waving at him. "Never mind the table, Walter. Mr. Wheeler is going to sit with me."

"Yes, sir," Walter said. "Sir?"

"I can find my way," Matt said.

"And bring him a beer and a steak," Parker called to Walter.

The other diners had looked up during the disturbance, then watched Matt walk across the room to Parker's table.

"Matt Wheeler," Parker said again, looking up at Matt but not smiling. "Have a seat, Marshal."

Matt sat, and the other diners went back to their meals.

"Not a marshal anymore, Judge," Matt said. "Not even a lawman."

"I heard about what happened," the judge said. "Your wife and your prison term. I was sorry to hear it all."

"Yeah, thanks."

"What are you doing now?" Parker asked.

Up close Matt could see the lines on the other man's face, much like the ones on his own. But Parker was wearing his age better than Matt was.

"Not much," Matt said. "Just . . . drifting."

"You never used to do that," Parker said. "You've always been a man with purpose."

"Prison changes a man," Matt said, "changes his priorities."

"Not you," Parker said.

He paused while a waiter came over and set down Matt's plate and beer.

"Best steak in town," Parker said as the waiter left. "Let's eat and catch up. What do you say?"

"Sure, Judge," Matt said, "but from what I hear, it looks like you're up to your old tricks, doing what you do."

"That's true," Parker said, "but I've got these young marshals working for me who've got bad attitudes. Not like the old days when I had you and Bass Reeves. Bass is still out there," Parker said, "but he's the only one I can count on at the moment. Tell me, why are you here?"

"I'm just passing through, Judge."

"Without stopping in to see me?"

"Well, I didn't know how you'd feel about that, with me being an ex-con and all."

"You never should've gone to prison, Matt," Parker said. "I'm sorry it took me so long to get you out."

"What?" Matt put his fork down. "It was you who got me the pardon?"

"I might've gotten you out sooner, but I wanted it to be with a pardon so your record would be clean. You see, technically, you're not an ex-con. Your arrest and conviction have been expunged."

"Judge," Matt responded, "I don't know what to say. . . ."

"Eat your steak," Parker said, "and say you'll come to work for me."

"You'd put a badge on me again?" Matt asked. "Now?"

"Why not?"

"I'm fifty years old, Judge."

"So am I," Parker said. "So's Bass Reeves. I need you, Matt. And you need a badge."

"Do I?"

"If you're going to get the other two men who shot you and your wife, you'll need it."

"And what makes you think that's what I'm going to do?" Matt asked.

"Because you're Matt Wheeler," Parker said. "Oh, you've suffered some and probably changed a bit, but you're still Matthew Wheeler. You're not about to let those two go free."

Parker reached into his pocket, took out a US deputy marshal's badge, and put it on the table.

"You're carrying that with you?"

"I've been expecting you, Matt," Parker said, "ever since you got out. I knew you'd get here sometime or other. As soon as you got the rest of it out of your system."

"The rest of it?"

"Yes," Parker said, "depression, despair, leaving the stink of Yuma Prison behind, becoming yourself again."

"I don't know that I am myself again, Judge."

"You're here, aren't you," Parker said, "pretending to meet me by accident?"

Matt decided to play it straight. "You knew that?"

"I told you," Parker said. "I've been waiting for you. I spotted you across the street from my office. I just figured all I'd have to do was wait." He pushed the badge across to Matt. "Go ahead, take it. We'll do the paperwork later."

Matt chewed his steak and stared at the hunk of metal. "If I take it—"

"You'll do the job," Parker said. "I know that. But whatever else you do with it is up to you."

"You're saying if I find those other two and I kill them, that's fine with you?"

"No," Parker said, "I'm saying if you find them and bring them to me, I'll hang them. Of course, if they resist . . ." Parker shrugged.

Matt still couldn't believe it was Judge Parker who had gotten him out of Yuma with a clean record.

"Take your time making up your mind," Parker said. "Finish your steak, pick the badge up after, or leave without it. It's up to you."

"You haven't changed a bit, have you?" Matt asked.

"No," Parker said, "I'm still the smartest man you'll ever know."

Matt stared down at the badge, wondering if Judge Parker really was doing the smartest thing by giving it to him. The last thing he would want to do was bring shame to it, but he knew he couldn't trust himself to do the right thing if and when he came face-to-face with Jason Pardee.

But during his trek from Fairview to Fort Smith, he had come to terms with what he had to do. The years in prison had forced him to wait for his revenge. And more time was lost reestablishing himself out in the real world. But now he felt he was back on track, and one of the things he needed to get the job done was that badge at his elbow.

He finished his steak, put his knife and fork down, and picked up the badge.

"Good man!" Parker said. "Pie?"

CHAPTER TWENTY

Dᴇᴘᴜᴛʏ ᴜs ᴍᴀʀsʜᴀʟ Matt Wheeler was assigned roughly the same area as Bass Reeves, the Western District of Arkansas, which included Indian Territory. It was such a large and diverse area, though, that during the first two months, he still had not crossed paths with the black deputy marshal.

In the course of his duties, he asked questions and kept his ears open, hoping to hear or learn something about Jason Pardee. He could not accept that Pardee had pulled that payroll job in Fairview and then gone into hiding. A man like that would pull as many of those jobs as possible, and he could not do so without word getting out about his escapades.

But after that payroll job, Pardee had probably gotten as far away from Montana as he could. That would indicate he might have gone south. Every miscreant Matt tracked down underwent a thorough grilling before they were taken in to face Judge Parker's court.

None had any information about the whereabouts or activities of a Jason Pardee.

Two and a half months into his second term of service to Judge Parker, Matt was in Fort Smith, having just brought in the Taylor brothers. The three men had been on a killing spree for half a year, and when Matt finally tracked them down, he brought two back alive and one slumped over a saddle. He hadn't killed him, though. The man had fallen from his horse and broken his neck.

Matt's second term was marked by his unwillingness—not inability—to bring outlaws back dead. He had used the stipend given marshals to supply himself with a new pistol and rifle—a Colt and a Winchester. But he used both sparingly, as he wished to question his captives, not kill them. At the same time, he was socking away his pay for a time when he would have to travel to finally track down Pardee and the third man, Corbin.

Matt took himself to task for not searing Corbin's face into his brain. All he had been able to remember during his initial search for the killers was the face of Pardee, the look of satisfaction on the man's face when he had gunned down Angie in the street. The face and name of Ed Corbin had come to him later. At least he had known Al Chester's name and had been able to track him down. Too bad he had killed him before he could question the man about Pardee's whereabouts. But he wasn't sure, if he were able to go back, he would have done it differently.

Every night he'd tell himself that was in the past. He had to concentrate on looking forward.

A FTER TURNING IN the Taylor brothers, Matt went to the small restaurant where he had decided to take his meals. He didn't want to keep running into the judge in the Bighorn Steak House. He was working on a succulent cut of venison when he saw Bass Reeves walk in.

Reeves, a big, mustachioed black man, was Judge Parker's top deputy. Matt was surprised to see him, because there had been no word that Reeves was bringing somebody in. Of course, he could have come in just after Matt. But for two and a half months their paths had not crossed, and now here the big man was.

More to the point, Reeves looked around, spotted Matt, and came walking over.

"You mind if I join you?" he asked.

"Not at all," Matt said. "The venison's great."

A waiter came over, and Reeves said, "I'll have what he's havin'."

"Yes, sir."

As the waiter left, Reeves leaned on the table and stared at Matt.

"I was happy to hear the judge recruited you again," he said. "These kids he's got now . . ." He shook his head.

"So he said."

"With you back on the job, I won't have to do all the heavy liftin'."

"I'm happy to help."

"Unless . . ."

"Unless what?"

"Unless you hear somethin' that takes you away from your appointed job."

"Like what?"

"Like where a certain man might be."

"What man?"

"The man you're lookin' for," Reeves said. "You know, I couldn't believe it when I heard you were sent to Yuma. I never thought you'd come out alive."

"I had my doubts, too," Matt said. "In fact, for a while, I didn't want to come out alive."

The waiter came with a plate and set it down in front of Reeves, accompanied by a glass of beer.

"Thanks," he said.

"You're welcome, Deputy."

"So," Matt asked, "what man are we talking about?"

"What man are you lookin' for?"

Matt finished chewing, then put his utensils down and looked across the table at Reeves, who had just started cutting into his venison.

"Are we playing a game?" Matt asked. "Did the judge send you here?"

"Judge Parker doesn't know I'm in town," Reeves said. "He thinks I'm off tracking an Indian Comanchero named Pale Blue."

"But you're not."

"I was," Reeves said, "and as far as the judge is concerned, I still am. But I came back because I heard somethin'."

"Something I should know?" Matt asked.

"I don't know what your arrangement is with the judge," Reeves said, "but if I tell you this, I don't want him to hear about it."

"He won't hear it from me," Matt said.

Bass Reeves sat back, took a deep breath, and said, "All right, then. All I know about what happened to you in Fairview is that a man named Jason Pardee shot your wife."

"That's true."

"I heard that a man named Pardee is riding with Pale Blue and his bunch."

"He's riding with Indians?"

"Pale Blue is Cherokee, but he's not ridin' with other Cherokees. He's ridin' with a band of Comancheros the judge wants me to track down."

"And you heard that Pardee is with them?"

"Pardee and another man named Slim Johnson. Do you know him?"

"There was a third man who shot me in Fairview," Matt said. "His name is Ed Corbin, but I have no idea where he could be. I guess Pardee is going to have to tell me that when we catch him."

"When *we* catch 'im?"

"Well, I assume you're telling me this because you want me to come along."

"You can ride with me," Reeves said, "but like I said, I don't know what your deal is with the judge. If Pardee is there when we catch 'em, I'll back your play to the limit of the law. If we agree on that, you're welcome to come."

"We agree," Matt said.

"I'm serious," Reeves said. "I won't help you kill 'im or stand by while you do it."

"Got it," Matt said. "We're agreed. When do we leave?"

"In the mornin'," Reeves said.

"What do you want me to tell the judge?"

"Just tell 'im you're goin' out to do your job," Bass Reeves said.

"Well," Matt said, "that is what I'm going out to do."

A FTER SUPPER THEY left the restaurant together, stopped just outside.

"Drink in the saloon?" Reeves asked.

"I don't think we should be seen together again," Matt said. "We don't want it getting back to the judge, do we?"

"Good point," Reeves said. "Then I'll meet you just west of town. There's a huge bur oak there that used to be for hangings."

"Not anymore?"

"Not since Judge Parker started hanging outlaws here in town," Reeves said.

"I know the place," Matt said, remembering it now. "I'll meet you there just after sunup."

"Good," Reeves said. "Bein' in town when the judge doesn't know it makes me nervous."

Matt had a feeling Judge Isaac Parker was the only man Bass Reeves had ever feared.

"Make sure you're outfitted to travel," Reeves said. "We're gonna have to ride well into Indian Territory to find your man. And that's if he's still there."

"Whether he's there or not, I'll be closer to him than I've been in years."

CHAPTER TWENTY-ONE

T HE NEXT MORNING, as Matt rode up to the oak hanging tree west of Fort Smith, he saw Bass Reeves sitting on the ground with his back to the tree, smoking a pipe. He also had a fire going with a pot of coffee on it.

"Light and set a spell," Reeves said. "Coffee's hot and strong."

"Trail coffee usually is," Matt said, pouring himself a cup. "You get out of town without the judge knowing you were there?"

"I think I did," Reeves said. "I guess I won't find out for sure until the next time I see him."

"Tell me about Pale Blue," Matt said. "He wasn't around during my first tenure in the judge's court."

"No, he came along later," Reeves said. "He's a fairly young buck. The blue comes from his eyes, which he supposedly got from his white mother."

"Sounds like Quanah Parker," Matt said.

"He hasn't earned the respect among the Cherokee that Quanah Parker has among the Comanche. Quanah was a chief. Pale Blue's a renegade. He leads a group that includes Indians, whites, and Mexicans."

"So Comancheros."

"Basically."

"Why would Pardee join up with them?" Matt wondered. "He's a bank robber, not a Comanchero."

"Who knows what he's gone through during the nine years since that robbery," Reeves said.

"And the murder of my wife."

"Oh, yes," Reeves said. "I didn't mean—"

"Never mind," Matt said. "It's fine. I know what you meant. Hopefully his nine years were as rough as mine."

"Did your wife have any kin?" Reeves asked.

"No," Matt said, "that was one of the things we had in common. It was just us."

"And she's buried up in Fairview?"

"Yes," Matt said, "on their boot hill. I . . . I've never seen the grave, though."

"What?"

"I saw her body at the undertaker's and swore to her that I'd bring the men who killed her and shot me to justice. I—I can't go to her grave until I've done that."

"Did you go back after you got out of Yuma?"

"Eventually," Matt said, "I worked my way back there, but the town's completely changed. And I couldn't walk up that hill to her grave. And I won't be able to until I take care of Pardee."

"Take care of 'im?" Reeves repeated. "You mean kill 'im?"

"I mean, see to it that he pays for what he did," Matt said.

"And what about the other man?"

"He didn't shoot Angie. He shot me," Matt said. "If I can catch him, I will. If not, so be it. It's Pardee I really want."

"To kill," Reeves said again.

"Bass," Matt said, "I'm not going to leave you hanging, no matter what happens."

"No, you're not," Reeves said. "If you kill him and the judge finds out I helped you, then you might as well hang me from this here tree."

"That's not going to happen," Matt assured him.

Actually, Matt didn't know what was going to happen, but he was sure of one thing. He would never cause Bass Reeves any misfortune or discomfort, no matter what.

"Well," Reeves said, getting to his feet and knocking his pipe against the hanging tree to dislodge the burned tobacco, "are we ready to go?"

"We are," Matt said. "And, Bass, if I haven't thanked you for this, I thank you now."

"Thank me if and when we find him, Matt."

M ATT HAD BOUGHT a new horse in Fort Smith, this time a Morgan. It was a breed that had been used extensively during the Civil War. They were muscular and compact, usually with well-arched necks. The six-year-old chestnut was the best horse Matt had ridden since getting out of prison. It still had trouble, however, keeping up with Reeves' big gray.

The night of the first day on the trail they camped in a clearing so they'd be able to see all around them. They built a fire, after which they made some beans and coffee for supper. They took turns standing watch in case some renegades or outlaws rode by.

Matt took the second watch, sat at the fire, making sure not to look into it for fear of destroying his night vision. Even a glance into the fire would cause the need to become accustomed to the darkness again. In those moments, anything could happen.

He had been camping alone during his time in Indian

Country over the past two and a half months. Having Reeves along had enabled him to get a solid four hours of sleep without having to worry about being snuck up on by four-legged or two-legged animals.

Matt and Reeves got to know each other much better than they would have liked during the four-day ride to the Western Indian Territory. They had stopped in only one small town along the way to reoutfit themselves with coffee and beans. Finally, they came to a town called Elk City.

"City" was a grandiose claim, considering the town they rode into.

"This is where you heard something about Jason Pardee?" Matt asked.

"It doesn't look like much, but apparently Pale Blue and some other gangs outfit in the mercantile and drink in the saloon here."

"Where did you hear Pardee's name?"

"I ain't sure," Reeves said. "It was sometime after I left here and heard that you were back wearin' a badge that I realized I'd heard it."

Matt looked around as they continued to ride in, attracting no attention at all. If outlaw bands used the place, it made sense that the citizenry would avoid new arrivals.

"I guess we'll just have to ask in both places," Matt commented.

"That's fine," Reeves said, "I could use a beer anyway." He pointed. "There."

Matt saw the saloon. Above the door was a crudely written sign that read THE TERRITORY SALOON. They rode up to it, dismounted, and tied their horses off.

"Are they going to know you when you walk in?" Matt asked.

"I'm not sure," Bass Reeves said, "but they'll know our badges."

"Maybe we should take them off," Matt suggested.

"No, not out here," Reeves said. "These badges act like a shield most of the time—sometimes like a target, but mostly a shield."

Matt shrugged and gave in to Reeves, who had been wearing the badge longer than he had.

They went through the batwing doors and stopped just inside. There were no other horses out front, but at least half a dozen men were inside, all with pistols in their belts or rifles at their sides.

Matt and Reeves walked to the bar, where three of the men were standing, nursing drinks. They had been conversing but suspended their talk when the two marshals approached.

"You marshals gotta come into my place?" the bartender complained. He was a tall man with a shock of white hair sticking almost straight up. He could have been fifty or eighty.

"Is there another place in town?" Reeves asked.

"No."

"Then we'll have beer."

The bartender drew the two beers and set them down with a bang, spilling some from each mug.

"Drink it and get out before you ruin my business."

At that moment two men who had been sitting together at a table stood and hurriedly left.

"See what I mean?" the bartender said.

"We'll camp out here," Reeves said, "unless you tell us somethin' we wanna know."

The bartender scowled. "You wanna turn me into a stool pigeon?" he demanded. "That'd really kill my business."

"We just need information about somebody's whereabouts," Matt said, "whether or not he's been in here and where he might be now."

"How would I know any of that?" the bartender barked. "How the hell do I know where you're goin' when you leave here?"

"Maybe," Reeves said, "you listen when men talk."

The other man scowled again, mightily this time, as if he had just eaten something that had gone bad. "Who're ya lookin' for?" he demanded.

"A man named Pardee," Matt said. "Jason Pardee."

Without hesitation, the bartender said, "Don't know 'im, never heard of 'im. Finish your beer."

The bartender started to turn away, but Reeves grabbed his upper arm in a viselike grip.

"Ow!" the skinny man said. "What the hell?"

Reeves released his hold. The man rubbed his arm.

"What's your name?" Reeves asked.

"Kelsey."

"What about Pale Blue, Kelsey?"

The bartender's eyes narrowed. "What about 'im?"

"You've heard of him," Reeves said.

"Everybody in the territories has heard of 'im," the barman said. "So what?"

"We heard Pardee might be riding with him," Matt said. "So when was the last time you saw Pale Blue?"

"I don't serve no Injuns in here!" the bartender blustered.

"Oh, you serve him," Reeves said. "If you didn't, he'd've burned this place down long ago. Now, when is the last time you saw him?"

"Weeks," Kelsey said. "Gotta be weeks."

"How many men did he have with him?"

"Ten, maybe more."

"And?" Reeves asked.

"And what? They came in, they drank, they left, which is what I wish you'd do."

"We will," Matt said. "Just give us a little more."

"And don't give us any reason to come back," Reeves said.

"A couple of the men who were with him were standin' at the bar, complainin' that Pale Blue was talkin' about goin' into Texas."

"Where in Texas?" Matt asked.

"How would I know?" Kelsey said. "They said somethin' about a bank."

"What bank?" Reeves asked.

"I dunno!"

"Come on, Kelsey," Reeves said. "We need more than that."

Kelsey looked around, then jerked his head at Matt and Reeves and led them down to the far end of the bar, away from the three men standing at the other end.

"Look, this can't get out," he said. "I'm serious. Nobody can know I gave you this."

"We don't have reason to tell anybody," Reeves said. "Now, what are you talkin' about?"

"Pale Blue wanted to get out of the territories and move his action into Texas."

"Why?" Matt asked.

"That I really don't know," Kelsey said.

"Do you know where he intended to start?"

Kelsey shook his head. "Just someplace in East Texas."

"That's a big area," Matt said.

"Maybe not when you discover how big Texas really is," Reeves offered.

"So we just ride into Texas and hope for the best?"

"Ain't that what you been doin' since gettin' out," Reeves asked, "ridin' around, hopin' for the best?"

Matt couldn't argue with that.

"Besides," Reeves said, "we ride into Texas, and our badges are worth shit."

Matt didn't agree. Because they wore US badges,

they gave them some semblance of authority, no matter what happened.

But he couldn't expect Bass Reeves to feel the same way.

They finished their beer, paid for them—which surprised Kelsey—and left the Territory Saloon.

Outside, they untied their horses and prepared to mount when a man came through the batwings, looked around, and, seeing them, hurried over.

"You're the fellas lookin' for Pale Blue, right?" he asked.

"You should know," Reeves said. "You were in the saloon when we were."

"Um, well, what's it worth to ya?"

"What's what worth?" Reeves asked.

"To know where Pale Blue and his bunch were goin' from here?" the man said.

"What's your name?" Matt asked.

"Me? I'm—Folks just call me Lippy."

Reeves and Matt could see why. The man's lower lip seemed three times the size as his upper, like he'd been hit.

"Lippy, if you're trying to take us for a few dollars, we'll be back this way—" Matt warned.

"Look," Lippy said, "I wanna get out of this town. I know if I lie to ya, you can track me down. All I want's a horse."

"You want us to buy you a horse," Reeves said.

"No," Lippy said, "I'm just gettin' the price of a horse together."

"So what are you doin' in a saloon?"

"I swamp out the saloon, and he gives me a dollar and a few drinks," Lippy said. "Look, Marshals, I gotta get outta here. A few dollars would go a long way to gettin' me the price of a horse."

Reeves looked at Matt.

"Tell us what you know," Matt said. "If it sounds good, I'll give you a few dollars."

"Well," Lippy said, "I can tell ya one thing for sure."

"What's that?" Matt asked.

"There was a fella named Pardee with them."

CHAPTER TWENTY-TWO

MATT GAVE LIPPY a few dollars.

Oh, not at first. First, he had Lippy describe the man called Pardee, and then he forked over the money. The description matched the man Matt had seen at the Fairview bank robbery all those years before, but somewhat older.

"And where were they goin'?" Reeves asked.

"They was all goin' to a place called Copper River."

Reeves looked at Matt. "That's a small town in East Texas that outlaws use," the black marshal said.

"Only I gotta tell ya one more thing," Lippy said.

"What's that?" Matt asked.

"That feller Pardee? He may not be goin' there with 'em."

"Why not?"

"He was talkin' to another man, sayin' he wasn't sure he wanted to stay with Pale Blue's bunch."

"What'd this other man look like?" Matt asked.

Lippy gave Matt a description that fit the third man from the bank robbery.

"Did you hear a name for him?" Matt asked.

"I just heard somebody call him Ed."

That confirmed for Matt that he was talking about the third man, Ed Corbin.

He gave Lippy another dollar.

"Thanks, Marshal," Lippy gushed, and ran back into the saloon.

"You didn't believe all that about a horse, did ya?" Reeves asked. "He's gonna spend it on whiskey."

"I don't care," Matt said. "He got Pardee's description right and that other name? Ed? I remember it from the bank that day. Ed's the other fella that shot me."

"So whataya wanna do?" Reeves asked.

"Me, I want to go to Copper River," Matt said. "I don't expect you to come with me, Bass. We'd have to cross over into Texas—"

"Not that far in," Reeves said. "It's right on the border. If Pale Blue's anywhere near there, it's worth it to me."

"But if Pale Blue and his bunch are in Texas, and not in Indian Territory, wouldn't the judge be satisfied with that? You could tell him you drove him out."

"And that's what I'll tell him if the trail goes cold in Copper River," Reeves said. "But we ain't gonna know that till we get there, and we ain't gonna get there if we stand here jawin' all day."

So they rode. . . .

I⟨T TOOK SEVERAL⟩ days before they crossed the border into East Texas and made camp a couple of miles outside of Copper River.

As they ate their beans and washed them down with

coffee, Matt asked Reeves, "Have you ever been to Copper River before?"

"No," the black deputy said, "I've only heard stories about it being an outlaw stronghold."

"So how do you think they'll react to having two marshals ride in?"

"They'll either gun us down before we dismount," Reeves said, "or they won't want to kill two marshals, only to have twenty more show up in retaliation."

"Interesting," Matt said. "I vote for the second."

"You think that's the way to play it?"

"I just meant I vote against getting gunned down in the street before we even dismount," Matt said with a grin.

"Well, that gets my vote, too," Reeves said, shaking his head, "but how do we wanna play this? We could also take off our badges and ride in undercover."

"We're not Pinkertons, Bass. We're deputy marshals," Matt pointed out.

"So you say ride in and be bold," Reeves said.

"That sounds like you, doesn't it?" Matt asked.

"It does," Reeves said. "What about you? Are you feelin' up to that?"

"I'm feeling better than I have in years," Matt said. "I'm going to have the chance to keep my promise to my wife. I'll take any chance to get that done."

"Okay, then," Reeves said. "In the morning we ride in bold as brass, and whatever happens"—he shrugged—"happens."

"Agreed."

Matt took the first watch and poured himself some more coffee while Reeves wrapped himself in his blanket and bedroll.

Matt wouldn't have asked Bass Reeves to risk his life this way, but Reeves was after Pale Blue, so the situation could benefit both of them.

* * *

IN THE MORNING they had a quick breakfast of bacon and coffee and got on the trail. The first signpost they came to read COPPER RIVER ONE MILE in black print and, beneath that in red, STAY AWAY!

"Do they really think that's gonna put folks off more than make them curious?" Bass Reeves asked.

"Who knows?" Matt said. "Right now the sign doesn't matter one way or the other."

They rode on. . . .

COPPER RIVER WAS a small group of buildings, many of them boarded up, but obviously operational were a hotel, a saloon, a trading post, and—surprisingly—a church. Another building they passed had a second-floor balcony, and on it were several scantily clad women who simply watched Matt and Reeves ride by.

"They look too tired to wave," Reeves commented.

"Or they can see our badges," Matt said.

"Good point."

The street was empty, and the whores seemed to be the only people who were outside.

They reined in their horses in front of a saloon that had a sign over the door: SALOON. They dismounted and looked around. They checked rooftops, windows, and doorways, but they did not see any rifle barrels pointing at them.

"Are you sure about this town?" Matt asked. "I thought they'd have some shooters on lookout."

"I told you, I've only heard about this place," Reeves said. "I've never been here. Maybe things have changed."

"I hope we didn't come here for nothing."

"Let's go inside and find out," Reeves suggested.

They mounted the boardwalk and entered the saloon. It had had batwing doors at some point, but they were long gone. Inside, they found much of the same things they had found in the Territory Saloon in Elk City. There were a diminutive bartender and a few customers in a dark, small interior. No girls, no gambling.

When they went to the bar, the bartender's eyes went straight to their badges. "You fellas must be crazy," he said.

"Is the beer that bad?" Reeves asked.

The bartender leaned in and lowered his voice. "Do you know where you are?" he asked.

"We've got a pretty good idea," Matt said.

They became aware of one of the customers heading out the door in a hurry.

"He's puttin' out the word you're here," the bartender said. "There's gonna be a dozen guns here in five minutes."

"That oughta give us time to have a beer," Reeves said.

"It's your funeral, friend." The barkeep straightened up, drew them two beers, and set them down.

Matt and Reeves picked up their beers, turned their backs to the bar, and looked around. There were three men there staring at them. If they were interested in making a move, they were waiting for help to arrive. The marshals turned back to the bartender.

"Pale Blue," Reeves said.

"Who?"

"Come on!" Reeves snapped. "Everybody knows who he is."

"The Cherokee," the bartender said.

"Yeah."

"What about him?"

"When was the last time he was here?" Reeves asked, rather than "if" he'd ever been there.

"What makes you think he's been here?"

"Because he's an outlaw," Matt said, "and this is Copper River."

"This used to be Copper River."

"What's it called now?" Reeves asked.

"It don't have no name now," the bartender said. "We're just a mud puddle in the road."

"Well, as far as we're concerned, it's still Copper River," Reeves said. "Now, answer my question, or I'm gonna burn this place to the ground."

"You wouldn't," the man said.

Reeves took a lucifer out of his pocket. "Pale Blue," he said. "Who's gonna miss this place if it's just a mud puddle?"

Chairs scraped along the floor as the other three men in the place stood up. Matt looked over at them, putting his hand on the butt of the gun in his belt. At that point more men poured through the front entrance, and by the time they stopped, there were ten in all, staring at the two marshals standing at the bar.

"Let's just all take it easy," Matt said. "Gunning down two marshals is only going to bring you more trouble, and we're not here for any of you."

Reeves kept his eyes on the bartender, leaving the other ten men to Matt. He held his thumb to the lucifer.

"Pale Blue," he said.

"He was here last month," the bartender said. "Stayed a couple of weeks, then left."

"What'd he do while he was here?"

"He spent time in here, at the hotel, and in the whorehouse," the bartender said. "When he was in here, he didn't talk, only drank."

"With who?"

"He always sat alone at that back table," the man said, pointing.

"And who rode in with him?" Matt asked, without taking his eyes off the other ten men.

The bartender shrugged and said, "A bunch of men."

"Names," Reeves said.

"I didn't hear—I heard one fella called Abbott. Another called . . . I think it was Harmon. . . . Well, and then there was Ed."

Now Matt looked at the bartender. "Did you hear the name Pardee?" he asked. "Jason Pardee?"

"Pardee," the bartender repeated. "Yeah, I mighta . . ."

"Was he here?"

"No," the man said, "but they was talkin' about him. . . ."

Matt turned to face the man, so Reeves turned to watch the others, but still kept the match at the ready. His other hand was on the butt of his pistol.

"What'd they say about him?"

"I think that feller Ed said Pardee went off on his own, but he didn't wanna go with him. . . . Yeah, that was it. They were ridin' together but split up."

"Where'd Pardee go?" Matt asked anxiously.

"I dunno," the bartender said. "I didn't hear that. Uh, can you get him to put that match down? This place'd go up like a tinderbox."

"You can't tell us where Pale Blue or Pardee went?" Reeves asked.

"I would if I could, Deputy," the man said. "Believe me."

Reeves looked at Matt, who nodded, and Reeves lowered the match.

"Of course," the bartender said, "you could ask Ed."

"What?" Matt asked. "He's still here?"

"Probably at the whorehouse," the bartender said. "He splits his time between here and there."

CHAPTER TWENTY-THREE

L ET'S GO," MATT said to Reeves.
  They both turned to face the ten other men in the room. Some of them looked nervous; some looked bored. None of them looked like they particularly wanted to draw their guns.

"We're walkin' out," Reeves said. He put some money on the bar. "You fellas have a drink on us."

The other men watched as the marshals headed for the door. The few who were barring their path moved aside. The situation was tense, but Matt and Reeves were able to make it out the door without incident. Once they were outside, they could hear all the men heading for the bar.

"How do you wanna play this?" Reeves asked.

"We've got to get to Ed before somebody warns him," Matt said, "but the last time I tracked a man to a whorehouse, I ended up in Yuma."

"So you wanna wait for him to come to the saloon?"

"Not with all those guns in there," Matt said. "Why don't we just wait outside the whorehouse?"

"I've got a better idea," Reeves said.

M ATT WENT AROUND behind the whorehouse while Bass Reeves went inside. He knew Reeves hated places like that, so Matt appreciated his willingness to go in.

He waited out back for about twenty minutes, and then suddenly a second-floor window opened and a man's legs appeared. The drop from the window was not far, but the man grunted when he hit the ground. He had his pants on, but his shirt fluttered down from the window behind him, followed by his hat and boots. Then the window closed with a slam.

Matt walked over to where the man was sitting on the ground, trying to collect himself.

"Hello, Ed," he said. "Remember me?"

The man stared up at him, then shielded his eyes with his hand and stared longer. Suddenly, recognition dawned and he opened his mouth.

"Wait," he said. "You . . ."

Matt leaned over and plucked the man's gun from his belt. "Put on your shirt and boots, Ed," Matt said. "We're going to have a talk."

W HEN MATT CAME around the building with Ed in front of him, Reeves was waiting.

"Okay," Reeves said, "where do we take 'im?"

"There's a livery at the end of the street," Matt said. "Let's go there."

"H-hey, what's this about?" Ed stammered. "I ain't done nothin'."

Matt pushed the man ahead of him and said, "You must've been going out the window for a reason, Ed."

"I—I didn't know who was askin' about me."

When they reached the livery, Matt gave Ed a big shove and said, "Inside."

"Hey!" Ed staggered forward and into the stable.

Matt and Reeves followed, saw an older man who must have been the hostler.

"We're borrowing your place for a while," Matt said. He gave the man two bits. "Go get a beer."

"Ya don't gotta tell me twice," the man said, and left.

As the hostler left, Ed turned on them and asked, "Are ya gonna kill me? You can't. You're lawmen."

"We're out of our jurisdiction," Matt said. "Now we're just two fellas."

"So whataya want with me?" Ed asked.

"Come on, Ed," Matt said as Reeves let him do the talking. The big black deputy walked over to the door to keep watch outside. "You recognized me."

"Yeah, you're that sheriff from Fairview," Ed said. "Look, if Kaufman sent ya to get his money back—"

"That was a long time ago, Ed," Matt said. "I'm sure that money's gone, and the Double-K is out of business."

"Then whataya want?"

"What do you think I want?" Matt asked. "You, Al Chester, and Jason Pardee shot me and killed my wife."

Ed's eyes went wide. "I never shot no woman!"

"No, but you shot me," Matt said.

"Did we?" the man asked. "I—I don't remember."

"I remember," Matt said. "You and Chester shot me, and Pardee shot my wife. I already killed Chester. Now I want to know where Pardee is."

"You killed Al?" Ed asked. "I heard he was dead, but I didn't know you done it. B-but that was years ago. Why are ya here now?"

"I took some time off," Matt said. "Now I'm back, and I want Pardee."

"I ain't seen him in years."

"That's a lie," Matt said. "You and him have been riding with Pale Blue. Now you've gone your own ways."

"We had to. That Injun is crazy!"

"Well, Deputy Reeves and me, we want to know where Pale Blue and Pardee are."

"I dunno! I swear!"

"You gotta do better than that, Ed," Reeves said from the door.

"What's your last name?" Matt asked.

"It's Corbin. . . . Why?"

"I want to know what to put on your headstone," Matt told him.

Ed's eyes went wide again. Matt remembered the man vaguely from over nine years before, but he looked to have aged twice that much since then.

"Aw, gee, look, I—I ain't got nothin'. I'm stuck here in this nothin' town. . . ."

"You want some money?" Matt asked.

Now the look of despair turned to one of hope. "You gonna gimme some? I could get outta here?"

"You give us some information, and we'll see," Matt said. "First, when Pale Blue left, did Pardee go with him?"

"No," Ed said, "Pale Blue left, and I stayed here."

"Where did Pale Blue go?" Reeves asked.

"He said he was gonna rob some white men's banks in Texas before he went back to Indian Territory."

"How many banks?" Reeves asked.

"I dunno," Ed said, "but it was gonna be more than one, that's for sure."

"What about Pardee?" Matt asked. "Where was he going?"

Ed hesitated, his eyes got shifty, and he said, "Uh, I dunno—"

"That's a lie," Reeves said. "I can see it from here."

"Maybe I should let Deputy Reeves get it out of you," Matt said.

Ed looked over at Reeves, who was glaring at him.

"If I do it," Matt went on, "I just might kill you for shooting me."

"It wasn't my idea!" Ed said. "Besides, I don't think I shot you. It was Al Chester."

"I was shot by two different guns, Ed."

"Then Pardee did it!"

"I saw Pardee shoot my wife," Matt said, "while you and Chester turned your guns on me." Matt looked at Bass Reeves. "Deputy Reeves, he's all yours. Break anything you want, but don't kill him yet."

"I'll try not to," Reeves said, taking a few steps, "but you know how I get when I start. Sometimes, I just can't stop until they're dead."

"No, wait!" Ed yelled. "Keep him away!"

Matt put his hand out to stop Reeves' progress.

"I dunno where Pardee is, but I got an idea where he might've gone."

"Where?"

"Mexico."

"Mexico?" Matt said. "Why Mexico?"

"There's always a revolution brewin' down there," Ed said, "and they're always lookin' for mercenaries. Pardee said he was gonna go down there and sell his gun, if not to Porfirio Díaz, the president, then to whoever was tryin' to overthrow him."

"Díaz has been in power for four or five years now," Reeves said to Matt. "He's pretty stable."

"So where exactly in Mexico was Pardee going?" Matt asked.

"He was gonna start in Mexico City," Ed said.

Matt looked at Reeves, who shrugged. Then he looked at Ed Corbin.

"If I find out you're lying—"

"I ain't!" Ed said. "I know you'd track me down. I mean, Jesus, ya tracked me here after more than nine years! That's . . . crazy!"

Matt touched his gun, but didn't take it from his belt. "You tried to kill me, Corbin," he said. "I should shoot you right now."

"No!"

"Matt . . . ," Reeves said.

Matt looked at Reeves.

"I can't just stand by and watch you shoot 'im," Reeves said. "Either take him back to Fort Smith, or let 'im go."

"I can't take him back to Fort Smith," Matt said. "I have to go to Mexico."

"Matt!" Reeves said.

"Bass, you can take him back to Judge Parker," Matt said.

"And tell him what? That you crossed the border? That badge won't do you any good down there."

"I'll go and present myself to the *federales*," Matt said. "I'll get their permission to hunt for Pardee. The judge can't argue with that."

"Yeah, he can if he wants to," Reeves pointed out. "But maybe he won't."

"He said if I brought the guilty parties from Fairview back, he'd deal with them."

"You talkin' about Judge Parker?" Ed asked. "Hangin' Judge Parker? He'll hang me!"

"Maybe, maybe not," Matt said. "Deputy Reeves will tell him you cooperated with me in trying to find the man who killed my wife. That should work in your favor."

"So—so you ain't gonna kill me for shootin' you?" Ed asked.

Matt studied the other man for a moment. It would

have been so easy to just draw his gun and plug the man in the heart, but he couldn't do it in front of Bass Reeves. He'd end up in prison again, and Judge Parker might even hang *him*.

"No," Matt said, "I won't shoot you. But you're going to Fort Smith." Matt turned and looked at Reeves. "Bass?"

"I'll take 'im back," Reeves said. "I can't go into Mexico with you."

"That's all I ask," Matt said.

"You know," Ed Corbin said as they started for the door, "back in Fairview I had no idea you was the Matt Wheeler who rode for Judge Parker."

"Would that have made a difference?" Matt asked.

"I dunno," Ed said. "Maybe."

"You got a horse in here?"

"Yeah."

"Let's get it saddled."

A S THEY LEFT the livery, walking their horses, they stopped short. Once again, there were ten men with guns in their way, and this time they looked ready to use them.

"They ain't gonna let ya take me outta here," Ed Corbin said with great satisfaction. "They never do."

"How many US deputy marshals have they had ride in here?" Reeves asked.

Ed didn't answer.

Matt stepped behind Ed and drew his gun from his belt. "Ed, if they don't let us take you out of here, I'll kill you where you stand."

"Then they'll kill you," Ed said with a lot less satisfaction.

"Maybe," Reeves said, "but you won't be around to see it."

"Plus if they kill us, they're going to have to deal with a lot more marshals coming here," Matt said. "Judge Parker knows where we are."

"The Hanging Judge," Reeves pointed out loudly.

The ten men had been able to hear everything being said, and they started to exchange glances.

"I don't know if you fellas have a leader," Matt said, "but you'd better make a decision soon. We're mounting up and riding out."

While the ten men watched, Matt, Reeves, and Corbin all mounted their horses, Matt keeping Corbin covered the entire time.

When they were ready to ride, Matt looked at the outlaw band and said, "Well?"

Slowly, reluctantly, the men began to move aside until, finally, there was a path cleared. Matt rode through with Ed ahead of him and Reeves taking up the rear. There were now outlaws on both sides of them, but none seemed ready to draw their guns.

When the three riders had cleared the ten men, Matt slapped Ed Corbin's horse on the butt, and the three of them lit out of Copper River before the outlaws could change their minds.

CHAPTER TWENTY-FOUR

Mexico City, Mexico

THE STREETS OF Mexico City were alternately alive with merriment and celebration or quiet during siesta time, only to come to life again.

Matt had been there for three days and still was not used to the changes in climate.

It had taken him almost three weeks to ride from Copper River to Mexico City, which was toward the southern tip of the country.

He'd had to deal not only with several troops of *federales* stopping him to investigate him, but also a few bands of *bandidos* trying to rob him. Neither the *federales* nor the *bandidos* had been impressed by his badge. In fact, it was after he flashed the badge at one particular band of *bandidos* that they tried to kill him rather than just rob him.

Once he arrived in Mexico City, he tried to present himself to the *federales*, as well as to the president himself. He had applied for a meeting with *El Presidente* Porfirio Díaz in the National Palace, and he had been waiting three days for a reply. For the sake of Judge Parker, Matt felt he had to meet with the authorities in Mexico so they would not only know he was there but why.

He took to the streets each day, just walking, knowing that chancing upon Jason Pardee was next to impossible. He stopped in a collection of cantinas, drank half a beer while he scanned faces and listened to conversations (most of which, unfortunately, were in Spanish). He tried not to get drunk, but by day's end, he would unsteadily make his way back to his small hotel.

On the evening of the fourth day, as he entered the cramped lobby of the hotel, a man in *federales* uniform confronted him.

"*Señor* Wheeler?"

"That's right."

"I am Colonel Esteban Corranza Obregón of *El Presidente* Díaz's personal guard."

"Nice to meet you."

"You have applied for a meeting with *El President*, stating that you are a lawman from *los Estados Unidos*."

"That's right."

The tall, handsome soldier in his forties stuck out his hand. "May I see your papers?"

"I'm afraid I don't have any papers."

"Hmm," the colonel said. "Then perhaps you have a badge?"

"Yes, I do." Matt reached into his shirt pocket, took out the badge, and handed it to the soldier.

"Hmm," the colonel said again, examining the badge, "it looks genuine. And who do you serve?"

"I ride for Judge Isaac Parker in Indian Territory," Matt said.

"And why are you here?"

"I'm tracking a man who killed my wife," Matt said.

"So you are not here officially," the colonel said, handing the badge back, "with your judge's permission."

"Not exactly," Matt said. "I'm still a marshal, and if I find the man, I'll take him back to Fort Smith for the judge to . . ."

"Hang?"

"Sentence. I just don't want to do anything in your country without letting your president know about it."

The colonel studied Matt for a few moments, then said, "Please, be at the palace tomorrow morning at eight a.m."

"To see the president?"

"For breakfast," the colonel said. "Then we will see about a meeting."

The man gave Matt a crisp salute and then left the hotel.

Matt looked over at the desk clerk, who had been very nervous the entire time the colonel was there. Now, suddenly, he was heaving a sigh of relief.

"Everything okay?" Matt walked over and asked him.

"*Sí*, it is now, *señor*," the man said. "When the colonel comes around, bad things often happen."

"Not today, I guess."

"No, *señor. Gracias*. You must be a very important man."

"I don't think that was it," Matt said, "but I guess I'll find out."

He went to his room.

M ATT WAS SURPRISED that the invitation to the palace was for breakfast. What he didn't know was whether or not it was actually breakfast with *El Presidente*. That hadn't been anywhere near what he'd been looking for. He'd been hoping for five minutes, just to smooth the waters and maybe ask about Jason Pardee.

Porfirio Díaz was in his second four-year term, although it had not run consecutively with the first. There had been four years in there where he was out of office. Now he was back, and the palace looked as if it had been redone. The awnings over all the windows looked brand-new. As Matt reached the front entrance, he saw the statues of female forms on either side.

Matt gave his name to the guards at the door and waited. He was surprised when it was Colonel Obregón who came to get him.

"*Buenos días*, Marshal Wheeler," the soldier said.

"Good morning, Colonel."

"I will need your gun, Marshal," Obregón said, "before I take you inside."

"Of course." Matt removed his pistol from his belt and handed it over.

Obregón handed it to one of the guards and said, "Please, come with me. *El President* is waiting to have breakfast with you."

"The president himself?" Matt asked, thinking he should probably show some degree of being impressed.

"*Sí,*" the colonel said, "he is very interested in meeting you."

Matt hoped that the hotel desk clerk wasn't right about the colonel, and that he wasn't being led to a dungeon or a cell.

Along the way the colonel gave him instructions.

"You will speak only when spoken to. You will refer to *El Presidente* as *El President* or Your Excellency...."

Matt listened intently to it all, as he wanted to be sure he didn't say anything wrong.

As they walked through a high-ceilinged room that appeared newly furnished, the colonel said, "This is the Ambassador Room. *El Presidente* has had this room redone, along with the kitchens, the stables, the lounge, and—as you will see—the dining room."

Finally, they entered the dining room, and Matt could see what the colonel was talking about. It gleamed with crystal and gold. The French had been gone for over twenty years—ever since Emperor Napoleon III had recalled his troops, because he had grown weary of the war in Mexico—but French architecture was still very popular in Mexico City.

There was an extremely long wooden table in the center of the room, and a single man was seated at the head of it. Matt thought if the colonel sat him at the other end of the table, he wouldn't be able to hear *El President* speak. But that was not the case. The colonel walked him to the head of the table and stopped him mere feet from the president.

Matt was impressed in spite of himself. He had never been in the presence of a political leader before. The most authoritative man he had ever met was Judge Parker. This was totally different. This man had the fate of an entire country in his hands.

Matt was surprised that the man rose. He was tall, and he stood proudly erect. He was wearing a uniform festooned with medals and ribbons. His hair and beard, both dark but shot with gray, had been expertly trimmed.

"*El President* José de la Cruz Porfirio Mori Díaz," the colonel said, "may I present Deputy US Marshal Matthew Wheeler."

"*El Presidente,*" Matt said, wondering if he was supposed to bow, "this is an honor."

"Marshal Wheeler," Díaz said, and again surprised Matt by extending his hand. They shook briefly. "Please, be seated."

"Thank you, sir."

Matt sat in a chair the colonel pulled out for him, which put him at the president's left. Obregón then walked around the table and sat at the president's right—which Matt presumed was fitting for Díaz's right-hand man.

A man dressed entirely in white was standing off to one side, and the president looked at him and nodded. Before long, that man was leading an army of others carrying food to the table.

"I have arranged for American as well as Mexican breakfast items," Díaz said.

Matt saw eggs and bacon as well as tortillas, rice, ground beef, and beans.

"It all looks and smells delicious, Your Excellency," he said. "Thank you."

The man in white supervised the setting of the plates on the table, then poured everyone coffee before withdrawing.

"Please," the president said, "eat."

"After you, sir."

That seemed to please Díaz, and he began to put food on his plate.

"You are probably wondering why I invited you here, *señor*," Díaz said.

"I am, sir."

"Well, I must tell you," the president said, "I needed to meet and speak with you before I decided if we would tolerate your presence in our country . . . or execute you."

CHAPTER TWENTY-FIVE

M ATT PAUSED IN loading his plate with food, but then continued. He was determined not to show surprise or fear to this man.

"What would you like to know, Your Excellency?" he asked.

"First," Díaz said, "you are the Matt Wheeler who rode for Judge Isaac Parker years ago?"

"I am."

"And you ride for him again?"

"I do."

"But he did not send you here."

"He did not."

"And during the time you did not ride for him," Díaz asked, "what did you do?"

Matt decided that the only way to play this was to tell the truth. "I was the sheriff of a small town in Montana," he said.

"Why would a man of your stature accept such a lowly position?" Díaz asked.

"My stature?"

"*Señor*, during your time with Judge Parker, you became quite well-known."

"Did I?"

The president stopped fiddling with his plate and stared at Matt. "Are you being modest, *señor*?"

"I don't think so, sir," Matt said. "During that time, I simply did the job the judge asked me to do."

"And quite well, I am told," Díaz added.

"I thought so."

"Then I ask again, why did you leave to take such a lowly position?"

"I got married."

Matt rolled meat and beans into a tortilla and took a bite. The flavors that burst into his mouth were unlike anything he had ever tasted before.

"Ahhh," Díaz said, nodding. "I see. But now you are back with Judge Parker?"

"I am."

"And why is that?"

"My wife was killed."

"After many years as sheriff in Montana?"

"No," Matt said, "during the first two years."

"But what have you been doing since then?"

"I started by hunting the men who killed her," Matt said. "I found one and killed him. As a result, I was sent to Yuma Prison. After seven and a half years there, I was pardoned."

Díaz sat back and regarded Matt solemnly. "This is very interesting," he said. "Perhaps we should get to the big question, though. What are you doing in my country?"

"There were three men that day. I was shot. She was killed. The one who actually shot her is still at large."

"He is here?" Díaz asked.

"That's what I'm trying to find out," Matt said, "but

I didn't want to do anything without checking with you first."

Díaz looked at the colonel, who was eating heartily.

"So you are not here as a United States marshal," Díaz said, "at the behest of your Judge Parker?"

"No," Matt said. "I'm following the trail of a man named Jason Pardee. I'm hoping that I don't find he's working on your behalf here in Mexico."

Díaz looked at the colonel again, who shook his head.

"We have some Americans who have come down here to fight with us," Díaz said, "but no one by that name."

"He might be using another name."

"That is true," Díaz said. He started to eat. "I presume you know what he looks like?"

"Oh, yes."

"The murder of your wife," Díaz said, "it took place ... how many years ago?"

"More than nine," Matt said, "during a bank robbery."

"Ah," Díaz said again. "So this is why you are not wearing your badge?"

"The badge is meaningless here, sir," Matt said. "I know that."

"Nevertheless," Díaz said, "your reputation is not."

"Sir?" Matt said. "Does this mean you won't have me executed?"

"I suppose that will depend on your behavior while you're in my country," Díaz said, "but for now, no."

Matt felt relieved.

"At least," Díaz continued, "not until you finish breakfast."

A FTER BREAKFAST THE table was cleared except for a coffeepot and some cups.

"Deputy—," Díaz started, but Matt cut him off.

"You don't have to call me that, sir."

"Do not interrupt—," the colonel started to snap, but then Díaz interrupted him.

"It is fine," he said, waving his hand. "*Señor*, I will have the colonel arrange for you to see all of the gringos we have working with us. If your man is here, you may take him back with you."

"Thank you, Your Excellency."

"I assume that is what you intend to do," *El Presidente* went on, "take him back to face justice?"

"Yes, sir."

"Then you are a better man than I am," Díaz said, "for if it were me, I would kill him on the spot."

Matt didn't respond.

"The colonel will show you out of the palace," Díaz said. "You will hear from him when he has arranged for you to see the men."

"Thank you."

They all stood, and Díaz extended his hand. They shook, and he said, "We will not meet again."

"I understand," Matt said, "and I'm grateful to you."

"If you should kill any of my people while you are here," Díaz said, "you will not be." He turned and left the dining room.

"This way, please," the colonel said.

"Lead the way."

Obregón took him back to the entrance of the palace, where he retrieved Matt's gun from the guard and gave it back to him.

"I will come to your hotel when I have the men assembled," the colonel said.

"How many are there?"

"I am not sure," Obregón said.

"Well, how long do you think it'll take?"

"I am not sure of that, either," the soldier said. "But I suggest you be patient."

"Patient," Matt said. "Well, I've been waiting over nine years. I guess a few more . . . hours—days—won't be too much to ask."

"Excellent," the colonel said. "I will see you soon."

He went back into the palace and closed the doors. The two uniformed guards there never looked at Matt.

B ACK AT HIS hotel, the clerk smiled as Matt went to the stairs.

"Everything is fine," he said to the young man.

"Muy bien," the clerk said.

Matt went to the door of his room and stopped. He pressed his ear to it, heard nothing. Nevertheless, he took the gun from his belt, opened the door, and stepped in, holding his gun out in front of him. He didn't know what he expected to find, but the room was empty.

Matt thought the desk clerk had looked nervous, but it was possible the man always looked that way. He surveyed the room one more time to see if anything had been touched, then checked the hall before closing the door.

He thought about changing hotels, but he was waiting for Colonel Obregón to contact him. Was he foolish to think the soldier wouldn't know if he did switch? They probably knew every move he made.

He went back downstairs to talk to the desk clerk.

"Sí, señor?"

"Are you always nervous?" Matt asked.

"Oh, *sí, señor,*" the clerk said. *"Lo siento.* It is always my way."

"Tell me about Colonel Obregón," Matt said.

"Oh, *señor*, he makes me very nervous," the clerk said.

"Why?"

"He is—how do you gringos say—not predictable."

"What do you mean?"

"He does not always do what *El Presidente* wants him to do."

"I thought he was President Díaz's right-hand man?"

"Oh, *sí, señor,*" the clerk said, "but—How do you gringos say about right and left hands?"

"One doesn't always know what the other is doing," Matt replied.

"*Sí, señor,*" the clerk said. "*Exactamente!*"

CHAPTER TWENTY-SIX

A CCORDING TO *EL Presidente*, Colonel Obregón would allow Matt to look at all the gringo mercenaries who were working with the Mexicans. According to the hotel desk clerk, the colonel would do whatever suited him.

Would President Díaz lie? Well, yes, he was a politician, and that was what they did.

Would the desk clerk lie? Possibly, but why? What reason would he have? And what of the colonel? When you were the right-hand man to a great leader, didn't that mean you were loyal to him? But if the colonel was using his position to pad his own pockets, would he go to a man like Jason Pardee and offer to sell him the information that Matt was in Mexico City looking for him?

Matt had one more question for the desk clerk.

"Where are the *federales* and the gringo mercenaries lodged?"

"At the garrison, *señor*, next to the palace."

"Gracias," Matt said, and handed the young man a dollar.

"Muchas gracias, señor!"

Matt left his hotel and headed for the palace again, this time with the intention of having a look around.

H E FOUND THE garrison, but it was enclosed with a guarded gate. However, he didn't need to get inside. He only needed to see if someone left. If Pardee was there, and the colonel had warned him, would he leave immediately? Would one of them wait until after dark: Obregón to issue the warning, Pardee to leave? Would Pardee be able to leave before paying the colonel?

Or was Matt being overly suspicious? Maybe all he needed to do was wait at his hotel like he was told, and the information would come to him.

He was about to leave the doorway from where he'd been watching the garrison when a smaller door next to the gate opened and two men came out. They were both gringos. They were laughing and slapping each other on the back. Matt decided to follow them and see where they were going. Perhaps there was a place in town where the gringo mercenaries gathered.

T HE TWO *AMERICANOS* led Matt through the darkening streets of Mexico City to a small cantina that was not on any main road. There was no identifying name anywhere on the building.

He watched as they went inside, and when he thought he had let the right amount of time go by, he went inside himself.

He had been correct. There was a small gathering of men there, and they all appeared to be Americans.

Matt went to the bar and said to the bartender, *"Cerveza."*

"Sí, señor."

He saw the two men who had left the garrison standing at the bar, only feet from him. He picked up his beer and turned his back to the bar.

"Guess my hotel clerk was right," he said aloud. "This looks like the place for a lonely gringo."

"You got that right, friend," a man said.

With satisfaction, he saw that it was one of the men from the garrison.

"You just get to town?" the man asked.

"Yup, rode in this morning. I was already getting lonely for my own language when the desk clerk told me about this place."

"Well, you came to the right place," the second man said. "Nothing but *Americano* spoken here."

"Except for Jesús," the first man said. "Best damn bartender in Mexico City."

"Gracias, señor," the portly bartender said with a smile.

"You know what else I'm looking for?" Matt said.

"What's that, friend?" one of the men asked.

"Work," Matt said. "A job. Some way to make money."

The two men exchanged a glance.

"Well," one said, "if you was to spring for a coupla more beers, we might be able to help ya with that."

"Jesús," Matt said, "set my friends up with fresh beers."

"Sí, señor!" Jesús said happily.

M ATT DRANK WITH the two men most of the evening, while others came and went. According to Sam Maxwell and Irv Bracken, there was nobody else in the place from the garrison.

"We're not even supposed to be here," Maxwell said. "We sorta snuck out to wet our whistles."

"They must be pretty strict there if you had to sneak out," Matt said. "I'm not real good with discipline."

"Oh, it ain't that bad," Maxwell said.

"Not if ya don't get caught," Bracken said, and laughed.

Matt knew if he hadn't taken the time to notify the *federales* and the president of his presence in their city, he could have simply tried to join them as a mercenary and get a look at all the gringos that way. Now the best way to go would probably have been to drink with these fellows for a few nights before starting to ask questions. But he didn't feel he had time for that.

So he decided to go ahead and make his move and see what happened.

"You know," he said, "I had a couple of friends who said they were going to come down here and join up because the pay was pretty good."

"The pay's better when there's a war goin' on," Bracken said, "but there are still some revolutionaries out there and bandits, so it ain't bad."

"Who're your friends?" Maxwell asked. "Maybe we know 'em."

"Let's see," Matt said, acting like he had to try to remember their names. "One was a fella named Ed Corbin and the other was . . . Who was it? Oh, yeah, Jason Pardee."

The two men looked at each other owlishly, trying to make their way through a drunken haze.

"I don't know any Corbin. Do ya, Sam?" Bracken asked.

"Naw," Maxwell said, "never heard of no Ed Corbin—but that other fella . . . wasn't he here?"

"Pardee," Bracken said, pronouncing the name very carefully, "Jason Pardee."

"Yeah," Maxwell said, "yeah, he was here. Said he came down after ridin' with some Comanchero bunch. Remember?"

"Now that you mention it," Bracken said, "I do remember him."

"Is old Jace still here?" Matt asked, his heart beating faster. "I'd sure like to see a familiar face. Did some riding with an outlaw bunch myself for a while."

"Naw," Maxwell said, "he ain't here now. He left . . . What was it? A week or two ago?"

"Yeah, yeah," Bracken said. "He was complainin' that the pay wasn't good enough, said maybe he'd get more ridin' with some *bandidos*."

"Say," Maxwell said, "why don't you join up? You already got friends." He slapped his chest. "Us!"

"You know," Matt said, "I might just do that."

Bracken nudged his buddy and said, "We gotta get back before bed check."

"There's bed check?" Matt asked.

"Yeah," Maxwell said drunkenly and lowered his voice, "but we stuffed pillows under our blankets."

"These *federales* ain't the smartest buncha guys," Bracken said.

"We gotta go," Maxwell said. "Maybe we'll see ya at the garrison."

"Maybe," Matt said.

They started for the door, then turned.

"Hey, what's yer name?" Maxwell said.

"They call me Jud," Matt said, "Jud Parker." He'd almost said "Judge" Parker, but one of these fellows might have recognized the name.

"See ya, Jud!"

The two men staggered out. Matt wondered how they were going to get back into the garrison without getting caught.

"More *cerveza, señor*?" Jesús asked.

"No, thanks," Matt said. "I think I'll just sit and finish this one."

Matt made his way to a table in the back and sat. He had managed to only drink about half what Maxwell and Bracken had, but he still felt a bit woozy.

He looked around at the other men in the room, seated alone or in twos. At the moment there was no one standing at the bar. He wondered how many might have heard his conversation with Maxwell and Bracken, but men were coming in and out the whole time. Maybe no one had heard the entire conversation.

He thought about what the two men had told him. If it was true that Pardee had left to join up with some *bandidos*, wouldn't Colonel Obregón have known the name? Or perhaps the man wasn't acquainted with every gringo mercenary in the Mexican's employ.

Matt thought about his next move. Should he continue to wait to hear from Colonel Obregón or simply leave and start looking for *bandidos*? But what *bandidos*? There had to be many bands of them out in the hills. Which one would Pardee join up with?

He realized he was drunker than he had thought, as the words of President Díaz, Colonel Obregón, the hotel clerk, Maxwell, and Bracken swirled about in his mind. Who to believe and who not to? What if everyone was lying to him? Or could they all have been telling the truth?

His best bet seemed to be to go back to his hotel and get a good night's sleep, try to make sense of all of it in the morning.

He left the cantina and started back, hoping he would be able to find his hotel in his current condition. He took a wrong turn, found himself in a very dark alley, and turned to go back the way he had come when he heard the first shot.

Hot lead whizzed by his ear and, before another

shot could be fired, he dove for cover. He banged his knee painfully on something, but found the cover he needed behind some crates when the second shot came. The bullet smacked harmlessly into the crates.

It suddenly got very quiet. With his gun in hand, he risked peering out from behind the crates. The only light he could see was at the front of the alley, which was where he needed to be. He looked around him, saw only pitch-black. The shots had to have come from the lit end of the alley. He started to get to his feet, and pain shot through his bruised knee.

He pressed himself against the wall on one side of the alley, began to inch his way toward the light. If anyone stepped out to fire at him again, he would be sure to see them. He looked up, wondered if the shots might have come from a window or a rooftop, but the way the second bullet had struck the crates, it seemed to have been fired from the ground.

Matt reached the mouth of the alley without any further shots being fired. As he limped out into the street, he stuck his gun back into his belt, turned, and began to find his way to his hotel, suddenly sobered by the experience.

CHAPTER TWENTY-SEVEN

HE WOKE THE next morning with a mouth that felt like it was full of sand. He rolled off the bed, intending to drink some water from the pitcher, but his leg buckled, and he almost fell. He sat back down on the bed and looked at his knee. There was a huge mottled bruise covering it. He flexed the leg, trying to work some life into it, then finally stood and limped to the pitcher. He drank directly from it. The water was warm, but it did the job, washing the sandy feeling from his mouth.

He poured some water into the basin and washed his face and hands, then ran his wet hands through his hair. That done, feeling more awake, he went back to the bed and sat to try to recall all the events of the previous day.

Anybody he had talked to the day before could have taken a shot at him. Were Maxwell and Bracken not as drunk as he had thought? Had they fired at him? No, the shots had come from one gun, and he was certain the two men were too drunk to have done it. That left anyone else in the cantina who might have heard their discussion. Or someone sent by Colonel Obregón for his own reasons. Or better still, simply someone intending to rob him after they had killed him.

It was futile to give the incident any more thought. Someone had shot at him, and it was not the first time it had ever happened. He would just have to keep a sharp eye out, watch his back, and not drink so much again.

He moved on to what he had found out about Jason Pardee. Apparently, he *had* been a member of the Mexican garrison, but had since moved on to try to join up with a band of *bandidos*. Matt wondered how in hell he could find out which one, since the hills were crawling with them.

And what of Colonel Obregón? Had he truly not recognized Jason Pardee's name? Perhaps Pardee hadn't been signed on long enough to make an impact.

Matt was putting on a clean shirt, intending to go downstairs for some breakfast, when there was a knock at his door. When he opened it, he saw a young soldier with two stripes on his sleeve standing there.

"*Señor,*" the soldier said, saluting smartly, "Colonel Obregón would like you to come to the garrison this afternoon."

"Did he say why, Corporal?"

"*Señor*, he said you would know the reason."

There was only one. Obregón had managed to gather together all the gringos in Mexico's employ. Despite what he'd been told about Jason Pardee leaving, Matt didn't see any harm in taking a look. And maybe he would be able to question the colonel again about the man.

"Did the colonel say what time I should come by?" Matt asked.

"*Señor*, he said noon," the corporal said, "before siesta time."

"All right, Corporal, tell the colonel I will be there at noon."

"*Sí, señor.*"

"Oh, Corporal," Matt said as the man started to walk away.

"*Sí, señor?*" the man said, turning.

"What time is siesta time?"

"Usually between one and four, *señor*."

"Thank you."

"*Por nada, señor.*"

The soldier left to deliver the message. Matt grabbed his hat and went down to find some breakfast.

N O MATTER WHERE he ate, it would be a poor substitute for the breakfast he'd had with President Díaz. He settled for a small cantina a couple of blocks from his hotel. Indeed, the ambience was no match, but he found the food to be almost as good, as he ordered Mexican breakfast tacos.

While eating, he rubbed and flexed his sore knee, hoping that the stiffness would abate, but the heavily bruised area continued to cause him pain. He just hoped it wouldn't continue to impede his movement, as he had limped all the way there from the hotel. If he was going to avoid being shot or continue his hunt for Pardee on the trail, he'd need to be in good health.

"*Señor?*"

He looked up at the motherly waitress who had served him his food. "Yes?"

"You have injured your leg?" she asked.

"Hmm? Oh, yes, I . . . fell and bruised it," he said, rubbing it again.

"You would like a . . . *médico*?"

"Médico?" he repeated. "Oh, you mean a doctor?"

"Sí," she said, smiling, "a doctor."

"No," he said, "thank you, but I don't think I need a doctor. I don't know what he'd do. I'll be fine, as long as I can keep it from stiffening up."

"Then you would like more food? More *café*?"

"More coffee, yes, thank you."

She nodded, went to the kitchen, and returned with another pot of coffee.

Matt had two more cups, then stood up to leave, staggering slightly on his bad knee. He regained his balance and settled his bill with the woman, who smiled at him.

"Por favor," she said, "I hope your leg gets better."

"Thank you."

He limped out the door.

A FTER SPENDING THE rest of the morning exercising his leg, he managed to present himself at the gate of the garrison without too much of a limp.

"I'm here to see Colonel Obregón," he told the two guards. "I'm Matt Wheeler."

"Sí," one of them said, "you are to follow me, *señor*."

"Fine."

Rather than open the large gate, the guard opened the smaller door Matt had seen the two men use the night before. He followed the guard through and then across an open field toward two structures, one large, one small. He assumed the larger was a barracks, so the smaller must have been the headquarters for Colonel Obregón.

Matt followed the guard to the smaller building, where he stopped and knocked before entering. Matt followed him. Inside he found the colonel standing at a large table. On the table was what looked like a map.

"Ah, *Señor* Wheeler," Obregón said. "Welcome."

"Good afternoon."

"I have collected all of our gringos for you to look at," the colonel said. "It was not very hard, as they are all here in the garrison at the moment."

Matt realized that as soon as Maxwell and Bracken saw him, they would know they'd been fooled.

"Colonel," Matt asked, "is there a way for me to see them without them seeing me?"

Obregón frowned a minute, then seemed to understand.

"I see," he said. "If your man Pardee is here, you do not wish him to see you."

"That's right."

"Of course," Obregón said. "I will have them line up outside. You can look at them from this window. Will that do?"

"That should do just fine," Matt said. He went to the window and looked out. "Yeah, this should do."

"You have hurt your leg?" Obregón asked.

Matt had thought he was covering up his injured knee pretty well. "I just twisted my knee a bit," he said. "I'll be fine."

"Bien," Obregón said. "I will have the men in a line just outside this window shortly."

"Thank you."

Matt watched from the window as Obregón went to the barracks, then came out, followed by six men, all Americans. He put them in a line, as promised, so Matt could inspect them from the window. They all stood, shifting their feet nervously, since they didn't know why they had been called out. Matt recognized Maxwell and Bracken from the night before. But he had never seen any of the other four men.

After a short time, Obregón dismissed the men and came back inside.

"So?" he asked. "Is your man there? What was his name?"

"Pardee," Matt said. "No, he's not there. But I have a question."

"Yes?"

"Could he have been here recently but left before I arrived?"

"That is possible."

"Do you have a list of men who worked for you but have since left?"

"Alas, we do not. We have a list of our soldiers so that they may receive their salaries, but mercenaries are paid separately and in cash. There is no record of such men."

Matt didn't know whether that was true or not, but he couldn't call Obregón on it. That would've been tantamount to calling the man a liar.

"Well, all right," Matt said. "I appreciate your help, Colonel, and please give President Díaz my thanks."

"I will do so, *señor*," Obregón said. "But . . . might you not be persuaded to join us while you are here?"

"Is there a revolution coming?" Matt asked. "Or would this be to battle local *bandidos*?"

"Perhaps both."

"How many bands of them are there at the moment?" Matt asked, hoping to get something that would aid him in tracking Pardee.

"There are several," the colonel said, "but the ones we are dealing with right now, more than any others, are being led by Juan Carlos de la Plata. He is growing in support and so may be the next such bandit to challenge *El Presidente* for leadership of our people."

"De la Plata, huh?" Matt said. "I've never heard of him. On the way here, I was chased by a couple of gangs. Might his have been one?"

"If they were chasing you to rob you, they would not

have been de la Plata's men. He is beyond petty crimes at this time."

"Well," Matt said, "I thank you for the offer, Colonel, but I do have to continue my hunt for Jason Pardee."

"He killed your wife more than nine years ago—is that correct?"

"It is."

"And yet you continue to pursue him with the same passion?"

"More," Matt said, "much more. I admit, during my incarceration, and for a short time after, I doubted my ability to continue the search, but I no longer have such doubts."

"It would seem your Judge Parker agrees with your assessment of your abilities," Obregón said, "or why else would he have once again given you a badge?"

"That's true enough," Matt said.

"*Señor*, if you change your mind, please feel free to come back and join us."

"I'll keep that in the back of my mind, Colonel."

"But while you are here," Obregón went on, "please remember *El Presidente*'s warning. Do not feel the need to kill any of our people."

"Does that include bandits who may try to attack me?" Matt asked.

"If you were to kill Juan Carlos or any of his men," Obregón said, "I believe I could be persuaded to look the other way."

"Understood. And would you be able to give me anything in writing I might produce if I'm stopped by your *federales*?"

"Alas, no such written document would be permitted," Obregón said. "But you may invoke my name if such a time arises. Just do not speak the name of *El Presidente*. The meeting between you and he must be kept confidential."

"I understand," Matt said. "I'll do my best to stay out of trouble."

The colonel clicked his heels and executed a slight bow. "My guard will show you to the gate, *señor*," he said. *"Vaya con Dios."*

Matt nodded, turned, and followed the guard from the shack to the gate.

CHAPTER TWENTY-EIGHT

T HE VISIT TO the barracks to inspect the gringo mercenaries had resulted in one good piece of information. The *bandido* leader causing the most trouble
at the moment was Juan Carlos de la Plata. So who else
would Jason Pardee offer his services to? Matt's next
move to find Pardee was to find de la Plata.

He figured he could head out in the morning, leaving Mexico City to ride into the hills, seeking the bandit leader. But he was going to need a very good reason
for de la Plata not to kill him, whether on sight or afterward. And even though he had been warned not to
invoke the name of *El Presidente*, it seemed to him
that was the only card he had to play.

When he got back to the hotel, he sat on his bed and
counted his money. He'd been saving his pay from
Judge Parker, as well as much of the stipend he received for supplies. At the moment he still had enough
to get himself back to the United States, and possibly
all the way back to Fort Smith, when the time came.

He was just going to have to try not to get robbed or worse while he was actively seeking the de la Plata *bandidos*.

Matt decided to stop in a cantina after having supper to see if he could hear anything about the *bandidos*. Or he might even ask some questions. But after a couple of hours, he still had not discovered anything helpful. At that point he decided to go back to the cantina he'd followed Maxwell and Bracken to, hoping they had once again snuck out of the barracks for some drinks.

When he got there, he saw several men he had seen the night before, but not the two mercenaries. Also, he did not see any of the men he had looked over at the barracks that afternoon. He went to the bar and ordered a beer.

"You're Jesús, right?"

"*Sí*, that is my name."

"Have you seen my friends tonight?" he asked when the bartender brought his drink.

"Your friends, *señor*?"

"The two men I was here with last night," Matt said. "I thought they might come back tonight."

"I have not seen them today, *señor*," the man said.

"Will they be in later?"

"Who can tell?" the barman said with a shrug.

"Well, do any of these men know them? Perhaps I can find out—"

"I do not know, *señor*," the bartender said. "I serve drinks, and I mind my own business. *Comprende?*"

"Yes," Matt said, "I understand."

"But you can feel free to ask," Jesús said. "It is of no matter to me."

"Okay, thanks."

Matt turned and studied the room. Men had come and gone the night before while he was there, but he recognized a couple who were sitting together. Then he recalled thinking that it could have been one of the men from this cantina who had shot at him when he left.

He was pressing his luck, but what could he do about it now? He was there.

With his beer, he walked over to the table. "'Scuse me, gents."

They looked up at him.

"You want somethin'?" one asked.

"Just to ask a question," Matt said. "I'm looking for some fellas I met in here last night named Maxwell and Bracken. Would you know them?"

The men looked at each other, then back at Matt.

"Never heard of 'em."

"Do you fellas come in here a lot?"

"What's it to ya?" the second man asked.

"Hey, look," Matt said, "I don't want any trouble. I was just looking for my two friends to drink with again. I need some Americans to talk to, you know?"

"Yeah?" the first man said. "What's wrong with us?"

"You fellas want to have a beer with me?"

"That depends," the second man said. "You buyin'?"

"I am."

"Then have a seat, friend," the first man said. "I'm Gage, and this is Fred."

"Jesús!" Matt called out. "Beers for my friends, Gage and Fred!"

"Sí, señor."

Matt sat, and Jesús brought the beers over.

"You make friends very quickly, *señor*," he said to Matt.

"Ain't that the truth?" Gage said, grabbing a beer.

T HE FIRST THING Matt noticed about Gage and Fred was that they weren't carrying guns. It turned out they were day laborers, going out each morning to see

if they could find work digging or chopping or carrying.

"Whatever we can get," Fred said. "These friends of
yours, where do they work?"

"They're over at the barracks."

"Ah," Gage said, "mercenaries. You a mercenary?"

"Me? No, I'm just somebody trying to stay out of
trouble," Matt said.

"You got trouble back in the States?" Fred asked.

"Some," Matt said, trying to sound reluctant about
revealing much.

"Say no more," Gage said. "We've all got somethin'
that chased us down here." He raised his glass.

They drank to that and more.

M ATT EVENTUALLY RAISED the subject of *bandidos*.
"We try not to take any work that puts us near
those hills north of town," Gage said.

"North?"

"That's de la Plata country," Fred said.

Matt couldn't believe his luck. "Is he the one the
federales are worried about?" he asked.

"Oh, yeah," Fred said, "he's gettin' himself some
followers. Díaz is afraid of him, all right."

"What about gringos?" Matt said. "Does he have
any with him?"

"Mercenaries, you mean?" Gage said. "Hell, I guess
so. They ain't all down here workin' for Díaz. They're
goin' where the money is."

"Wait," Fred said. "You ain't thinkin' about goin' to
work for de la Plata, are ya?"

"I don't know," Matt lied. "I never heard his name
till just a minute ago. Would he pay more than the
federales?"

"Who knows?" Fred said. "You'd have to ask your two friends—your other two friends—about that."

Gage and Fred were getting very drunk, and Matt didn't want to follow. He thought he'd found out enough information for one night, so he finished what was in his glass and started to get up.

"Hey, you done?" Fred asked. "We got more drinkin' to do."

"Not me," Matt said. "I'm heading out in the morning."

"Back to the States?" Gage asked.

"I don't know," Matt said. "I just know I can't stay here anymore."

"Why not?" Gage asked.

Matt decided to toss something out and see how the two men reacted. "Somebody took a shot at me last night after I left here," he said, studying their faces.

"What?" Fred said.

"You fellas saw me here last night, right?"

"Sure, we did," Gage said.

"Did you see me leave?" Matt asked. "See anybody follow me, maybe?"

"Hey," Fred said, "in this cantina, we're all in the same boat. Ain't nobody from here woulda shot at you."

"Damn right!" Gage said. "You musta already been set on by *bandidos*."

"De la Plata's men?" Matt asked.

"Naw," Fred said, "they got bigger fish ta fry. Some street bandit was after your poke, is all. Some other fellas have been robbed a time or two after leavin' here."

"You're probably right," Matt said. "Well, my thanks to you fellas for the company."

"Thanks for the beers," Gage said, lifting the remnants of his last one.

Matt tossed a look in Jesús the bartender's direction. The man gave him a baleful look while halfheartedly cleaning a glass with a dirty rag.

Not as drunk as he had been the night before, Matt didn't take any wrong turns, but he did pay special attention to his back trail as he walked the streets. He was sure somebody was following him, and this time he wanted to be the one springing a surprise.

CHAPTER TWENTY-NINE

THIS TIME WHEN he turned down that dark alley where he'd been shot at the night before, he did so deliberately. But as soon as he ducked into it, he flattened himself against the wall and waited. Sure enough, a figure stopped just at the mouth of the alley and seemed to be peering in. Matt reached out from the darkness, grabbed the front of a wiry man's shirt, and yanked him in. He slammed him against the wall, drove his fist into the man's stomach, and relieved him of the gun he had in his hand.

Allowing the man to slump to the ground, Matt leaned over, struck a match so he could see the man's ratlike face, and said, "Okay, now we're going to talk."

"*Señor—*" The Mexican gagged. "You have made—a mistake."

"You made the mistake, amigo, when you took two shots at me last night." Matt dropped the match and didn't bother lighting another one.

"*Señor—*"

"Don't bother denying it," Matt said. "And don't bother denying that Jesús sent you."

Still attempting to catch his breath after the punch to the stomach, the man said, "Jesús?"

"The bartender in the cantina I just came from," Matt said. "Considering I'm in Mexico, I'm going to guess he's your brother or cousin—"

"He—he is married to my sister, *señor*," the man admitted, sounding sad about it.

"And how many gringos has he sent you out to rob after they've been in his place?"

"Many, *señor*," the man said.

"And how many have you killed?"

"*Señor*," he said, "if I did not do as he asks, he would kill *me*."

"Well, how about if I turn you over to the *federales* over at the garrison, and you can tell them your story?" Matt suggested.

"Oh, *señor*," the man said, actually starting to blubber, "*por favor*, I have a family."

"I'm sure some of the men you've killed had families, too," Matt replied.

"I—I have not k-killed anyone, *señor*," the man said. "I swear." He made the sign of the cross.

"Then why take two shots at me last night?"

"Jesús," the man responded, "he said you would be a dangerous one."

"So why not leave me alone?"

"He said you had money."

That was what he got for buying Maxwell and Bracken drinks—and he'd done it again tonight with Gage and Fred.

"I am n-not a killer, *señor*," the man said. "I swear!" He crossed himself again.

"Well," Matt said, "you're sure as hell not any good at it."

The man rolled himself up into a ball on the ground and asked, "What will you do to me now, *señor*?"

"I happen to be friends with Colonel Obregón," Matt lied. "Do you know him?"

"Oh, *sí, señor*," the man said. "The colonel, he is *muy malo.* Very bad!"

"What's your name, amigo?"

"*Señor*, I am Santino."

"Well, Santino," Matt said, "I'm going to give the colonel your name and Jesús' name and let him know what the two of you have been up to. I don't know what he will do then. Do you?"

"No, *señor*," Santino said, "but whatever it is, it will be very bad."

"Maybe you'll want to get out of town as fast as you can without warning your brother-in-law. Let him deal with the *muy malo* colonel instead of you."

"*Sí, señor*, I will do that. *Señor*? You will be letting me go now?"

Matt stood up straight and said, "Yes, Santino, I will be letting you go. But if you don't get out of town and stop robbing gringos—"

"Oh, I will, *señor*," Santino said. "*Madre de Dios*, I swear!"

Matt reached down, grabbed little Santino by the back of his collar, hauled him to his feet, and pushed him out of the alley.

"Get out of here!" he shouted as the man ran. Matt tossed the little bandit's gun into the darkness of the alley and headed for his hotel.

IT DIDN'T TAKE much packing, since all he had were his saddlebags and rifle. Some beef jerky and coffee were all he would need to camp at night. His shirts could've used washing, but there was no time for that.

Once he had everything packed, he set his saddle-bags aside and thought about the little no-name cantina run by the bartender named Jesús. Should he actually go to the garrison to report the man? Or was this something the *federales* were already aware of— gringos being robbed on their streets? And would they even consider that a problem when they had to deal with *bandidos* and would-be revolutionaries?

He actually didn't want to have any more contact with the *federales*. He preferred to get out of Mexico City with his purse and his life intact. He had already left both *El Presidente* Porfirio Díaz and Colonel Obregón on good terms. Why risk another meeting?

His final decision was a quick breakfast come morning and then getting the hell out of Mexico City.

M ATT CHECKED OUT of the hotel the next morning and paid his bill.

"*Señor*, did not have any trouble," the clerk asked, "with the colonel?"

"I did not," Matt said, "so far. But I'm leaving town this morning."

"That is good, *señor*," the clerk said. "This is not a good place for gringos."

"Thanks for the warning," he said. He wondered if there was some specific trouble the clerk had expected him to run into?

"*Vaya con Dios,*" the clerk wished him.

Matt had breakfast at the same little café he'd eaten before, where the motherly waitress had asked him about his leg.

"You are better today?" she asked before taking his order.

"Much better, thank you."

She looked at his saddlebags. "You are leaving Mexico City?"

"Yes," he said, "I just wanted to have breakfast here one more time."

He had a small Mexican breakfast, which did not put a big dent in his purse, and then left to walk to the livery stable to retrieve his horse.

"Vaya con Dios, señor," the waitress bid him as he walked out.

"Thanks."

At the livery he had the hostler saddle his horse, then double-checked the cinch himself before putting his saddlebags and rifle in place and mounting up.

"Vaya con Dios, señor," the hostler said to him as the clerk and the waitress had.

"Say," he asked, "exactly what does that mean?"

"Señor, it means 'go with God,'" the man told him.

"So everybody says goodbye like that?"

"Not everyone, *señor,*" the hostler said, "but it is a kindness to do so."

"Well . . . then, thanks."

Matt mounted his horse and headed out, wondering if God would really go into the hills with him?

CHAPTER THIRTY

H<small>E MADE IT</small> out of Mexico City with no trouble. He didn't know what kind of trouble he was expecting. Santino might have gone back to his brother-in-law, Jesús, and told him what happened the night before, but Matt thought he had sufficiently scared the skinny bandit.

Was he expecting the colonel to pull something? Matt was sure the man was an opportunist, but what could he possibly have expected to get from Matt?

Maybe it was all the *vaya con Dios* he got on the way out of town that protected him. If only they would continue to keep him safe as he searched for Juan Carlos de la Plata up in the hills.

Looking into the distance, he figured it was half a day's ride before he had to worry about being seen. Still, he kept a sharp eye out in case de la Plata had scouts out. After all, the bandit leader would want to know if a company of *federales* was coming for him, wouldn't he?

Matt knew he was taking a big chance, hoping the *bandidos* wouldn't just shoot him from a distance when they did see him coming. If he got the chance to talk first, he'd have to convince them that he was trying to sell his gun. His only trouble would come if Pardee was there and recognized him when he rode in.

As he approached the hills north of Mexico City, he realized he could wander through them for days without seeing anybody. Rather than finding de la Plata, he decided to try to let the man find him.

He dismounted and made camp for the night, even though there was plenty of daylight left. After making sure his horse was settled, he got a fire going, put on a pan of beans and a pot of coffee, then hunkered down to eat. That done, he spread his bedroll and stretched out to go to sleep.

He did that for three days, and the reason he stayed put and repeated it was that he knew he was being watched. Finally, on the fourth day, while he was sleeping, somebody eased into camp and nudged him with their foot.

"Finally," he said, sliding his hat up from his eyes so he could see. The sun had gone down, but there was still some daylight. He found himself looking up at a Mexican with a big sombrero and a large rifle that was pointed down at him.

"*Señor,*" the man said, "if I was you, I would not move."

"I ain't moving," Matt said. "I'm just wondering what took you so long."

"*Señor?*"

"To come down here and wake me," Matt said.

"You expected this?" the man asked.

Matt sat up and said, "I was inviting it."

The man frowned mightily, scrunching up his face

and then scratching his mustache. "Ay-yay-yay, a crazy gringo," he said.

"Not crazy," Matt said. "You mind if I stand up?"

"Slowly, *señor*," the man said. "Please to leave your gun where it is."

The gun had been on the ground next to Matt. He stood up and left it there. The Mexican took a step back when he saw that Matt was bigger than he was, kept his rifle trained on him.

"Are you with de la Plata?" Matt asked.

"*Señor?*"

"Juan Carlos de la Plata," Matt said. "Is he your boss?"

"*Sí*, Juan Carlos is my *patrón*."

"Then good," Matt said. "I'd like you to take me to him."

"*Señor*, you want me to take you to see *El Chacal*?"

"El . . . what?"

"*Chacal,*" the man said. "He is the Jackal."

"Well, I haven't heard him called that, but yeah, okay, take me to see the Jackal."

"I do not know if I can do that, *señor*."

"Why not?"

The man just shrugged, and before he could say another word, someone else spoke.

"Rodrigo, what is the problem?"

Rodrigo looked up the hill at the speaker, another man holding a rifle. "He wants to be taken to *El Chacal*."

"Ay-yay-yay," the man said. "Another crazy gringo."

"*Sí.*"

"Why do you say another crazy gringo?" Matt asked. "Was there another man who wanted to be taken to *El Chacal*?"

"Oh, *sí, señor*," Rodrigo said, "many weeks ago. He came up here, as you did, and said the same thing."

"And did you take him?"

"*Sí.*"

"So then take me," Matt said. "What's the problem?"

The other man had come down to the camp and heard the question. "*Señor,*" he said, "that time it did not go very well."

"Look," Matt said, "all I'm looking to do is offer my gun to *El Chacal.* I'm sure he needs good men." Seeing these two, Matt was sure their leader could use his help.

"What do you think, Carlos?" Rodrigo asked the other man.

"Where have you come from, *señor*?" Carlos asked.

"Just now I came from Mexico City. I didn't like it there. Too many *federales.*"

"*Es verdad,*" Carlos said, "too many." He and Rodrigo laughed. "But you have been camped here for four days. For what are you waiting?"

"I was waiting for you," Matt said, "or somebody like you to come along and take me to see de la Plata."

"But, *señor,*" Carlos said, "what if we had just killed you?"

"Then that would be very bad," Matt said, "for me."

The two men thought about that, then laughed.

"*Sí,*" Rodrigo said, "that would be very bad for you, *señor.*"

"On the other hand," Matt said, "what have you got to lose? I might end up being of some help, and if I'm not, you can kill me then."

"*Sí, sí,*" Carlos said, "this makes sense." He squared his shoulders. "Rodrigo, I have made a decision. We will take the gringo to see *El Chacal.*"

"But, Carlos," Rodrigo said, keeping his voice low, "what is his name?"

"*Sí,*" Carlos said, "what is your name, *señor*?"

"My name is Parker, Jud Parker."

* * *

THEY WAITED WHILE "Jud" broke camp and saddled his horse, then walked him up the hill to where their horses were.

"*Señor*," Carlos said, "we must tie your hands and blindfold you."

"Is that really necessary?" Matt asked. "What's the difference if I see where your camp is? I'm either going to join you or you're going to kill me."

The two men exchanged a glance, but then Carlos said, "No, we must blindfold you. If we do not, *El Chacal* will be very angry."

"Oh, all right," Matt said. "Go ahead."

"*Gracias, señor,*" Rodrigo said.

THE GOING WAS very rocky; the hill sloped upward at a steep angle. Matt thought, if the need arose, he might be able to figure out the route they had taken. But why would that ever be the case? After a few miles, he stopped trying to figure it out and just went for the ride.

Before long the ground flattened out, and he thought they had reached a plateau of some sort. He heard other voices speaking Spanish, and he knew that Carlos and Rodrigo were explaining their decision to bring him in. Matt kept wondering if the other "crazy gringo" had been Pardee, and why things had not gone well for him? He hoped that *El Chacal* had not already killed Jason Pardee. If that was the case, then Matt had come a very long way either for nothing . . . or to die at the hands of the bandit leader.

The discussion turned into an argument, and then rough hands suddenly grabbed Matt and pulled him from his horse. He landed on the ground with a thud. If he was going to die, he wanted to see it, so with his bound hands, he reached up and pulled off the blind-fold. He found himself encircled by Mexicans, all glaring at him.

"I'm looking for Juan Carlos de la Plata," he said loudly.

All of the men—there had to be a dozen of them, all Mexicans, all wearing sombreros—began to laugh.

"*Silencio!*" another voice shouted, and they all fell silent.

The man came into view as those surrounding Matt fell away. He was not wearing a sombrero, but a bandanna was wrapped around his head. He had twin cartridge belts crisscrossing his chest. He walked over to where Matt was still sitting on the ground and looked down at him.

"I am Juan Carlos de la Plata."

Matt was surprised. This fellow wasn't even yet thirty.

"And what is your name?"

"Jud Parker."

De la Plata laughed. "That sounds like Judge Parker, your famous hanging judge."

"Um, yeah, it does," Matt said, aware that he still had his deputy marshal's badge in his shirt pocket.

De la Plata looked at Rodrigo and Carlos, pointed at them. "You and you, bring him."

He then turned and walked off.

CHAPTER THIRTY-ONE

Rodrigo and Carlos lifted Matt to his feet and then half dragged him across an open area to a shack, which de la Plata had entered. They took him inside.

"There," de la Plata said, pointing to a chair. He had a bottle of tequila in his hand, and he poured himself a drink. "Now, get out," he said.

"Do you want us to tie his hands behind his—," Rodrigo started.

"He's fine the way he is," de la Plata said. "Out!"

The two men left.

"Tequila?" de la Plata asked.

"Sure."

The bandit leader filled another glass, walked over, and handed it to Matt, who held it in his bound hands.

"You speak English very well," Matt said.

"I went to school in the United States," de la Plata said. "I was going to start a career there in law."

"What happened?"

"I realized somebody had to come back here and oppose Díaz."

"Why oppose *El Presidente*?"

There was a wooden table in the center of the room. De la Plata planted a hip on it. "Have you seen the palace?" he asked.

"I have, yes."

"He spent a fortune redoing it to his specifications," de la Plata said. "And he's hiring mercenaries from the United States. That's not where he's supposed to be spending money. Somebody has to stop him."

"I have to say, I'm surprised."

"That I'm so well educated," de la Plata asked, "or that I'm so young?"

"Well, for one thing, that I'm still alive."

"Why would I kill you?" de la Plata asked. "Because you're an American lawman?"

"What?"

"I see there's something in your shirt pocket, something weighing it down. If I reach in there, will I find a badge?"

"Yes."

"And considering the name you decided to use, I'd say you're working as a deputy US marshal for Judge Parker."

"Right again."

De la Plata put down his glass and walked over to Matt. He took a knife from his belt, cut the bonds that were holding Matt's hands.

"Thanks." Matt drank his tequila.

"What can I do for you, Deputy?" de la Plata asked, going back to the table and pouring himself another drink. He held the bottle up to Matt, who shook his head.

"I'm not here as a deputy," Matt said. "Judge Parker doesn't even know I'm here."

"What's your name? Your real name?"

"Matt Wheeler," Matt said. "I'm tracking a man named Jason Pardee. I think he might have come up here a few weeks ago."

"He did," de la Plata said.

"Your men Rodrigo and Carlos, they said it didn't go well for the other 'crazy gringo.' What did they mean by that?"

"He wanted to join us," de la Plata said. "I didn't want him."

"So he's not here?"

"No."

"Do you know where he went?"

"Well, considering he had already tried working for the *federales*, there was only one other place *for* him to go."

"Back to the United States."

De la Plata nodded. "That's my guess."

Matt's shoulders slumped.

"Disappointed?" de la Plata said.

"Yes."

"How long have you been tracking him?"

"Over nine years."

"He must have done something truly serious," the young *bandido* said.

"He did," Matt said. "He killed my wife."

"Oh. I'm sorry."

"Say," Matt said, "how did you get all these bandits out there to accept you?"

"A lot of them aren't bandits," de la Plata said. "I've got storekeepers, farmers, ranchers, men who have lost their livelihood because of Díaz and his *federales*. They just needed somebody to pull them all together."

"How did you get the name *El Chacal*?" Matt asked.

That made de la Plata laugh. "I called myself that,"

he admitted. "I needed some sort of intimidating name."

"I don't know that it's scaring Colonel Obregón," Matt said. "He never mentioned it to me."

"You saw Obregón?" de la Plata said, surprised.

"And Díaz."

"What?"

"I had breakfast with him in the palace."

"Breakfast with the president!" de la Plata exclaimed. "Oh, you have to tell me about that!" He took his hip off the table, stood up straight. "Look, I know you've got no choice but to head back to the United States and try to pick up Pardee's trail again. But stay here overnight. We'll feed you and give you a place to rest, and you can get an early start."

"And in return?"

"Tell me everything you saw in the palace, everything Díaz and Obregón said to you."

"You think that's going to be helpful?"

"It can't hurt." He picked up the tequila bottle again. "Another drink?"

"Why not?" Matt said. "I'm not going anywhere."

MATT HAD SUPPER with de la Plata in the shack while the rest of the men ate around campfires outside. The meal was beef, beans, and tortillas—simple but tasty. They washed it down with more tequila.

While they ate, Matt told de la Plata all about his conversation with President Díaz and his different encounters with Colonel Obregón. Matt told him what he had seen in the palace and in the barracks. And he even told him about his conversations with the two mercenaries Maxwell and Bracken.

Over coffee Matt asked, "Has any of this been helpful?"

"All of it," de la Plata said. "I wasn't sure how many men they had in those barracks, how many mercenaries they were paying. Now I do."

"You know," Matt said, "I'm impressed. For one so young—"

"How long have you ridden for Judge Parker?"

"Well," Matt said, "there's a story there, too. . . ."

S EVEN AND A half years in Yuma Prison?" de la Plata said when Matt had finished. "And you are impressed? How did a lawman stay alive that long in a place like that?"

"I had to learn," Matt said. "And when I came out, I had to learn to be me again."

"So you went to Parker, and he took you back?" de la Plata asked.

"He's the one who got me out," Matt said. "And he gave me a badge that I thought would be useful when I did find Pardee."

"Even here in Mexico?"

"President Díaz said he knew who I was," Matt said. "He recognized my name from my previous years with Judge Parker."

"So Parker was willing to let you do what you had to do," de la Plata said, "while wearing his badge?"

"Not quite," Matt said. "I don't think he expected me to disappear and go to Mexico."

"What will you tell him when you get back?" de la Plata asked.

"Hopefully," Matt said, "I'll ride into Fort Smith with a prisoner."

"Or a body," the young bandit said.

"Yes."

De la Plata showed Matt where he could spend the night, away from the prying eyes of his men, and told Matt he would see him at breakfast.

Matt spent a fitful night, not sure that all of *El Chacal*'s men would adhere to his wishes and leave him alone. Although if most of them were storekeepers and farmers, he probably didn't have much to worry about.

But frustration also kept him awake. This was probably the closest he had been to Jason Pardee in all the years that had passed since Pardee had killed Angie. But now Matt was forced to go back to the United States and start again. Even though he was no longer the man he had become in Yuma, and the shakes had left his hands, he wasn't sure he still had what it took to continue. It was only when he thought of Angie's grave that his determination prevailed.

He finally fell asleep, but dreamed he was at the base of boot hill, still unable to ascend to Angie's grave site.

I N THE MORNING Matt's meal with de la Plata once again took place in the man's shack while the other men ate outside.

When Matt was ready to ride, a man came up to him and handed him a sack. He recognized the other man as the cook.

"*El Chacal* said you should have some food for your trip, *señor*."

"*Gracias,*" Matt said, using one of the few words he had picked up while in Mexico.

He tied the sack to the saddle horn, thinking about *El Chacal*. How long would the educated young man be able to continue living out here in the hills? Hoping to overthrow a president who not only seemed firmly entrenched in office, but loved by his people, would be close to impossible.

De la Plata approached as Matt prepared to mount up.

"I could still use a man like you, Deputy," the young man said. "If you change your mind, come on back."

The two men shook hands. Matt realized he might have been twice de la Plata's age.

"I don't know how much more time you're going to give to this, *El Chacal*," Matt said, "but remember, you still have a long life ahead of you."

"My people need me," the young man said simply.

"Then I wish you luck," Matt said, and mounted up.

El Chacal looked up at him and said, *"Vaya con Dios, amigo."*

CHAPTER THIRTY-TWO

Matt had to ride into Fort Smith empty-handed. He had been back in the US for a month and could no longer justify staying away. He had to face Judge Parker and see if the man wanted to take back the badge he had given Matt. Hell, if it was Matt, he'd take it back in a minute.

He also hadn't run into Bass Reeves since his return from Mexico. But he knew that Bass was still out there, doing his job.

Matt didn't bother freshening up when he reached Fort Smith. He went directly to Judge Parker's chambers.

"You look like shit," the jurist told him.

"I feel like it, too," Matt said.

"Sit," Parker said. He poured a whiskey and handed it to Matt. "Drink it."

Matt drank it down, then set the empty glass down on the judge's desk. "Judge, I'm sorry—"

"Don't apologize," Parker said. "Bass came back

with that miscreant you caught and told me what was going on. I'm not surprised you went all the way to Mexico City in pursuit of the man who killed your wife. I'm just sorry you didn't get him. You didn't, did you?"

"No."

"Then give me a rundown of what happened," the judge said. "I think I deserve that much."

So Matt related it all, and Parker listened silently until he was done.

"That's impressive," Parker said, "meals with *El Presidente* and a bandit leader."

"I believe it was the president's respect for you that kept him from executing me," Matt said.

"Balderdash! The man had no reason to execute you. And if he had done so, he surely would have had me to deal with." Parker folded his hands over his vest. "Why don't you get cleaned up, fed, get some rest, come back here tomorrow, and we'll discuss your next assignment?"

"Yes, sir," Matt said, standing. "I appreciate you not just yanking this badge off my chest, Judge."

"That day might still come, Deputy," Parker said, "but not until after you've made that long-overdue apology to your wife at her grave."

Matt left the judge's chambers, surprised at how many men—hard men—softened when it came to his late wife. President Díaz, *El Chacal*, Bass Reeves, and even Judge Parker all understood his need to exact justice for her.

Matt didn't have a regular room in Fort Smith, and he preferred not to bunk in the barracks with the other deputies, so he got himself a hotel room and boarded his horse before going for a meal. After a steak, he stopped in a saloon for a couple of beers. At that point the fatigue overtook him, and he just made it back to his room in time to fall on the bed, fully clothed, and drift off to sleep.

T HE NEXT MORNING Matt once again presented himself at Judge Parker's chambers, this time after a bath and some fresh clothes.

"Here," Parker said, pushing an envelope across the desk at him. "You haven't picked up your pay or your stipend in quite a while."

"Thank you, sir." Matt put the envelope in his pocket without checking it.

"Judge," he said before the jurist could speak, "has Bass brought in Pale Blue yet?"

"No," Parker said, "that renegade is still out there, wreaking havoc."

"He's back in Indian Territory from Texas?" Matt asked.

"Yes," Parker said. "Apparently, Texas didn't agree with him."

"How would it sit with you if I want to go out and try to help Bass?" Matt asked.

"Why would you want to do that?"

"Bass went out of his way for me," Matt explained. "He even risked your wrath to do it."

"Believe me," Parker said, "I chewed his ass out when he got back, but he did have that third man with him, Corbin."

"What happened to him, by the way?"

"He's in a cell," Parker said. "I still need your story concerning his part in the whole Fairview debacle before I decide what to do with him."

"That's easy," Matt said. "He was in on the robbery, and he put a bullet in me."

"Not enough to hang him, I'm afraid," Parker said,

"but I can put him away for a long time. Now that only leaves Pardee. You didn't come back from Mexico with any idea of his whereabouts?"

"None," Matt said.

"But you still intend to find him?"

"Oh, yeah."

"Well, all right," Parker said. "If you want to help Deputy Reeves with Pale Blue, go ahead, but I'm afraid you're going to have to find him, first."

U S DEPUTY MARSHAL Matt Wheeler rode out of Fort Smith the next day, in search of both the Cherokee outlaw Pale Blue and Deputy Bass Reeves.

He had made up his mind to pay Bass back for his help, assist him in putting away Pale Blue, and then continue his search for Jason Pardee. However, if during that time he got word of Pardee's location, all bets would be off. He did not want to get close again only to miss.

T HE INFORMATION HE had gotten from Judge Parker was that the last time Pale Blue had been seen, it was around a town called Lawton in Indian Territory. Of course, he wasn't going to be there when Matt arrived, but it was a starting point.

When Matt rode in, he presented himself to town sheriff Lance Randall.

"Deputy Reeves was here about a week ago," the sheriff said. "Pale Blue a few days before that. They just missed each other."

"What did you do about Pale Blue being here?" Matt asked.

The tall, middle-aged sheriff said, "Nothin'. He didn't

do nothin' while he was in town that I coulda arrested him for."

"And if he had broken the law, would you have arrested him?" Matt asked.

"I'm alone here, Deputy," Randall said. "No deputies. Whataya think?"

"What did you tell Bass?" Matt asked.

"The same thing."

"And where'd he go?"

"Out there," the sheriff said, pointing.

"Be more specific."

"Pale Blue tried Texas, and it didn't work for him. He came back over the border, beefed up his gang, and now he's workin' the border. He crosses over, robs a bank or a Wells Fargo office, then comes back across. He's got himself a hole out there somewhere. He goes in, pulls it in after him. Bass is out there lookin'."

"And how do you know all this?" Matt asked, looking into the man's eyes.

The sheriff stared right back. "I'm the sheriff," he said.

"If I find out you're working with Pale Blue—"

"You got a helluva lotta nerve comin' into my town and sayin' that to me," Randall said.

"We'll see," Matt said.

He mounted up and rode out of Lawton, looking for Bass Reeves and Pale Blue.

CHAPTER THIRTY-THREE

M ATT DECIDED TO ride the Texas border, remaining
on the Indian Territory side, keeping his eyes
and ears open. In a small border town, he was in a saloon when he heard the name Bass Reeves. According
to the conversation, Bass had been seen near a town
called Poverty.

"Rode in big as brass with that badge on his chest,"
the storyteller said.

"And then what?"

"And then they got 'im and took him to Pale Blue's
camp."

"Aw, shit, they gonna kill 'im?"

"Looks like," the man said, "but they're waitin' for
Pale Blue ta get back."

"Son of a bitch, I'd like ta see that," the second man
said. "That big black has been a pain in the ass fir
years. 'Bout time somebody did somethin' about him."

"I might just go and take a look at that myself," the
first man said.

"You know where Pale Blue's camp is?" the other man asked.

The first man shushed him, and that was all Matt was able to hear. No one else in the saloon seemed to be concerned.

Matt waited for the storyteller to leave the saloon and followed.

It was getting dark, shops were closing, and the streets were emptying out as people either went home or to a saloon. Matt wasn't sure where the man was headed—another saloon or his hotel—but he decided not to wait and see.

As the man approached the mouth of an alley, Matt closed the distance between and stuck his gun in the man's back.

"What the—"

"Just take it easy." Matt reached around and took the man's gun from his belt.

"I got no money," the man said.

"I don't want your money. Get in the alley."

"You gonna kill me?"

"Just move!"

They went into the alley, which was not quite totally dark but soon would be. Before that could happen, though, Matt took his badge from his pocket and showed it to the man.

"Goddamn deputy marshal!" the man spat.

"That's right," Matt said. "What's your name?"

When the man didn't answer, Matt hit him on the shoulder with the butt of his gun.

"Ow! Damn!"

"It's only going to get worse," Matt said. "Name."

"Tillis."

"Okay, Mr. Tillis," Matt said, "you're going to take me to Pale Blue's hideout."

"What makes you think I know where Pale Blue is?"

"You were bragging about it in the saloon," Matt said. "You said they had Bass Reeves, and you were going to go and watch them kill him."

"I was just talkin'—"

"And I was listening," Matt said. "You're going to take me there, or I'm going to kill you."

"You—you wouldn't do that."

"Why not?"

"You're a lawman. If you're gonna do anythin', you'd take me to Judge Parker."

"I'll just save him the trouble of hanging you."

"But . . . why?"

"Because I'm going to set Bass Reeves free," Matt said, "as soon as you take me there. If you don't and they kill him, then I'll kill you. An eye for an eye."

"Wait. Wait. . . . Okay," Tillis said. "I can take you there."

"How do you know?"

"I used to ride with Pale Blue," Tillis said. "I know a few of his hideouts. It's gotta be one of them."

"You don't know for sure?"

"I know they have Reeves, and I know it's gotta be one of three places."

"Well, you'd better hope you get me to the right one in time."

"I—I'll try."

"Come on."

"What, now? It's gettin' dark."

"Let's get your horse saddled. When we're out of town, we'll camp. I don't want to have to deal with any of your friends."

"Can't we just leave in the mornin'?"

"No," Matt said. "And if you make a fuss before we ride out, I'll put a bullet in you."

"Yeah, okay."

"Now, move!"

* * *

THEY WENT TO a livery stable, got Tillis' horse saddled, and then rode out of town without incident.

"Stop here," Matt said when they got to a clearing about a mile out of town. "We'll take care of the horses, then make a fire."

"Are we gonna eat?"

"Beans," Matt said, "and coffee."

"I coulda had a steak in town."

"Should've thought of that before you started mouthing off in the saloon," Matt said.

"Why don't you make the fire while I take care of the horses?" Tillis said. "We'll eat sooner that way."

"Nice try," Matt said. "Like I'd leave you alone with the horses."

They got the horses secured, unsaddled, and rubbed down, and then Matt held his gun on Tillis while the man started a fire.

"You want me to cook?" Tillis asked.

"I'll take care of that," Matt said. "I'm not going to trust you with a frying pan any more than I would with the horses. In fact, put your hands behind your back."

"Wha—Aw, come on," Tillis said. "How am I gonna eat with my hands tied?"

"I'll untie you when supper's ready," Matt said.

He tied Tillis' hands behind his back, then made him sit on the ground. "If you try to run, I'll take your boots away from you."

"I ain't gonna run."

Matt got the coffeepot going, then made a pan of beans. He spooned them out into two plates he had in his saddlebags, and then he untied Tillis. He gave Tillis a cup of coffee, a plate, and a spoon rather than a fork. Then Matt sat across the fire from him and ate.

"Don't make me have to take out my gun, Tillis," Matt warned.

"I'm too hungry," the man said.

By the light of the fire, Matt could see that Tillis was a rough-looking forty, maybe forty-five, tall, and thin. When Matt had tied him, the other man had felt like a bag of bones.

"What's with you and Reeves?" Tillis asked. "I thought he didn't have no friends."

"He's not a friend exactly," Matt said, "more like a brother of the badge."

"So what's your name?" Tillis asked. "You look like you been ridin' for Parker a long time."

"Matt Wheeler."

Tillis looked surprised. "I heard of you," he said. "I also heard you quit."

"Well, I'm back," Matt said.

"You and Reeves gotta be Parker's oldest marshals."

"Probably. How long did you ride with Pale Blue?"

"Maybe six months."

"Why'd you leave?"

"To tell you the truth," Tillis said, "he scares me. That Cherokee is crazy. When he gets back and sees that his men got Reeves, he's gonna take 'im apart, slow-like."

"Not if I can help it," Matt said. "You finished?"

"Yeah."

"Hands behind your back."

"You gonna make me sleep like that?" Tillis complained.

"Yup."

Matt moved around behind Tillis and tied his hands again, then helped him to his feet and took him over to his bedroll.

"You gonna sleep?" Tillis asked.

"I'll stand watch for a while, make sure nobody's on

our trail. Somebody might have seen us riding out of town."

"You don't have to worry about that," Tillis said. "I didn't have any friends in that town."

"We'll see."

Matt went back to the fire and poured himself another cup of coffee.

"You're gonna be pretty tired tomorrow," Tillis warned.

"I'll get some sleep," Matt said. "Now, you just shut up until morning."

Tillis shifted about, trying to get comfortable with his hands behind his back. He finally settled on one side.

Matt stayed awake for a while, didn't hear anything out in the distance, and finally decided to simply close his eyes while he sat by the fire so that anyone from a distance couldn't tell if he was asleep or awake.

CHAPTER THIRTY-FOUR

A FTER THREE DAYS of riding around in Indian Territory and checking two locations, Matt lost his
patience. He reached out and knocked Tillis out of his
saddle. The man, still with his hands bound behind
him, landed awkwardly and cried out in pain.

"Jesus Christ!" he yelled. "What'd you do that for?"

"I'm tired of you running me around out here,"
Matt said. "Unless you tell me right now that you can
take me to Pale Blue's Comanchero hideout, I'm going
to put a bullet in you and leave you out here to bleed to
death." To punctuate his remark, he drew his gun from
his belt.

"Okay, okay," Tillis said, holding his hands up in
front of his face. "Wait."

"You've got ten seconds," Matt said, cocking the
hammer on his gun.

"Aw right, aw right," Tillis said, "but I gotta tell ya
somethin'."

"Go ahead."

"I can take ya there, but if they see me, they're gonna kill me."

Matt studied the man, then got it. He put the gun back in his belt. "So Pale Blue didn't let you leave," he said. "You just lit out."

"Yeah, that's right," Tillis said. "Once you join his gang, he don't like ta let ya leave."

"Wait a minute," Matt said. "Pardee left."

"But Pale Blue liked Pardee. Tol' him he could leave and come back whenever he wanted to. I never heard 'im tell anybody else that. In fact, I seen him kill two men who wanted to leave his gang."

"Look," Matt said, "you've got a choice of dying now, or maybe dying later when we catch up to them. But if you help me get Bass Reeves away from them, I'll let you go."

"How do I know that?" Tillis asked. "How do I know you won't just kill me when we're done?"

"You have my word," Matt said, "and I'm not Pale Blue."

Tillis drew his legs up so he could lean on his knees, took a few minutes to make up his mind.

"Okay," he said finally. "There's a box canyon not far from here. It's hidden. Pale Blue has lookouts posted, but I think I can get you in."

"Get *us* in," Matt said, dismounting to help Tillis to his feet and back into his saddle.

"Lead the way," Matt said. "And remember, this is your last chance."

T HERE," TILLIS SAID, "and there. See 'em?"

Matt stared off into the distance. "I see them."

Tillis was pointing at two lookouts holding rifles. They had positions on either side of a pass that led to the hideout.

"They can't see us?" Matt asked.

"Not here," Tillis said. "There's an outcropping of rock that hides us, but I know how to look around it."

"And now what?" Matt asked. "How do we get by them without being seen?"

"There's a way," Tillis said. "But we'll have to leave our horses."

"That's dangerous."

"Yeah, it is. But we should be able to get Reeves out and come back and get them."

"Then Bass won't have a horse."

"He'll have to ride double with you or me," Tillis said. "You, I think, since you have a better horse."

"That won't be a problem," Matt said.

"You should remember one thing, though," Tillis said.

"What's that?"

"If Pale Blue is back, Reeves is dead. And it won't be my fault."

"You ran me around out here for three days," Matt said. "So it certainly will be your fault."

"Then if Bass is dead, you'll kill me?"

"We'll have to see," Matt said, "just how badly I take it. Come on, now. Lead the way. We've still got plenty of daylight."

T ILLIS TOOK MATT on a rocky route where at times they were still able to see the lookouts, who were standing up on top of rocky points.

"Why can't they see us if we can see them?" Matt asked again.

"One reason is the sun," Tillis said. "And another is, they're not looking over here. They're watching for riders. Okay, around this bend, it gets tricky."

The path narrowed, and at one point, they had to turn sideways to get through an even narrower pass.

"How did you find this route?" Matt asked.

"Once I decided I wanted to leave, I knew I had to find a way out where I wouldn't be seen."

"So you walked this way and then what? You had no horse."

"I was able to arrange with a friend to meet me not far from here with a horse."

"Then we could've done that again to get Bass a horse."

"No," Tillis said, "that friend's dead."

They continued to walk. When they came around the bend, a canyon suddenly appeared below them.

"Keep low," Tillis said.

They ducked down, then kept moving until they saw a couple of shacks and some campfires. Off to one side was a makeshift corral made from logs, and inside it were several horses.

"Doesn't look like Pale Blue is back," Tillis said, "or there'd be more horses in that corral."

"Looks like . . . five," Matt said. "So with the two lookouts, that leaves three Comancheros down there."

"Bass will be in that shack, the smaller one." Tillis pointed. "They use it for a jail."

"And the other one?"

"It's Pale Blue's when he's here," Tillis said. "When he's not here, nobody goes near it."

"That's good," Matt said.

"Why?"

"That might come in handy."

"How?" Tillis asked.

"I don't know yet. How do we get down there?"

"There's a path up ahead, leads down to the canyon floor. You'll come out behind the shacks."

"*We'll* come out behind," Matt said. "And if you sound an alarm, I'll kill you."

"If I sound an alarm, *they'll* kill me," Tillis said.

"Okay," Matt said. "You first."

T ILLIS TOOK MATT to the path, which they used to descend to the canyon floor. As Tillis had said, it took them behind the two shacks.

Matt could see three men around a campfire, drinking coffee and laughing. They weren't bothering to look around, since they had two lookouts posted.

"The small shack," Matt said. "Move."

"Don't you think you'd better untie me first," Tillis asked, "and give me a gun?"

"I'll untie you," Matt said, then did so. "But I can't give you a gun, since I only have one. The others—yours and my rifle—are on my horse."

"That's great," Tillis said. "If there's shootin', what am I supposed to do?"

"Keep low," Matt said. "Let's move."

They ran quickly to the back of the small shack, where Matt was able to look in a window. On the floor, trussed up like a pig, was Bass Reeves. There was some blood on his face, but Matt could see he was breathing.

There was only one door.

"I'm going to have to go in the door," Matt said, "and get him out."

"They might see you."

"If they do," Matt said, "use this." He handed Tillis his gun.

"You're trustin' me with a gun?"

"Why did you leave Pale Blue in the first place?" Matt asked.

"He's crazy," Tillis said. "He kills people for no reason. I couldn't take it anymore."

"I don't think you want to join up with him again," Matt said. "I think I can trust you with the gun."

"Yeah," Tillis said, "you can."

"Okay," Matt said. "Hopefully there's no padlock on the door."

"There ain't," Tillis said. "It's just barred by a piece of wood."

"Okay, then I'm going in."

"Good luck," Tillis said.

As Matt went around to the front of the shack, Tillis took cover along the side, keeping an eye on the men at the campfire. Matt kicked away the piece of wood that was jammed against the door and opened it. With difficulty, Bass sat up to have a look.

"Matt!"

"You okay?" Matt asked.

"I am now," Bass said. "Get me out of here."

Matt crouched down next to him and untied his hands and then his legs.

"Can you walk?" Matt asked.

Bass flexed his legs. "I think so."

"We've got a ways to go on foot," Matt said. "Can you make it?"

As Matt helped Bass to his feet, the black man's legs buckled. "I don't think so."

"Okay, then," Matt said, "we'll have to take them."

Bass looked him up and down. "You don't have a gun?"

"I gave it to a friend. Come on."

They moved toward the door, where Matt peered out. He could see the Comancheros at the fire, still looking the other way. With Bass leaning on him, he went out the door and around to where Tillis was standing.

At that point one of the men looked over and saw the open door.

"He got out!" he shouted, and the other men turned, clawing for their guns.

"Shit!" Tillis said.

He fired once and missed. At that point the three men started shooting. Matt, Bass, and Tillis ducked behind the shack.

"We'll never make it back to that path," Matt said. "Bass' legs won't take it."

Tillis handed Matt back his gun.

"I say we make for Pale Blue's shack," he said. "There gotta be guns in there. Then we'll be on even terms."

"Unless the lookouts get here," Matt said.

"They're not supposed to leave their posts, no matter what," Tillis said.

"Okay, then," Matt said, "you take Bass and make for the shack. I'll cover you. On three. One . . . two . . . three!"

With Bass hanging on him, Tillis started for the shack. Matt peered around the shack and fired at the three men, who were scrambling for cover.

Then he started for Pale Blue's shack.

CHAPTER THIRTY-FIVE

MATT ENTERED THE shack just as bullets struck the door behind him. Bass was sitting at a table in the middle of the room, trying to catch his breath. Tillis was searching.

"Any guns?" Matt asked.

"I haven't—Wait. Yes!" Tillis had opened a trunk and brought out two Navy Colts.

"Those will have to do," Matt said. "Are they loaded?"

"No," Tillis said, "but there's ammo here." He set about loading the guns.

Matt went to a window and looked out. The three shooters had spread out and dropped down on their bellies.

"They're waiting," he said, "or planning."

"Nobody plans without Pale Blue," Tillis said. "They won't know what to do but wait." He handed Bass a gun.

"Thanks," Bass said.

"Is there any food here?" Matt said. "Or something to drink?"

Tillis looked around, came up with a hunk of beef jerky and half a bottle of whiskey. He gave them both to Bass, who consumed them ravenously.

"We gotta move quick before Pale Blue gets back," Tillis said.

"We'll take care of those three," Bass said, "and the lookouts, and then we can wait for Pale Blue."

Matt looked at Tillis. "How many men will Pale Blue have?" he asked.

"That depends on whether or not he picked up more along the way."

"He left here with ten," Bass said. "So he'll be coming back with at least that many."

"Ten against three, that ain't good odds," Tillis said.

"We'd better not worry about our odds right now," Bass said.

"He's right," Matt said. "Let's take care of this situation first."

"How?" Tillis asked.

Bass set the empty whiskey bottle aside, picked up one of the Navy Colts, and stood up. "The way we always do it," he said. "Just go out and get it done."

Matt looked at Tillis. "Three on three," he said. "Why not?"

"When?" Tillis asked.

"Now," Bass said. "Can't waste any more time."

"Are you up to this, Bass?" Matt asked.

Bass still looked unsteady. "I'll be fine. Let's go."

"How do we get out?" Tillis asked. "These windows are too small." They were hardly more than gunports in the walls.

"Out the front door," Bass said. "It'll surprise them and give us an advantage."

Tillis looked at the Navy Colt in his hand. It needed cleaning. "These things had better fire," he said.

Bass unloaded his, then pulled the trigger to be sure

it would work. He then reloaded it. "They're twins," he said, pointing to Tillis'. "They'll be fine."

"Okay, then," Matt said. "It's agreed. Out the front door."

"On three?" Tillis asked. "One . . . two . . ."

Bass let out a banshee yell and ran for the door.

"Three," Tillis said.

He and Matt followed Bass out the door. The big black deputy was already firing his gun.

The three Comancheros fired back. As they saw Matt and Tillis come out, they got to their knees to take better aim. That was their mistake. Tillis was firing wildly, but Matt and Bass fired straight and true, and the three Comancheros fell to the ground.

Bass and Matt checked the bodies to be sure they were dead, then exchanged their Navy Colts for the dead Comancheros' better weapons.

They now had guns and horses.

"We need to take care of the lookouts," Tillis told them, "or Pale Blue will know we're here."

"What if he comes back and sees there are no lookouts?" Matt asked.

"That would sure warn him all right," Bass said. "I suggest two of us take turns as lookouts just so he sees men on duty. Then, when he and his gang ride past, we can come in behind them. Between us and the one inside the camp, we'll have them in a cross fire."

"But first we need to take care of the men on lookout now," Tillis said.

"How do we get close to them without them knowing we're not Comancheros?" Matt said.

"I can do it," Tillis said. "They might recognize me and not realize until it's too late that I left."

Bass gave Matt a look, which Matt was able to read. Could they trust this man?

"We'll come up behind you," Matt said. "We just have to catch them off guard for a few moments and get the drop on them."

"Okay," Bass said, "but there's no time to waste. We need to do it now."

The three of them went to the corral to saddle a horse each.

T HEY HAD THE Comancheros' pistols *and* rifles. Matt and Bass each took a Winchester with them when they followed behind Tillis.

The first man on watch spotted Tillis coming toward him, pointed his rifle, then stopped. As Tillis had hoped, the man seemed to have forgotten that Tillis had left.

"What the hell was all that shootin'?" he called out to Tillis.

Before Tillis could give him an answer, Matt shot the man off his high perch.

The man on the opposite perch saw what happened and raised his rifle to retaliate, but Bass had already gotten into position to take care of him. He fired, and the second Comanchero fell to the ground.

They checked the two men to make sure they were dead, then hid the bodies behind some rocks.

"Tillis and I will stand watch out here," Matt suggested to Bass. "Why don't you just get back to the camp, see if you can't find something else to eat? You need to get your strength back. Besides, they might wonder why there's a black man on lookout."

"That's a good point," Bass said. "If I hear shots, I'll be ready."

Matt turned to Tillis, pointed, and asked, "Which rock you want?"

* * *

AFTER TWO DAYS of changing shifts on the rock—
even Bass took a turn just so Matt or Tillis could
have a rest—Matt was starting to wish they'd kept one
Comanchero alive to question. When was Pale Blue
expected to return? Had he given any idea how long
he'd be gone?

"He's gotta be back soon," Tillis said. "I'm sure they
woulda sent him a message tellin' him they got Bass.
He'd come back for that."

Later in the day, as Matt and Bass crossed paths,
Bass asked, "Do you really trust this fella, Tillis? I
mean, he was a Comanchero."

"I can't say I trust him completely," Matt said. "But
he's already had several chances to light out, and he's
still here. That's got to count for something."

"I s'pose," Bass agreed.

Late in the day, Tillis and Matt were on lookout.
Tillis' spot gave him the first look at the approach, and
he suddenly turned and started waving at Matt. Somebody was coming; Matt hoped it was Pale Blue and his
bunch. He was also hopeful that the Cherokee hadn't
picked up too many new men.

The plan was to wave the bunch on and then come
in behind them. Matt only hoped somebody didn't recognize Tillis and remember that he had left, or even
recognize himself as not being a Comanchero.

But as the bunch came into view, he actually counted
eight instead of ten, meaning Pale Blue had lost a couple instead of picking up new men. Tillis waved first and
got a return wave, and then Matt waved. For a moment
he thought the jig was up, but finally he got a return
wave, and the bunch moved on through the pass, led by
a long-haired man wearing a blue shirt.

Both Matt and Tillis scrambled from their perches to their horses and followed the bunch in. There was no way to warn Bass, but the big black deputy was ready every moment for Pale Blue to show up. He'd spot the riders coming in if he didn't hear them first.

Now they would find out if this plan was going to work.

CHAPTER THIRTY-SIX

"Was he there?" Matt asked Tillis as they rode through the pass.

"Yep," Tillis said. "Pale Blue was right out front."

Matt had never seen Pale Blue before this day, and he was happy when Tillis identified him.

This was what Bass Reeves had been working toward for months.

Bass Reeves heard the horses before he saw them. He took cover behind the shack he'd been held in. When the riders came into view, he saw Pale Blue right out front, and his heart began to race. With a gun in each hand, he stepped from cover to face the man he'd been hunting for so long.

The riders stopped as Pale Blue raised his arm. Then he rode close to Bass while the others stayed back and waited.

"I should have known you would get loose," the Cherokee said. "My men?"

"All dead."

Pale Blue frowned. "Then who was on lookout—" Suddenly, he turned to yell a warning to his men, but it was too late. . . .

M ATT AND TILLIS reached the canyon floor in time to see Bass Reeves facing Pale Blue.

"What's he doin'?" Tillis asked. "The plan was to get 'em in a cross fire, not face 'em like that."

"Bass usually has his own plans," Matt said. "We'd better get this done."

Shooting men in the back was not something Matt liked doing, but Bass, Tillis, and he were outnumbered and didn't have much choice.

They raised their rifles and began to fire. . . .

A S LEAD FLEW onto the canyon floor, Bass Reeves joined the fray. He extended both arms and began to fire. Pale Blue surprised him, though, and instead of trying to get away, the Cherokee rode right for him.

Pale Blue's Comancheros were confused; their reactions were dull. They were being fired on from front and back, and by the time they could figure out which way to turn, half of them were already on the ground.

"Let's get outta here!" somebody yelled.

But in order to get out, they would have to turn around and go back through the pass, which was blocked by Matt and Tillis. They tried, anyway, and rode right into blazing guns.

Pale Blue seemed to be a man possessed. Bass' bullets didn't seem to be hitting him, and as he reached the black deputy, he launched himself off his horse and onto the other man.

The two men rolled, came up standing, facing each other.

Pale Blue was six feet tall and built well, but at that moment, he looked considerably smaller than the six-feet-two, one-hundred-eighty-pound deputy.

Bass Reeves had dropped one of his guns. Unfortunately for the Cherokee, he hadn't dropped the other one.

Pale Blue drew his knife. "This has been a long time coming," he said to Reeves.

"Too long for me to mess it up," Bass Reeves said, "so just drop the knife and put your hands in the air." He pointed the gun at the Comanchero leader. "It's all over."

"Put that gun down and fight me like a man," Pale Blue said.

"Not a chance," Reeves said. "I'm not takin' any chances. You're gonna have your meetin' with Judge Parker."

The Cherokee screamed and charged at Bass Reeves with both his knife and his teeth flashing. Reeves calmly shot him in the leg. The man went down, dropped the knife, grabbed his leg, but refused to cry out.

Across the way, both Tillis and Matt were walking among the dead bodies.

"He's not here," Matt said. "Pardee's not here."

"And they came back with less men than they left with," Tillis said. "Something must've gone wrong."

"Let's get these buried and then see what we can find out from Pale Blue."

TILLIS AND MATT buried the dead while Bass Reeves sat at the fire, preparing something for them all to eat. It would be dark soon, so they couldn't leave until the next morning. Pale Blue was off to one side, trussed up and bandaged so they could get him back to Fort Smith for his reckoning with Judge Parker.

Matt and Tillis came over to the fire and tossed their shovels aside. As they sat at the fire, Reeves passed them plates of bacon and beans and cups of coffee.

"What about him?" Tillis asked, indicating Pale Blue, who was glaring at them.

"Let him go hungry," Bass Reeves growled.

"You doing okay?" Matt asked Bass.

"I'm fine," he said. "I've gotta thank you both for savin' my ass."

"You're welcome," Matt said.

"Deputy Wheeler forced me into it," Tillis admitted, "but I'm glad I done it. At least he won't be out there killin' people for no reason anymore."

Matt finished eating, accepted another cup of coffee from Bass, then stood up. "I'm going to talk to him," he said. "I need to find out what he knows about Pardee."

"Try to get it out of him without mentioning the name," Bass said.

"If I can."

Matt went over and crouched down next to Pale Blue. "Are you hungry?" he asked.

"I will not eat with lawmen and traitors."

"Suit yourself," Matt said. "It looks like you had some trouble before you even got here. I heard you had more men."

"Traitors are everywhere," the Cherokee spat.

"Ah, somebody betrayed you out there?"

Pale Blue spit on the ground. "I should know better than to trust a white man," he said.

"What happened?" Matt asked.

Pale Blue didn't answer.

"Come on," Matt said, "it's gnawing at you. I can see that."

"A man I trusted formed his own force and fought against me. I will kill him!"

"I don't think so," Matt said. "I don't think you're going to be able to do anything about it."

Pale Blue fumed.

"Unless . . ."

The Cherokee looked at him sharply. "Unless what?"

"Well," Matt said, "if he was in the next cell or even the same cell as you, you'd be able to get your hands on him."

"You expect me to help you catch him?"

"Why not?" Matt asked. "You're going to prison. He betrayed you. I'd think you wouldn't want him going free."

Matt had no idea whether or not they were talking about Jason Pardee. He could only hope that they were and that Pale Blue was going to tell him where to find the man.

"Think it over," Matt said, and went back to the fire.

"Anythin'?" Tillis asked.

"He says somebody he trusted turned on him," Matt said.

"Pardee?" Tillis asked.

"I don't know, but he says it was a white man."

"Did he trust Pardee?" Bass asked.

"He liked 'im," Tillis said. "He let Pardee leave. He don't usually do that. You only leave Pale Blue feet-first."

"You left," Bass said.

"I snuck out," Tillis said. "I knew he'd kill me before he'd let me go. But even before I went, Pardee left, and Pale Blue told him to come back if he wanted to."

"It seems this white man formed his own gang and turned it on Pale Blue," Matt said. "That's why they returned with less men than when they left."

"He didn't give you a name?" Bass asked.

"No," Matt said, "but I planted a seed in his head. Let's see if it takes root."

THE NEXT MORNING they had a quick breakfast. A couple of meals and a good night's sleep had Bass Reeves on the mend. He had a cut on his head he received from a gun butt, but it had scabbed over.

They saddled four horses for the ride back to Fort Smith. As Matt and Reeves lifted the trussed-up Pale Blue into the saddle, the Cherokee said, "Pardee."

"What?" Matt asked, trying not to seem anxious.

"The white man who turned on me is named Jason Pardee," Pale Blue said. "He is leading a force of about twelve."

"And where are they going?" Matt asked.

"They are going to start hitting banks in Texas. Small towns, at first, but if you get to Beaumont before they do, you can be there waiting for them." Pale Blue stared hard at Matt. "Bring him in and put him in a cell next to me. That's all I ask."

"I'll do my best."

"Your best was good enough to catch me," Pale Blue pointed out. "I will be waiting."

Matt and Bass Reeves walked away from the Cherokee, leaving Tillis to watch him. Pale Blue glared at the man he considered a traitor.

"You did not have to turn on me," he said.

"If I tol' you I wanted out, you woulda killed me," Tillis pointed out. "And this wasn't my choice."

"Then help me escape," the Comanchero leader said.

"Can't do that," Tillis said. "You'd kill me the first chance you got, especially after what Pardee's done. Now you'd kill anyone before you let them leave or give them a chance to betray you."

"And what do you think will happen to you when they get you back to Fort Smith?" Pale Blue asked.

"Forget it, Indian," Tillis said. "I trust them more than I trust you."

S TANDING WHERE PALE Blue and Tillis couldn't hear them, Bass Reeves asked, "What are you gonna do?"

"I'll head straight for Beaumont," Matt said. "This might be the best chance I'll ever have."

"If he's got a dozen men—"

"I'll make contact with the local law as soon as I get there," Matt cut in. "Maybe we can set up a nice reception committee for them."

"If they believe you and go along with your plan," Bass said. "I suggest you telegraph Judge Parker when you get there. He might be able to convince them to help you."

"Good idea," Matt said. "And you can do something for me?"

"What's that?"

"Before you get to Fort Smith, let Tillis go."

"Why?"

"I couldn't have saved you without his help," Matt said. "I don't want the judge tossing him in a cell."

"Maybe I can get the judge to offer him amnesty for his crimes," Bass said.

"Then offer him that choice," Matt said. "Let Tillis decide if he wants to take that chance."

"I will. And you watch your back."

"I will."

Matt walked over to Tillis and shook the man's hand. "Thanks for going along with me."

"You didn't leave me much choice," Tillis said.

"Maybe not in the beginning," Matt said, "but you came around on your own."

"What's gonna happen when we get to Fort Smith?" Tillis asked.

"Bass is going to talk to you about that," Matt said. "You'll have some decisions to make before you get there."

"Sounds fair. You watch yerself."

Matt nodded and mounted up. They had packed some provisions for the ride to Fort Smith. Because Matt had decided he was going to Beaumont, they divvied them up.

"Remember what I said," Pale Blue called out to Matt. "The cell next to mine!"

"Yeah," Bass Reeves said under his breath, "like that'd happen." He looked up at Matt. "You sure you wanna do this alone?"

"You have to go back," Matt said, "or I'd welcome you, Bass. Yeah, I've got to do this alone."

"Well," Bass said, "you're up to it. You're the Matt Wheeler I knew years ago."

"Not quite," Matt said, "but I'm close."

CHAPTER THIRTY-SEVEN

Beaumont, Texas

MATT WHEELER HAD never been to Beaumont. He had never been this close to an actual beach. But as much as the beach and the Gulf of Mexico were attractions to people, they were not why he was there.

Matt was surprised by the size of Beaumont as he rode in. It was a port town that depended heavily on lumber and rice for its livelihood. Matt truly felt like a man of the Old West, faced with all the modern conveniences Beaumont had to offer, including the major port.

But he couldn't be distracted by all of that. He was there to find Pardee; he hoped before the man and his gang robbed a bank.

Before trying to decide which bank might be targeted, he boarded his horse at the first livery stable he came to and himself at the first hotel he found, the Port Hotel, which was not located anywhere near the port.

That done, he went out to tend to his hunger and his thirst.

After eating at a small restaurant down the street from his hotel, he paid the bill and asked the waiter his question.

"Is there a sheriff or marshal in Beaumont? Or do you have a modern police department?"

"We have a sheriff and a police station."

"Who's the sheriff?"

"His name's Tom Friday."

Matt didn't know the name. "How long has he been sheriff here?"

The waiter, a man in his forties, said, "Jeez, Tom's been here as long as I have. . . . Maybe twenty years? He just has a lot less responsibilities now, what with the new police department."

"How's he feel about that?"

"Not good, but whataya gonna do? It's progress. We got some electric lights in the city, and they're sayin' that soon we're gonna have some of them telly-phone contraptions. It's goddamn progress."

"Yes, I saw some wires and poles while I was riding in."

"You just get here?"

"A little while ago," Matt said. "Where can I find the sheriff's office?"

"His office is on Sutter Street," the waiter said. "Used to be on Main, but they moved and knocked down the old sheriff's office to build the new police station."

"How do I get there from here? Can I walk?"

"Oh, yeah, just go out the door, turn right, walk about four streets, and that'll be Sutter. Make another right, and it'll be there. You can't miss it. There's a shingle."

"Thanks."

"I gotta warn ya, though, about Sheriff Friday."

"What about him?"

"He ain't a happy man," the waiter said, "and he tends to drink because of it."

"I'll keep that in mind. Thanks again."

Matt left the restaurant and followed the waiter's directions. Just as the man had said, he came to a shingle that read SHERIFF TOM FRIDAY. He opened the door and went inside.

He had passed many new buildings as he rode through Beaumont. But this one—and this street—was old. The inside smelled musty and looked dusty, so did the man sitting behind a small desk that leaned on one broken leg.

The man looked at Matt, one hand on a bottle and the other hand holding a coffee mug. He had a sheriff's badge on his chest.

"You're in the wrong place," the sheriff said. "If you're lookin' for law and order, go to the new police station."

"I'm looking for Sheriff Tom Friday."

Friday poured some whiskey into the mug. "You found him," he said. "You want a drink?"

"Coffee would do."

"Sorry. No coffee," Friday said. "Just whiskey."

"Then no," Matt said. He took his badge out and pinned it on. "My name's Matt Wheeler. I'm a deputy marshal assigned to Judge Parker's court."

"Ain't you a little out of your jurisdiction?"

"We've started covering parts of East Texas," Matt lied.

"And South Texas?"

"I'm here for a reason."

"And what would that be?" Friday asked. "Wait a minute." He sipped from the mug, then put it and the bottle down. "Did you say Matt Wheeler? Deputy Marshal Matt Wheeler?"

"That's right."

"Hell, you used to ride for Parker years ago," Friday said. "Then I heard you left."

"I'm back."

"I can see that," Friday said. "How old are you now?"

"Fifty."

"A little old to be ridin' the Indian Territory, ain't ya?" Friday asked.

"Look," Matt said, "I'm looking for a man named Jason Pardee."

"Pardee," Friday said. "I don't know the name. What's he wanted for?"

"Killing my wife," Matt said, "over nine years ago."

"Wait," Friday said. "Wait, wait. I remember that. Your wife was killed, and you were shot during a bank robbery. You recovered and started hunting the men who did it. You found one and killed him, and they put you in prison. Where was it?"

"Yuma."

"How long were you in?"

"Seven and a half years."

"Jesus," Friday said. "That must've been tough, an ex-lawman in Yuma Prison."

"It was," Matt said. "You know, I'll have some of that whiskey now."

"Sure thing. Have a seat."

Friday got up, fetched another mug from the top of the potbellied stove, and brought it back to his desk. He poured some whiskey for Matt and some more for himself, pushed one of the mugs across the desk.

"How did you get out?" Friday asked.

"I got a pardon from the governor."

"So you're not even considered an ex-con?"

"No."

"And Judge Parker took you back?"

"He worked on the governor to get me the pardon."

"So Parker wanted you back pretty bad."

"I suppose."

"And does he know you're here?"

"He does."

"Okay, then," Friday said, "tell me about this Jason Pardee."

A FTER MATT TOLD Friday everything that had happened so far, Friday sat back in his chair.

"So Pale Blue said he was coming here to rob a bank?"

"Yes."

"We have several banks," Friday said. "Which one?"

"That I don't know."

Friday looked at the whiskey bottle on his desk, then put the cap on it and stuck it in his desk drawer. He stood up, grabbed his hat, and said, "Why don't we try to find out?"

T HEY STOPPED AT three banks. All the managers seemed surprised to see the sheriff.

"Does Chief Montgomery know you're here asking these questions?" Martin Cameron, the manager of the Beaumont Bank, the largest in Beaumont, Texas, wanted to know.

"I'm tryin' to keep you from bein' robbed, Cameron," Sheriff Friday said. "Why would I need to go to the chief of police?"

"Because he's the top lawman in Beaumont."

Sheriff Friday stepped in close to the tall, expensively dressed dandy. Cameron was in his sixties and sat on the Beaumont town council.

"He's a blowhard and a fool," Friday said.

"Since when do you even come out of your office, Friday?" Cameron asked. "Did you run out of whiskey?"

"I'm Deputy Marshal Matt Wheeler," Matt said. "The sheriff is trying to help me discover which bank a band of Comancheros is coming here to rob."

"This man is sheriff in name only," the bank manager said. "He has no authority."

"I'd rather deal with him than some chief of some fancy police department."

"That's your mistake, Marshal," Cameron said. "I'm not worrying about a robbery threat brought to me by this man." He pointed at Friday. "Besides, I have plenty of security guards."

Matt looked around, saw two darkly clad security guards with shotguns.

Friday turned to Matt. "Come on," he said. "Let's get out of here."

Outside Friday put his hand on Matt's arm. "That's the place."

"How can you tell?" Matt asked.

"It's the biggest bank in town," Friday said. "Why else would a gang of Comancheros risk riding in here? Also, the bank manager's a fool if he thinks his security is going to save him."

"I've been through this before," Matt admitted, thinking back to Fairview. "Do you think we should go to Chief Montgomery?"

"He's not a lawman," Friday said. "He's a politician. But I'll leave that up to you. I've given you my opinion. This is the bank."

"Politician or not, if he's the top lawman in town and he has the men . . ."

"I get it," Friday said. "Go to see 'im, see if he even believes you. When he doesn't, then come back and see me."

"Will you be sober?" Matt asked.

"I'll be cleaned up and sober, Deputy," Friday promised, "and waitin' for you."

CHAPTER THIRTY-EIGHT

M ATT FOLLOWED SHERIFF Friday's directions to the
Beaumont police station. It was a new three-
story brick building, with a man in a tan uniform sitting
at a front desk as Matt entered.

"Can we help you, sir?" he asked.

"My name is Deputy Marshal Matt Wheeler," Matt
said, showing the man his badge. "I'd like to see Chief
Montgomery."

"Deputy marshal?" the officer said. "From where?"

"Indian Territory," Matt said. "Judge Parker's court."

"Judge Parker?" the man asked. "What're ya doin'
here?"

"I'm trying to head off a bank robbery."

"Bank robbery? Here?" The officer laughed. "This
ain't the Old West, Marshal."

"Still," Matt said, "I'd like to see Chief Montgomery."

The officer looked to be in his twenties, which explained why he said, "Well, okay, old-timer, let me see
if he's available. Have a seat."

Matt sat on a bench in front of the desk while the officer turned and went deeper into the building. He thought about what he could do if this Chief Montgomery didn't believe him.

When the young officer returned, he had an older man with him, tall, lean, gray haired, wearing a spotless tan uniform of shirt and trousers.

"Are you Deputy Wheeler?" the older officer asked.

"That's right," Matt said, standing up. "Chief Montgomery?"

"That's me. Why don't you follow me back to my office, Deputy."

"Sure."

Matt followed the chief through the building until they reached an office door that read CHIEF MONTGOMERY.

"Have a seat, Deputy," Montgomery said, "and tell me about this bank robbery."

Matt explained how he had come to be in Beaumont and why he expected one of their banks to be robbed.

"By this fella, Jason Pardee, and his gang?" Montgomery asked.

"Yes."

"And he's the man who shot and killed your wife."

"Yes."

"So you're really here to take your revenge," Montgomery said.

"No," Matt said, "I'm here to keep him from robbing a bank and to take him back to Fort Smith to face Judge Parker."

"Do you really expect me to believe that?"

"Why wouldn't you?"

"You're a dinosaur, Wheeler," Montgomery said. "Your code of the West calls for you to kill him."

"Dinosau—I'm younger than you are!" Matt said.

"But I'm an educated man," Montgomery said. "My decisions are based on intellect, not emotion."

"Chief, I'm trying to do you a fav—"

"And you say he's going to hit the Beaumont Bank."

"Yes."

"Based on the opinion of a drunken lawman who is also a dinosaur."

"Now, wait a minute," Matt said. "Can we do away with the dinosaur comments?"

"Sorry," Montgomery said, "but I'm not a fan of frontier justice."

"Chief," Matt said, "I suggest you put some men on the Beaumont Bank."

"They have their own security."

"Two men with shotguns are not going to do it," Matt told him.

"Look, Deputy," Montgomery said, "we appreciate your input. We'll take it from here."

Matt knew that he was being dismissed and that Chief Montgomery probably wasn't going to do a thing. He stood up to leave, but had to have one last say.

"I want you to remember I came to you with this, Chief," he said. "Remember."

"Thank you very much," Montgomery said. "I'm sure you can find your way out, Deputy."

Matt retraced his steps and made his way out of the building, satisfied that he had done his best. In truth, he didn't care if one of Beaumont's banks got robbed or not. He just wanted to finally catch up with Jason Pardee. If a bank got robbed, so be it. It would fall to Chief Montgomery to explain it.

W HEN MATT WALKED back into the sheriff's office, Tom Friday said, "No luck, huh?"

"The chief listened and then said thank you."

"And he's not gonna do a thing about it, right?"

"Right," Matt said.

"So that leaves it to us."

"Us?"

"You and me, Deputy," Friday said. "We're gonna stop a bank robbery."

"As long as you understand, I'm here to catch Jason Pardee and bring him back to Fort Smith."

"Is he guilty of somethin' in Indian Territory?" Friday asked. "Is there somethin' Judge Parker will charge him with?"

"I'm sure there is," Matt said. "That'll be up to the judge."

"But you are willin' to help me stop a robbery, right?"

"If we've even got the right bank picked out," Matt said.

"Of course we do."

"How can you be so sure?"

"There's more money in that bank than in all the others combined," Friday said. "Where else would they hit?"

"What if they think one of the others is an easier target?" Matt proposed.

"Is Pardee likely to go for the easy job," Friday said, "or the biggest?"

"I can't say for sure," Matt said. "I've been chasing him for some time, but I really don't know that much about him."

"But you'll know him on sight, right?"

"As long as he hasn't changed too much in nine years," Matt said.

"So you haven't seen him since . . . since that day?"

"No."

"Well," Friday said, "I hope you can recognize him. Until then, we'll just stop anybody who tries to rob that bank."

"As far as the bank's own security force goes . . . ,"
Matt said.

"Yeah?"

"That was Pardee's job when he robbed the bank in
Fairview."

"I'll keep that in mind. . . ."

THEY AGREED TO meet for supper that night so they
could formulate a plan of some kind. Matt told Friday he was staying at the Port Hotel, and the sheriff
told him what restaurant to meet at that was near there.

Matt resented being treated like the old-timer he
was, but on the other hand, every bone in his body ached
from all the time he had been spending in the saddle.
Riding the range, for whatever reason—lawman or
outlaw—was definitely a young man's game. What he
needed to do was soak in a hot tub, but he didn't think
he had the time for that. And he didn't dare take a nap
for fear he wouldn't wake up in time to meet Sheriff
Friday for supper.

Friday was another "old-timer." Would the two of
them be able to stop Pardee and his gang?

I HAD THAT THOUGHT, too," Friday said as they talked
over steaks. "Not because of our age but because
there're just two of us."

"You got something else in mind?"

"Yeah," Friday said, "I know some other good men
who've been put out to pasture before their time."

"Our age?"

"And older," Friday said, "but that don't matter.
They're still good men. A couple of them used to be
my deputies."

"What happened?"

"I had to let them go when there was no money in the budget for them, not with the city embracing that new, modern police force."

"So where are these men?" Matt asked.

"They're in the city," Friday said. "I can get them together."

"How soon?"

"Tomorrow."

"That quick?"

"They ain't doin' anythin' right now they'd rather be doin' than stoppin' a bank robbery. Let's meet in my office in the mornin'. Once you've seen the others, we can figure out our next move."

"Our only move," Matt said, "if we stick with your choice of banks, is to put a constant watch on it. Hopefully, they haven't cased the job already, and we can spot somebody looking the bank over."

"We can take care of that tomorrow when we're all together."

"You have a lot of faith in these men?" Matt asked.

"I have more faith in them than I've had in myself for some time," Friday said.

Matt noticed the sheriff was drinking coffee with his supper while he himself had a beer. "Tell me," he said, "have you stopped drinking?"

"Earlier today, when you saw me cap that bottle of whiskey in my office?" Friday said. "That was it—at least until this is all over."

"Then back to the bottle?"

"Who knows?" Friday asked. "If we can prove that a town sheriff can still do a better job than the police . . ." Friday shrugged.

"Well," Matt said, "for your sake, I hope you and me are both right." He lifted his beer mug.

"For both our sakes," Friday said, clinking Matt's mug with his coffee mug.

CHAPTER THIRTY-NINE

WHEN MATT ENTERED the sheriff's office the next morning, he had second thoughts.

Tom Friday was seated at his desk, drinking coffee and talking to three other men. They all looked older than his own fifty, but he decided he couldn't judge these men by their age or appearance. It wouldn't have been fair.

"Mornin', Sheriff," he said.

"Deputy," Friday said, standing. "Let me introduce you to these men." He walked to all three and put his hand on each of their shoulders. "This is Big Ed Rivers. He was my deputy for five years before the city made me fire him."

Rivers was a small man, around five five, with gray hair and a wrinkled face. He was probably sixty or more, but he still had sharp, intelligent blue eyes. He smiled at Matt and gave him a friendly wink.

"This is Banjo Ben Williams."

Williams was a black man of medium height in good

shape for a man in his fifties. He had big eyes, mostly whites, so they reminded you of banjos. "Hiya, Deputy," he said.

"And this fella is Pepper O'Shay."

The Irishman had probably once had red hair, but it had since gone gray. He was tall and beefy with very large hands. The freckles on his lined face made him look like somebody had sprinkled him with pepper. "Deputy," Pepper said with a nod.

"These are the three men we can count on, Deputy," Friday said.

"The sheriff told us your story, Deputy," Ed Rivers said. "We're here to back you up."

"And save the bank if we can," Pepper said.

"We look like old codgers," Banjo Ben said, "but we can get the job done."

"Well," Matt said, "since I'm an old codger myself, I can't really hold that against you."

Pepper, who appeared to be the oldest of them, cackled and said, "Compared to us, son, you're a young buck."

"All right," Friday said, "age ain't no matter, as long as we come up with the right plan. . . . You want a cup of coffee, Matt?"

"Yeah," Matt said, even though he'd had breakfast before he came, "that sounds good."

Friday went to the potbellied stove, poured a cup, and handed it to Matt.

"Okay," Friday said, settling in behind his desk, "let's talk this through. . . ."

PEPPER AND BANJO added whiskey to their coffee while Tom Friday, Ed Rivers, and Matt drank theirs clean. At one point, Matt found himself standing by the window when Ed Rivers came up alongside him. Behind them the other three were still discussing options.

"I know your reputation," Rivers said. "You were Judge Parker's top deputy."

"That was years ago," Matt said. "This go-round I don't think he'd say the same."

"Look," Rivers said, "we've all been through a lot. Ya gotta if you're gonna get this old, ya know?"

"I do know," Matt said.

"I just appreciate what you're doin' for Tom."

"What I'm doing for him?" Matt asked. "I just rode into town yesterday and told him my story, and he's turning his life upside down for me. Why would he even believe me?"

"He's believin' ya because he's got to," Rivers said. "You're givin' him somethin' he couldn't get anyplace else."

"What's that?" Matt asked.

"A reason to stop drinkin'," Rivers said, "and start livin' again."

"Hey, you two!" Friday called out. "Get over here. I think we got somethin'."

A FTER A COUPLE more hours, Matt said, "I think we've got our schedule down. Now we'd better move before that bank gets hit while we're in here flapping our jaws."

"The deputy's got a good point," Ed Rivers said.

"One thing before we leave this office," Friday said. He opened a desk drawer and took out three deputy's badges and dropped them on the desk. "All of you raise your right hand and say, 'I swear.'"

They all did it.

"Pick up your badges," Friday said.

As the three men picked them up and pinned them to their shirts, Matt said to Friday, "I thought you said there was no money in the budget for you to pay deputies."

Friday gave Matt a long look and asked, "Who says they're gettin' paid?"

T HEY ALL WALKED over to the Beaumont Bank.

"There's a front door," Friday said, "but no back door. When they built the bank, they didn't want there to be another way in."

"Well," Matt said, "at least that was smart."

"The last smart thing they did," Friday said. "The dumbest thing they did was hire that Cameron as the manager."

"Martin Cameron," Ed Rivers said, "what an idiot."

The five of them were standing across the street from the bank.

"This is a good vantage point," Pepper O'Shay said. "How many of us do you think should be on watch at a time?"

"Two, wouldn't you say, deputy?" Friday asked.

"Yes, I agree," Matt said. "At least two. And you and I should check in every hour, Sheriff. Will that be a problem?"

"I don't see why," Friday said. "I've got nothin' else to do."

"None of us do," Banjo Ben said. "We can give this all our attention."

"We'll spell each other for meals," Friday said.

With two men on watch, one would remain in position across the street, while the other would move around and be on the lookout for suspicious characters. They were all experienced enough to know when somebody looked suspicious.

Friday turned to the three recruits. "Either Deputy Wheeler or me will be around here every hour," he said.

"Who's in charge?" Ed Rivers asked.

Friday and Matt exchanged a look, and Matt just shrugged and raised his eyebrows.

"Let's call it a joint effort," the sheriff said. "We're both in charge. You take his orders as if they're mine."

"Okay," Ed Rivers said.

Friday looked at Banjo Ben and Pepper.

"If one of us isn't here, Ed will be in charge. Got it?"

"We got it," Banjo Ben said.

"All right," Friday said. "Pepper, you and Ed will take the first shift. Banjo and me, we'll spell you so you can eat."

"Since there are five of us," Matt suggested, "why don't I just . . . drift? I won't take a shift, but I'll always be around, except when I'm eating."

"Since you're the only one who might recognize Pardee, I think that's a good idea," Friday said.

"You say this Pardee rode with Pale Blue?" Ed Rivers asked.

"For a short time."

"Then he probably learned some things from the Cherokee," Rivers said.

"You're probably right," Matt said. "And Pale Blue always cased his jobs fully before he did anything. That's why he was so hard to catch."

"But you caught him," Banjo Ben said. "That's what you told the sheriff."

"Bass Reeves and me, we caught him," Matt said. "Deputy Reeves had been chasing him for months. He took him back to Fort Smith to face Judge Parker."

"Is he gonna hang 'im?" Pepper asked.

"That'd be a good bet," Matt said.

"Deputy," Friday said, "why don't you and me go get some lunch and then come back? Banjo, you wanna come along so you and me can spell these fellas, after?"

"Lunch on you, Sheriff?" Banjo Ben asked.

"No," Matt said, "it's on me." His finances were dwindling, but he had enough to spring for lunch.

Y OU KNOW," FRIDAY said at lunch, "if we do foil this bank robbery, there's liable to be a reward."

"It's yours," Matt said. "Split it with these other fellas. I'm just after Pardee."

"If it's enough of a reward," Friday said, "I could retire."

"What the hell would you do if you retired?" Banjo Ben asked.

"Go fishin'."

"You hate fishin'," Banjo said. He looked at Matt. "You like fishin'?"

"I hate it," Matt said.

"Me, too," the black man said. "You sit there and wait and wait and wait. . . ."

"Like we're doin' now?" Friday asked.

"Good point," Banjo said. "Either one of you ever read Edgar Allan Poe?"

"No," Matt said. "I don't have time to read."

"Don't look at me," Friday said. "I've been too busy drinkin' these days to read."

"Well," Banjo Ben said, "if you retire, you could spend your time readin'. It'd be good for you."

"Hmm," Friday said, "fishin' or readin'? Those my only two choices?"

"Or you could keep your job for as long as the city will pay you," Banjo said. "And if we stop a bank robbery, I bet they give you a raise."

"Maybe enough to hire back some deputies?" Matt said.

"Wouldn't that be somethin'?" Banjo asked.

"You want your job back?" Friday asked. "Why?"

"Hey," Banjo said, spreading his hands, "I'm tired of readin'."

CHAPTER FORTY

F OR TWO DAYS, Friday and his deputies took their shifts. On the third day, Matt walked up to Friday and Pepper as four o'clock approached.

"You know what I'm wondering?" he said.

"What's that?" Friday asked.

"What are the chances they might try for the bank after it closes?"

"What are the chances they ain't even comin' to Beaumont?" Friday asked.

"I told you, that was the tip I got," Matt reminded him.

"Yeah," Friday said, "from Pale Blue. You think he was tellin' you the truth?"

"I do," Matt said. "I did at the time. He seemed furious that Pardee turned on him."

"Hurt his feelin's, you mean?" Friday asked sarcastically.

Matt studied the man. He hadn't had a drink in days, and maybe that was what was going on with him now. He seemed worn out and on edge.

"Sheriff," he said, "why don't you take a break? I'll stay here with Pepper for a while. The bank's going to close in two hours."

"Yeah," Friday said, "yeah, okay." He started to walk away, then came back. "I'm just gettin' frustrated, is all."

"I know," Matt said.

The two lawmen stared at each other for a few moments, Matt wondering if he should go ahead and tell the sheriff not to drink.

As if reading his mind, Friday said, "Don't worry. I'm not gonna have a drink."

"I wasn't thinking about that," Matt said.

"Yeah, you were. I'll be back in a coupla hours."

"Right," Matt said. "I think I'm going to stick around here a bit after they close."

"That's gonna be up to you," Friday said. "I'll see you later."

As Friday walked away, Matt turned to Pepper and asked, "Is he going to drink?"

"Naw," Pepper said, "not if he says he ain't."

"I'm going to take a look around the sides and the back of the bank," Matt said. "I want to see if there's a likely way in."

"Okay. I'll keep an eye out here."

"Be right back."

T HE BANK WAS freestanding on a corner with no buildings around it. It was easy for Matt to just walk around it. There were windows, but they had bars on them. As he had been told, there was no back door. Nor could he see any access to the roof.

He was back across the street with Pepper within twenty minutes.

"There's no other way in but the front door," Matt

said, "and they won't be able to break in that way without being seen."

"Unless they shoot out those streetlights," Pepper said, pointing.

"And that would be noticed, too," Matt said. "No, the only way to do it is to go inside, rob the bank as quietly as possible, and get out."

"Which we're sure to see while we're standin' here," Pepper said.

"Right."

"So we wait."

Matt nodded. "We wait," he agreed.

W HEN SHERIFF FRIDAY returned, he seemed to have either walked or drunk the edge off. When he got closer, Matt realized he couldn't smell any liquor.

"You can go, Pepper," Friday said. "I'll see you in the mornin'."

"Right, boss." Pepper gave Matt a small salute and walked off.

Matt explained to Friday that he had walked around the bank, looking for a possible way in at night.

"I don't think they can do it," he finished. "I think they're going to have to go in the front door and rob it."

"Or forget the whole thing."

"Hopefully not," Matt said, "but that's a possibility."

"In which case, you'll have to go back on the trail looking for your man, and I'll have to go back to sittin' in my office, drinkin'."

"Sheriff—"

"Don't tell me I have value and should stay sober," Friday said, holding up his hand. "The fact is, if this doesn't happen, I can't prove my worth. I'm just a washed-up, fifty-five-year-old lawman who should probably retire."

"Then why not retire?" Matt asked.

"Because," Friday said, touching his badge while continuing to keep his eyes on the front of the bank, "this is the only thing keepin' me alive."

"Come on—"

"Wait!"

"What is it?"

"That man," Friday said, "the one comin' out of the bank right now. I've seen him before."

"A regular customer?"

"I don't know," Friday said. "I only know I saw him comin' out of the bank two days ago, at this same time."

"Him?"

The man in question was tall, in his forties, wearing dusty trail clothes, and carrying no gun. He didn't look like a man who would have an account in that bank.

"We've got to follow him, then," Matt said.

"No," Sheriff Friday said, "I'll follow him. You stay here and wait for the bank to close."

"But if he leads to Pardee—"

"I'll let you know," Friday said. "With both of us followin' him, he might notice."

"Then I'll go, and you stay—"

"My town, Deputy," Friday said. "I can do this without bein' seen. Can you?"

Matt clenched his jaw. The sheriff was right. And there was no more time to argue. The man had started off down the street.

"All right," he said. "I'll stay. Go!"

M ATT WATCHED UNTIL the bank manager, Cameron, came out and locked the front door. Then, rather than go back to his hotel, he played a hunch and decided to follow Cameron. The worst that could happen was the man would go home.

That wasn't the case.

Cameron went directly to a restaurant and had a leisurely supper alone. Matt was able to see this because, although the place was a large steak house, the man sat at a window table.

Matt took up position across the street, in the doorway of a business that had closed for the night. He folded his arms and watched, hoping that Sheriff Friday was having better luck than he was.

After more than an hour, he saw Cameron pay his bill, rise, and put on his jacket. When he came out, he turned left and began walking up the street. Matt remained on the other side and followed him in that manner. He bumped into several people on the street, as he was keeping his eyes on Cameron, and excused himself each time. After the third time, he started to take more care, not wanting to attract any attention.

Finally, after a fairly long walk from the bank—Cameron apparently liked walking—the manager reached a large two-story house in an area where there were similar homes, all with at least half an acre between them. Matt had to stop following, for as Cameron approached the walk that led to his door, there was no cover. From a distance Matt was forced to maintain, he saw a man waiting for Cameron on his porch. The two of them had a conversation that might have gotten heated, and then Cameron went inside, and the other man left.

He came up the walk and headed toward Matt, who had to scramble for cover behind a small shed. As the man walked by, Matt noticed he was dressed similarly to the man who had come out of the bank. He was tall, lean, and in his forties, and he didn't walk so much as stalk, like a hunting animal.

Matt fell into step behind him. . . .

* * *

AFTER ANOTHER LONG walk, Matt found himself in a run-down section of Beaumont where the buildings all looked either in need of repair or as if they had just been boarded up.

He trailed the man to a two-story hotel with an abandoned building across the street, from where he could observe. Could this man be one of Jason Pardee's gang? And if so, was this where the gang was staying? And even more, what had the heated exchange with the bank manager been about?

Matt realized there was one option he hadn't considered when thinking about the bank robbery. It was a way the robbers could get into the building after it was closed for business.

Somebody could let them in.

Matt was trying to decide if he should simply keep watching or actually go in and try to get a look at the hotel register. He still hadn't decided when he heard something behind him. He turned quickly, drawing his gun from his belt, and found himself looking down the barrel of a gun.

CHAPTER FORTY-ONE

J ESUS!" MATT SAID. "I almost shot you."

Sheriff Friday lowered his gun.

"I didn't know who you were at first," he said, sticking his gun back into his belt.

"What are you doing here?" Matt asked, also tucking his gun away.

"I followed my man to this hotel," Friday said. "I've been tryin' to decide whether or not to go inside. How did you get here?"

Matt explained about tailing the bank manager home and then following another man from the manager's house to here.

"They had a conversation I couldn't hear," Matt explained, "but it didn't seem like either one of them was happy about him being there."

"So you're tellin' me if these two men are here to rob the bank, that the manager's in on it?"

"It seems that way," Matt said. "That's a sure way for them to get into the bank at night and clean it out."

"Why would the manager of the biggest bank in Beaumont, who has a fancy house of his own, get involved in robbin' his own bank?" Friday wondered.

"Any ideas?" Matt said.

"Why don't we go and ask him?" Friday said.

"And if we go in there after him and there's shooting, a lot of innocent people could get hurt," Matt said.

Friday laughed. "You think there're innocent people in that place?" he asked. "That's a haven for outlaws, con men, and prostitutes."

"That doesn't mean they deserve to be shot," Matt pointed out. "And you're not going to keep your job by shooting the place up."

"Okay," Friday said, "you might have a point. So whataya wanna do now?"

"Let's go to Cameron's house and put the question to him," Matt suggested.

"Then nobody's watchin' this place," Friday said.

"They're not going anywhere until they've robbed the bank," Matt said.

"Which, if you're right, could be tonight."

"Not if we get to the bank manager first."

"I still think somebody should be here watchin' the hotel," Friday said.

"Okay, then, let's get two of your deputies to watch," Matt said, "while we talk to Cameron. How fast can you get them here?"

"Pretty quick," Friday said. "I know where they're eatin' supper."

"Okay," Matt said, "go get 'em."

"And leave you here alone?"

"I'm just going to watch," Matt said. "Just get back here fast."

"Half an hour," Friday promised. "No more."

He lit out as darkness began to fall, and Matt kept his eyes on the front door of the hotel. He wondered what he would do if he saw Jason Pardee going in or coming out?

T WENTY-FIVE MINUTES LATER, Matt had seen only several prostitutes going in and coming out with their customers. When Friday returned, he had Pepper and Ed Rivers with him.

"Okay," he said. "These guys will watch the hotel while we go talk to Cameron."

"What do we do if they come out?" Pepper asked.

"Just follow," Friday said. "Don't confront them."

"What if they go to the bank?" Rivers asked.

"Then we'll probably all be there," Matt said, "with the bank manager."

"If not," Friday said, "we'll meet you back here."

"Okay, Sheriff," Pepper said, "whatever you say."

Ed Rivers nodded his agreement, and Matt and Sheriff Friday headed for Martin Cameron's house.

W HEN THE BANK manager opened his front door, he frowned at Matt and Sheriff Friday. "What's going on?" he asked, jamming his hands in the pockets of his robe. "Why are you here?"

"We need to come in and talk, Mr. Cameron," Sheriff Friday said.

"About what?"

"About you robbing your own bank," Matt said.

"What?" Cameron asked, looking at Friday. "Is he serious?"

"We need to come in and talk to you, Mr. Cameron," Friday said again.

"You're not even the real law—," Cameron started, but Friday cut him off.

"I *am* the law, Cameron, and we're comin' in!" he said, and pushed past the man.

Matt followed. Cameron slammed the door and hurried to catch up.

Matt looked around and was surprised that a house so large had so little in the way of furnishings. They were in a sitting room, and there were impressions in the rug showing where furniture had once stood.

"Looks like we had the right idea," Friday said. "You been sellin' things off here, Cameron? Things go bad for you?"

"It's none of your business, Sheriff," Cameron said. "Or yours, Deputy. Just get out and leave me alone."

"Can't do that, Cameron," Matt said. "We believe you're workin' with a man named Pardee to rob your own bank."

"Pard—Who? What are you talking about?"

"Jason Pardee," Matt said. "He's the man who killed my wife. I want him, and he's here in Beaumont to rob your bank, isn't he?"

"And you're part of the plan, aren't you, Cameron?" Friday asked.

"Crazy," Cameron said but with less conviction. "You're both crazy. . . ."

Friday looked around. "Where can we sit down and talk, Cameron?" he asked.

"The kitchen," the bank manager said. "Let's go into the kitchen."

The two lawmen followed him. There were still a table and four chairs in there.

"I don't have anything but whiskey to offer you," he said.

"Never mind," Friday said. "Just sit."

Cameron sat heavily in a chair. The sheriff sat across the table from him, but Matt remained standing.

"How did you figure it out?" Cameron asked. He suddenly looked older to Matt, the pale skin of his face almost like parchment paper.

"We told you when we came to see you," Friday said. "The deputy here got a tip and followed up on it. He came to me and I believed 'im."

"I—I've been struggling for some time," Cameron said. "I started selling things off, and when I didn't have anything else, I started embezzling money from the bank. Then they came to me with the idea, and I . . . I jumped at it."

"They want you to let them into the bank at night, right?" Friday asked.

"Th-that's right."

"When?" Matt asked, feeling excited.

"Tomorrow night," Cameron said, putting his head in his hands. "I'll stay inside the bank after closing and let them in when it gets dark."

"What about your security guards?" Matt asked.

"One remains in the bank all night," Cameron said. "I—I'm supposed to get the drop on him. They—they gave me a gun."

"And Pardee?" Matt asked. "It's his plan?"

"Pardee?" Cameron dropped his hands and squinted up at him.

"Jason Pardee," Matt said, "the man whose gang you're working with."

"I—I'm dealing with a man named Boland."

"The man who was here on your porch tonight?" Matt asked.

"You—you saw that?"

"Yes."

"That was him. He came to tell me it would be tomorrow night. I—I tried to back out, but he said he'd kill me if I didn't do it."

So that was what the argument had been about.

"So you've never seen Pardee?" Matt asked.

"I—I don't know that name."

"All right," Friday said, "get dressed. Wear what you'll be wearin' to work tomorrow."

"Are we—are we going to the police department?"

"No," Friday said, "they don't want any part of this. You're comin' to the jail with me. Then in the mornin', you'll go to work like always. Just do your daily routine and stay in the bank after closing."

"And then what?"

"And then," Matt said, "we'll take it from there."

CHAPTER FORTY-TWO

T HE BANK MANAGER spent a fitful night in one of
Sheriff Friday's cells. The sheriff and Matt also decided to stay there overnight, each taking another cell.

Sleeping in a jail cell—even one with the door wide-
open—brought back bad memories for Matt, and when
he finally fell asleep, he dreamed that Angie was waiting for him, standing by her gravestone, when he went
back to Fairview.

"I've been waiting for you, Matt," she said, and he
woke in a cold sweat.

"You all right?"

He looked at the open door and saw Tom Friday
standing there.

"I'm fine."

"Coffee's ready," Friday said.

"I'll be right there. Where's Cameron?"

"He's havin' a cup of coffee before he leaves for the
bank."

Friday left the cellblock as Matt got to his feet. He

wouldn't be able to wash his face until he went back to his hotel, but he did the best he could to dry the sweat with his shirtsleeves.

Friday was sitting behind his desk, with the bank manager across from him. Both were drinking coffee. Matt went to the potbellied stove and poured himself a cup.

"We can't take him to the bank," Matt said.

"I thought of that," Friday said. "I already sent Ed to the bank. He'll be there when Mr. Cameron gets there."

"Nobody'll recognize him as your deputy?" Matt asked.

"Ex-deputy. Maybe," Friday said. "I told him to put his badge in his pocket."

"What about Pepper and Banjo?" Matt asked.

"They'll be outside with us later tonight," Friday said.

"Where?"

"We'll figure it out," Friday said. "We've got all day."

Cameron sat there, staring into his coffee.

"Is he okay? Is he going to go to the bank if we let him walk out of here?"

"I think so," Friday said. "We're the ones who're gonna keep him alive."

Cameron looked up from his coffee and stared into Matt's eyes. "I'll be there," he said. "I swear. I want this to be over."

"It will be," Friday said.

Cameron looked at the sheriff. "What happens to me when it's all done?" he asked. "Will I go to prison?"

"I'll tell the judge you assisted in preventing the robbery of your bank," Friday said. "I don't think you'll do any time. But you'll have to leave the bank."

"That's no problem," Cameron said. "I just don't know what I'll do after."

"You'll figure it out," Friday said. "At least you'll be alive and not in prison."

"Yes, well . . ." He stood up. "I guess I'd better get to work."

"Remember," Friday said, "just do your job like normal all day."

"Yes, I remember."

Cameron started for the door, but Matt stopped him. "Just one thing," he said.

"What's that?"

"You said your contact with the gang is a man named Boland," Matt said. "How do you know him?"

"Months ago he was a security guard at the bank," Cameron said.

"What happened?"

"I fired him."

"Why?"

Cameron hesitated, then said, "I thought he might have seen me one time when I took some money."

"Oh," Matt said, "okay. Thanks."

They both watched as Cameron left the office.

"I'm going to follow him," Matt said. "Nobody would recognize me except for Pardee, and I'm not even sure about that."

"That's okay," Friday said. "I was thinkin' the same thing. You can make sure he actually goes to the bank."

"Right." Matt put his coffee mug down and headed for the door. "Once he goes inside, I'll be back."

"Pepper and Banjo should be here by then, and we can make plans for tonight."

Matt was already out the door. . . .

H E TAILED CAMERON to the bank, watched as the man stopped in front of the door. There were other employees waiting for him to let them in and some customers, including Ed Rivers. For a moment, though,

Matt thought the manager was going to turn and run, but in the end, he unlocked the door and went inside, followed by all the others.

Once the business day was under way at the Beaumont Bank, Matt left and headed back to the sheriff's office.

WHEN HE WALKED into Friday's office, the three men turned and looked at him.

"Did he go in?" Friday asked.

"For a minute, I thought he was going to run," Matt said, "but he went in. Rivers went in after him, along with the other employees and some customers. None of them looked like one of Pardee's men, not unless he's dressing them better."

"Well," Friday said, "whatever happens, we have a man inside. Now that you're here, we can plan where the rest of us are gonna be."

"Once they go in, we've got 'em, don't we?" Pepper asked. "I mean, they can't get out with the four of us out front."

"The bank manager will still be inside and maybe even Ed," Friday said. "We have to be in position to take them when they come out."

"One on either side of the building," Matt suggested, "and two of us across the street."

"That's too far away," Friday said. "Even with the streetlights, it's still gonna be night."

"Well," Matt said, "once they go in, we cross the street and get closer. We wait for them to come out."

"Are we gonna take 'em without shootin'?" Banjo asked.

"If they're Jason Pardee's gang, not likely," Matt said.

"Whataya mean, 'if'?" Friday asked.

"Cameron says he's never seen Pardee or even heard his name," Matt said. "What if this isn't Pardee's gang but another one? Maybe Boland's gang."

"So you get a tip that Pardee's comin' here to rob a bank, and it turns out to be another gang?" Friday asked. "Ain't that too much of a coincidence?"

"Maybe not a coincidence at all," Matt said.

"Okay, whataya mean?" Friday asked.

"What if Pardee's plan is to rob one of the other banks while this gang is robbing this one?" Matt asked.

"Now that's a stretch," Friday said. "This's gotta be Pardee's gang, and you'll see him when they come out the front door."

"I hope you're right," Matt said.

"Hey," Friday said, "this whole thing ain't me bein' right. It's you bein' right."

"Yeah," Matt said, "yeah, I guess so . . . but just for argument's sake, which bank would be your next pick to be robbed?"

CHAPTER FORTY-THREE

T HEY HAD THE rest of the day to check the other
banks again. The managers insisted they didn't
have enough cash on hand at any time to satisfy the
kind of gang Matt and the others were talking about.

"You're more likely to find them robbing the Beaumont," one of them said.

"Yeah, that's what we figure," Sheriff Friday said.
"We just didn't wanna take any chances."

By five in the afternoon, Tom Friday was satisfied
that no suspicious characters had been seen at the
smaller banks. Matt was still uncomfortable about it
but couldn't argue. If he'd been wrong all along and
the gang planning to rob the Beaumont Bank wasn't
led by Jason Pardee, he didn't know what his next
move would be. For now, though, he had to see this
through. If it didn't help him, at least it would do Sheriff Friday some good. Matt liked the idea of helping
another old-timer get his life back on track.

"Okay," Friday said as they left the last bank, "we'd

better get ourselves set up at the Beaumont. It's almost closin' time."

They picked up Pepper and Banjo at the sheriff's office and headed for the bank.

A S DUSK FELL, Friday sent Pepper off to the left of the front door and Banjo to the right. He and Matt stayed just across the street.

After several people—including one security guard—left the bank, Banjo moved on down to the window to look in, then waved and went back to his position.

"No more customers," Friday said. "That leaves Cameron, a security guard, and Ed."

"Does Ed know not to try to take them himself once they're inside?" Matt asked.

"He knows," Friday said. "He's an experienced man."

"All right, then," Matt said. "Let's see how the gang is going to play this."

I T WAS COMPLETELY dark when a couple of men appeared. The foot traffic on the street had thinned out to a trickle as other businesses in the area closed. These two men crept along the front of the bank, looking over their shoulders until they reached the door. One of them knocked, and then the door opened to admit them.

"Whataya think?" Friday asked.

"That's two," Matt said. "There've got to be more. I say we wait."

"Let's hope Ed waits, too," Friday said.

"You said he would."

"Anybody can get antsy," Friday said, "but I think he'll wait, like we said, for them to start leavin' the bank."

"Now we've just got to hope Cameron keeps his nerve," Matt said.

They continued to watch, and sure enough, other men crept along the front of the bank and then slipped inside.

"That's six," Friday said. "How many more do they think they'll need?"

"They're going to have to post somebody outside to watch," Matt said. "That'll be the last one."

"Good thinkin'," Friday said. "Have you seen Pardee?"

"The streetlights don't reach the front door," Matt said. "I haven't recognized him yet."

"Think he changed that much?"

"I don't know," Matt said. "I know I've changed a lot, and I only saw him that one day."

"Aw right," Friday said, "we'll know after we grab 'em."

A seventh man moved along the front of the bank, knocked but didn't go in.

"There's the lookout," Matt said.

"They should be comin' out soon," Friday said. "Let's get ready. If we hear any shots from inside, we're gonna have to move fast."

"Like you said," Matt commented, "let's hope nobody loses their nerve."

"They got us outnumbered seven to five," Friday said. "Let's hope the element of surprise evens things up."

"Don't forget the security guard," Matt said.

"Yeah, but after what you said about Pardee bein' the security guard in that Fairview bank all those years ago," Friday said, "we can't be sure which side he's on, can we?"

"No, we can't."

Matt and Friday both drew their guns and waited.

W̲E GOTTA GET closer," Friday said about ten minutes later. He waved at Pepper.

"What are you doing?" Matt asked.

"I want Pepper to take that fella out, and then we can move closer."

Matt saw Pepper look around the side of the building, then start walking toward the door. The man on watch had no reason to believe he was anything but a passing pedestrian. But when Pepper reached the lookout, the big, beefy Irishman clubbed him with a big fist and dragged him back around to his side of the building.

"Okay," Friday said. "Let's go."

He and Matt broke from their doorway and crossed the street, pausing to let a buckboard pass by. The driver glared at them but kept going.

Friday and Matt kept checking both ways as well as up at windows and rooftops for other lookouts.

"I would've put a man on the roof," Matt commented, "maybe two."

"They've probably scouted the area well," Friday said. "It's mostly businesses that are closed after six. Not much in the way of any kind of activity."

When they reached the bank side of the street, they risked a look through the window. There were several men with their guns out, the bank manager with his hands up, and a dark-clad man—probably the security guard—prone on the floor.

"I hope he's not dead," Matt whispered.

"They should be comin' out soon," Friday said. "I'll go over by Pepper. You get over with Banjo. We'll get 'em in a cross fire."

"Right," Matt said.

He ran to the other side and stood next to Banjo, told him what they had seen inside.

"Where's Rivers?" Banjo asked.

"We didn't see him," Matt said. "Hopefully, he's hidden somewhere."

Suddenly the bank door flew open. Two men stepped out, each carrying a bag.

Matt ducked back, heard one say, "Where the hell's Peters?" The two men were looking around them.

"He's supposed to be on lookout," one said.

"This ain't right," the other said.

The two men turned as if they were going to go back inside the bank.

"Boland," one called, "Peters ain't here."

At that point Sheriff Friday stepped out with Pepper behind him. Too soon, Matt thought, but he had to back the man's play, so he and Banjo did the same.

"Hold it right there!" Friday shouted.

The two men's heads swiveled back and forth quickly as they tried to assess what was happening.

They had two options. They could duck back into the bank or go for their guns.

They went for their guns.

"Damn!" Matt swore, and pointed his.

One man faced Friday and Pepper while the other turned to Matt and Banjo. As they all began firing, Matt had no idea if the lead whizzing past him was from the bank robbers or cross fire from Friday and Pepper.

"Get down!" he told Banjo.

They both dropped to a knee and kept firing. The two bank robbers began to jerk and dance as lead struck them repeatedly. As they went down, Matt and the others rushed for the bank door. At that moment, just before they would've rushed in, there were shots from inside. Two bullets punched into Banjo's chest, driving him back against Matt, who caught him and lowered him to the ground. At the same time Pepper cried out in pain as blood spouted from his left arm.

"Goddamn it!" Friday yelled. "Down!"

Matt dragged Banjo to the right while Friday helped Pepper to the left of the door.

"How is he?" Friday asked.

Matt looked down at Banjo's prone form. "He's dead," Matt said.

He saw the pain on Tom Friday's face and knew just how he felt.

CHAPTER FORTY-FOUR

"HEY OUTSIDE!" A voice called.

"I hear ya," Friday said.

"We got hostages," the voice said. "The manager, the guard, and your man."

"Damn, they got Ed," Friday said.

"You let us leave with the money, or they're all dead."

"Boland? Is that you?" Friday called back.

There was silence. The outlaw was probably wondering how Friday knew his name.

"Who's out there?" the man called.

"I'm Sheriff Friday," the lawman said. "I've got a US deputy marshal out here with me and two deputies."

"I don't know how you know my name," Boland said, "but these people ain't walkin' outta here unless we are, too."

"There are four of you in there," Friday called back, referring only to the bank robber, not to the hostages.

"In minutes there are gonna be a lot of police here from the new department. You ain't got a chance."

"Then neither does your man!"

Friday looked at Matt on the other side of the door. "Whataya think?" he asked.

"I think the guard's probably dead," Matt said, "maybe Rivers, too."

"That would leave them with one hostage," Friday said. "The manager."

"And he was part of it."

"You're sayin' he knew what he was gettin' into," Friday said.

"That's what I figure."

Friday turned around. "Pepper, you okay?"

"I got the bleedin' stopped," Pepper said. "I'm with ya, boss."

Friday looked at Matt.

"It's your call," Matt said.

"I'm only worried about Ed, not that manager," Friday said.

"Then let's have them bring Ed out with them," Matt said. "If they can't, we'll have to figure he's dead."

"And then we can go in," Friday said.

Matt nodded.

"Hello in the bank!" Friday said. "We'll let you come out but with your hostages."

They were greeted by silence.

"He's dead," Pepper said.

"Wait . . . ," Friday said.

"We're comin' out," someone who was apparently Boland called, "but we're bringin' the bank manager."

"Never mind him," Friday shouted back. "He's one of you. Bring one of the other hostages. Bring my man."

There was silence again, and then Boland called out, "Sheriff, we're comin' out shootin'!"

"Come ahead!" Friday called back. He waved Matt

and Pepper back. This time they stood at angles so that their cross fire would not endanger one another.

That was when they heard windows breaking.

"They're comin' out the windows!" Pepper shouted, and started for the side of the building.

"No!" Matt shouted.

Pepper stopped.

"The windows are barred," Matt said. "They're trying to distract us. Stay where you are."

Matt was right. Moments later the four bank robbers came rushing out the front door, their guns blazing. There was nothing else for them to do except give up, and they weren't doing that.

Matt, Friday, and Pepper began to fire, and before the bank robbers were able to adjust to their positions, three of them were down. The last one dropped the bags of money he was carrying and his gun, then threw his hands in the air.

"I give up!" he shouted.

Matt quickly rushed to the bodies of the other three, turned them over so he could see their faces. Friday rushed into the bank to see what Ed Rivers' condition was. Pepper kept the remaining bank robber covered.

When Friday came back out, he said, "Ed's alive. He's got a bump on his head. So does Cameron. Is he here?" he asked. "Pardee?"

"No," Matt said. "He ain't."

Matt stepped up to the last bank robber and asked, "What's your name?"

"Layne," the man said.

"Which one of these is Boland?"

"That one," Layne said, pointing to the man in the middle of the three on the ground. He appeared to be the oldest.

"Where's Pardee?" Matt demanded. "Jason Pardee."

"H-him and Boland had a fallin'-out," Layne said. "They split up. Some of us came here with Boland. The others went with Pardee."

"Where?" Matt jammed his gun barrel into the man's rib cage, making him flinch in pain. "Where did Pardee go?"

"I dunno!"

"You know," Matt said. "And you're going to tell me."

"We'll take Layne to my office. I gotta get Banjo's body taken care of," Friday said. A crowd had started to gather. "And the police department is gonna show up."

"Why don't I take Layne and Rivers back to your office? You handle your chief of police when his men arrive, and look after Banjo. We'll meet you after."

"Deputy," the sheriff said, "don't do nothin' stupid."

"I'm gonna put Layne in one of your cells," Matt said. "Then we'll have a talk."

Rivers came out, his hand to his head, his hat in his other hand.

"Ed, go with Matt and put this man in a cell," Friday said.

"Right."

"The deputy is gonna question him," Friday said. "Make sure that's all he does."

"Right, boss."

They heard a sound.

"What the hell is that?" Matt asked.

"It's a bell the police use to announce the arrival of one of their wagons," Friday said.

"Stupid," Matt said, shaking his head.

"Go ahead, get movin'," Friday said. "If you're here when they arrive, they won't let you leave."

"See you at your office," Matt said. He grabbed Layne's arm, said "Come on!" and dragged him off, followed by Ed Rivers.

* * *

M ATT LOCKED LAYNE in a cell and came out of the cellblock to find Ed Rivers rubbing his head.

"You want to see a sawbones?" he asked.

"No, I'll be fine," Rivers said.

"How did you come by that bump on your head?"

"The stupid bank manager panicked and gave me away."

"Panicked? Gave you away . . . accidentally?"

"I ain't sure it was an accident."

"Well, he's in custody at the new jail. If you're all right to walk," Matt said, "why don't you go out and get us something to eat? I'm sure the sheriff'll be hungry when he gets here."

"I can do that." Rivers started for the door, then turned. "Wait. The sheriff told me to keep an eye on you."

"I'm not going to kill my only chance to find Jason Pardee," Matt said. "At least, not in the short time you'll be gone."

Rivers nodded and left.

Matt went into the cellblock and unlocked Layne's cell. The man sitting on the cot looked up at Matt.

"Stand up," Matt said.

"What?"

"You heard me."

Layne stood. "What do you want?"

"Jason Pardee," Matt said.

"I told you," Layne said. "I don't know where he is."

Layne was a young man in his twenties who probably wanted nothing more than to live longer. Matt stepped in and hit him once on the jaw, knocking him onto his back.

"Think harder," Matt said. "The only way you walk out of this cell alive is to give me something I can use to find Pardee. You have until Sheriff Friday gets here."

"H-he won't let you kill me," Layne said, still on his back.

"Don't count on that," Matt said.

He backed out of the cell and locked it, left the cell-block as Layne rose and sat heavily on the cot.

R IVERS RETURNED WITH sandwiches, and they made coffee before Sheriff Friday returned with Pepper O'Shay.

"What happened?" Matt asked.

"Chief Montgomery wasn't happy," Friday said with great satisfaction. "He took Cameron into custody, and he wants the other bank robber."

"Layne," Matt said. "Are you going to give him up?"

"I am," Friday said, "but we'll be going in front of a judge who'll know that we stopped the robbery and not Montgomery's modern police."

"When?" Matt asked.

"Tomorrow."

"But not until he tells me what I want to know."

"Which is?"

"Something, anything that will help me find Pardee."

"Didn't he say he doesn't know where Pardee is?" Friday asked.

"He's got to know something," Matt reasoned, "even if he doesn't realize he does."

"Well," Friday said, "you'll have all night to find out. I told Montgomery I'd meet him at the judge's chamber at nine a.m."

Friday, Pepper, and Rivers began to unwrap a sandwich each.

"What about Banjo?" Matt asked.

"He was taken to a morgue," Friday said. "He had no family, so the city will bury him. Has Layne told you anythin'?"

"Not yet," Matt said, suddenly realizing how hungry he was. "I'm going to have one of these sandwiches and then try again."

"Maybe," Friday said, indicating the food still on his desk, "if you give him one . . ."

"Yeah, maybe," Matt said, "once he talks."

CHAPTER FORTY-FIVE

M ATT DECIDED TO go back into the cellblock with a
 sandwich this time rather than a fist. He opened
the door and tossed the sandwich onto Layne's lap.

"Eat," he said.

Layne stared down at the food in his lap, then un-
wrapped it and took a bite.

"Um, thanks," he said. "I'm . . . hungry." He chewed
and swallowed. "What's gonna happen to me?"

"You're going to prison," Matt said. "You're a bank
robber."

"So you're not gonna kill me?"

"Okay," Matt corrected, "I should've said, you're
going to prison if I don't kill you first."

Layne bit into the chicken sandwich in his hand
again, but then set it down next to him as if he'd lost his
appetite.

"Look," Matt said, "all you have to do is tell me
something you heard, something that was said between
Boland and Pardee that you overheard."

"Pardee said he didn't wanna come all the way to Beaumont to rob a bank," Layne said. "He said because Boland had been fired, he had a personal score to settle. Pardee didn't want any part of that. He said when he pulls a job, there's nothin' personal in it."

"Except his desire for money."

"Yeah," Layne said, "that. Ain't that in all of us?"

"A desire for money, yes," Matt said, "but not other people's money."

"But . . . when other people have money and you don't . . ."

"You can't just take it."

Layne frowned and Matt suddenly realized just how young the robber was. He was probably eighteen or so.

"Then how else do you get it?"

"You earn it," Matt said, "by working."

"You mean . . . a job?"

"Right."

"Boland says jobs are for other people," Layne said.

"Layne," Matt said, "what's your relationship with Boland?"

"He's my father."

"Your father?"

"Well, my stepfather," Layne corrected, "but he raised me after my mom died." He looked down at his hands, then back at Matt. "He's dead, ain't he?"

"Yes, he is."

"So if I help you, could I not go to prison?"

"If you help me find Pardee and the rest of his men, I'll tell the judge. It should help you when it comes time to be sentenced."

Layne fell silent, mulling his situation over.

"Layne, how many men went with Pardee?"

The boy thought for a moment, then said, "Five."

"Do you know their names?"

"Yes."

"Good," Matt said. "If you tell me, that'll be a start."

"Okay."

"I'm going to get you some paper, and you can write them down," Matt said. "Meanwhile, finish your sandwich and think some more about what might have been said between Boland and Pardee."

"A-all right."

As Layne picked up his sandwich, Matt locked the cell again and left.

"Well?" Friday asked from behind his desk. He was working on his second sandwich.

"He's a kid," Matt said. "Boland was his stepfather."

"Well," Friday said, "he watched us kill 'im. Do you really think he's gonna help you?"

"Yes, I do," Matt said. "I need something for him to write on."

Friday gave Matt a pencil and a wanted poster for Layne to write on the back of.

"He's going to give me the names of Pardee's men."

"And Pardee's location?" Pepper asked.

"I don't think he knows it," Matt said, "but I'm hoping he heard something that'll help me track him."

"Will he give you some details by mornin'?" Friday asked.

"I think so."

"Ed, why don't you and Pepper go get some sleep?" Friday said. "Be back here tomorrow."

"Will we still have jobs tomorrow?" Ed Rivers asked.

"I think we all will," Friday said.

"Okay, then," Rivers said, "we'll see you tomorrow."

Rivers and Pepper left the office.

Friday rubbed his face with both hands and said, "Okay, he's still all yours—at least, until mornin'."

"I'll get what I can from him by then," Matt said.

"Gonna beat it outta him?" Friday asked.

"Like I said," Matt replied, "he's a kid."

"So no beatin'?" Friday asked as Matt went back into the cellblock.

Matt entered the cell, saw that the sandwich was gone. "Here," he said, "write down the names, and I'll get you some coffee."

This time when he left the cell, he closed the door but didn't lock it. When he came back, Layne was still sitting on the cot. They traded coffee for paper, and Matt looked at the list. He didn't know any of the names, but that didn't matter. What mattered was that Layne had given them to him.

"What now?" Layne asked, sipping the coffee.

"Now you tell me what you know," Matt said, "or what you heard."

Layne scratched his head. "Are you the deputy who's been chasin' Pardee?" he asked. "Deputy Wheeler?"

"That's right."

"I heard one conversation," he said. "Pardee told Boland he was tired of knowin' you was on his trail. He said he was gonna go and visit an old friend."

"An old friend," Matt repeated. "Who?"

"He didn't say."

"Where?"

"He said . . . Montana."

Matt breathed out one word. "Damn."

Y OU SURE ABOUT this?" Friday asked.
"No," Matt said, "but what other old friend in Montana would he be talking about? And according to the kid, Pardee knows I'm after him. He wants it over, and so do I."

Friday opened his drawer, took out the whiskey bottle he had closed the day he met Matt. He opened it, poured one slug into a mug, and held it out to Matt. Then he corked the bottle again and put it away.

"He knows I'm after him," Matt said, again, "and he's going back there to end it."

"After . . . what? Almost nine years now?"

"He's got no other reason to go back to Montana."

"But how's he supposed to know that you got word he's goin' there?"

"Like you said," Matt answered, "it's been more than nine years. He'll be patient, wait for me to get word. He'll just wait."

"So you're gonna ride back there, figurin' he's waitin' for you?"

Matt downed the whiskey and said, "That's what I'm going to do."

"So it'll end where it all began."

"I hope so."

"And then what?"

"I don't know," Matt said. "I guess that depends on whether or not I come out of it alive."

"And what if you're wrong," Friday asked, "and he ain't there?"

Matt waved his arms helplessly and said, "Then I'm right back where I started."

CHAPTER FORTY-SIX

Fairview, Montana

MATT WHEELER COVERED the sixteen hundred miles from Beaumont, Texas, to Fairview, Montana, in record time, replacing his horse twice along the way so that he didn't ride one mount to death. He hadn't bothered sending a telegram ahead, because he felt that could tip Pardee off.

He picked up a sheepskin jacket along the way, because he knew what winter would be like in Montana. Sure enough, as soon as he crossed the border, he was riding in snow.

Matt remembered how the people of Fairview hadn't recognized or remembered him when he got back there. He could only assume the same would be true of Pardee. So the man would be able to eat in the restaurants, drink in the saloons, and walk the streets without worrying about being identified.

What Matt had no way of knowing was if Pardee

would be there alone or have his men with him. And with Fairview being a bigger town now than it had been nine years ago, he might even decide to hit the bank . . . again.

Matt didn't know how long Pardee would wait, but it took him more than three weeks to get there. Maybe the outlaw would be relaxed by the time Matt rode in.

The only telegram Matt had sent was to Judge Parker in Fort Smith, telling him where he was headed. He didn't bother waiting for a reply, because there was nothing the judge could have told him that would've stopped him.

As Matt entered Fairview, he rode right down Front Street, not wanting to hide from anyone. The snow had stopped, but what was on the ground crunched beneath his horse's hooves. He was a different man from both the one who had been sheriff there and the one who had been there soon after Yuma. And yet *this* man still had the shakes when he thought about going to Angie's grave.

He reined in his horse in front of the sheriff's office. There was no reason to think Pete Brown wouldn't still be sheriff of Fairview, yet Matt found himself hoping not. Talk about being different, this man was just not the one he had known.

But when he entered, it was Sheriff Brown who looked up at him from his desk.

"You're back," Brown said. "He said you would be."

"Who said it?"

"Pardee."

Matt's stomach went cold. "He's here?"

"He was," Brown said, sitting back in his chair. His badge looked as if he had just polished it.

"And you let him go?" Matt asked. "You didn't arrest him?"

"For what?" Brown asked. "A bank job nine years ago? I ain't even sure he pulled that one."

"I'm telling you he did."

"Well, you ain't a lawman anymore, Matt," Brown said.

"Where is he, Pete?"

"He said he'd be back," Brown answered. "He told me to tell you to wait for him."

"How long ago?"

"He was here a few weeks back, said he was lookin' for you. Then he left. But when he said he'd be back, I believed 'im. He's tired of you doggin' his trail."

"So I heard," Matt said. "Did he say when he'd be back?"

"Soon."

"So I'm just supposed to wait?"

"That's what he wants," Brown said, "but it ain't what I want, Matt." Brown stood up. Matt noticed that since he had last been there, Brown had started wearing his gun in a holster on his hip. "I don't want you here, Matt."

"I don't want to be here, Pete," Matt said. "But this is where it's all going to end."

"For you maybe," Brown said. "And for Pardee. But when it's over, I want you gone.".

"You think I want your job, Pete?" Matt asked. "Is that what this is about?"

"You're wearin' a badge," Brown said. "Don't tell me you don't wanna be a lawman."

"Not after this," Matt said. "When this is over, I don't know what I want, but it's not your badge."

"Yeah, well," Brown said, putting his hand on his gun, "you'd have to go through me to get this badge."

"You've changed, Pete."

"So've you, Matt."

"I'm going to board my horse and get a room," Matt said, "and then I'm going to wait. Just wait."

"Fine." Brown sat back down. "But remember what I said. This is my town."

"You can have it," Matt said, and left.

A FTER MATT TOOK care of his horse and got himself a room in the Front Street Hotel—which hadn't existed when he was sheriff—he sat on the bed and thought about Angie. He realized that without meaning to, he thought of her every day. Sometimes she was only in the back of his mind. But she was always there. And she was in his dreams. Usually, he didn't mind dreaming about her, but the one where she was standing at her own grave, waiting for him . . . that one always had him waking in a cold sweat.

There was a knock on the door that startled him. When he answered it, a nervous-looking man in a dark coat stood in the hall, fidgeting. It could have been his nerves, the cold, or both.

"Can I come in?"

"Who are you?"

"Deputy Wheeler, I'm the mayor." He looked up and down the hall. "I'd like to come in before someone sees me."

"Come on in." Matt stepped back, allowed the man to move past him, then closed the door. The mayor was a short, middle-aged man holding a bowler hat in his hands.

"Okay," Matt said, "tell me what you want."

"I'm Mayor Andrew Hopper," the man said, "and what I want you to do is kill Sheriff Peter Brown."

M ATT LEFT THE man in his room and went down to the front desk.

"Sir?" the desk clerk said.

"Can you tell me who the mayor of Fairview is?" Matt asked.

"Yes, sir," the clerk said. "His name is Andrew Hopper."

"How long has he been the mayor?"

"Oh, it's only been . . . probably a month. He's very new to the job."

"Elected?"

"Oh, yes, sir."

"And what can you tell me about Sheriff Peter Brown?"

The clerk's demeanor changed at the mention of Brown's name. "Nothing, sir," the clerk said. "We, uh, don't talk about the sheriff."

"I see," Matt said. "Thank you."

He went back up to his room, found the mayor nervously pacing.

"Are you satisfied that I'm the mayor?" he asked.

"Yes. But . . . why do you want the sheriff killed?"

"Because he's not a lawman," Hopper said. "He's a dictator. He's got everyone in this town under his thumb."

"The hotel clerk was obviously afraid of him," Matt said. "He wouldn't even talk about him."

"We're all afraid of him and his gun," Hopper said. "Those of us on the town council would like to bring Fairview into the new century and out of the Wild West. Sheriff Brown doesn't want us to do that. He thinks he's the next big legend of the West."

"I know he always thought of himself as a hand with a gun," Matt said, "but—"

"He's killed people," Hopper said, "just for . . . nothing. For questioning his authority."

"Do you know who I am, Mayor?"

"Of course," Hopper said. "That's why I'm asking this of you. You were once the law here."

"Yes," Matt said, "once, a long time ago."

"You can be again," Hopper said. "If you get rid of Brown for us, I'll make you sheriff. You'll have your job back."

"I don't want that job back," Matt said. "I'm only here for one reason: to get the man who killed my wife and to finally see her grave."

"You—you haven't seen her grave site?" the mayor asked.

"Not until I can tell her I got the man who killed her," Matt said. "I know that sounds crazy—"

"No, no, it doesn't," Hopper said. "I understand that. Look, you're a deputy marshal, and I'm asking for your help."

"Why don't you just have Brown voted out?" Matt asked.

"The people are afraid to vote against him," Hopper said. "And besides, nobody will run against him."

"Then fire him."

"I—I can't."

"You're the mayor."

Hopper rubbed his hands together, looked away, and said, "I'm afraid of him, too."

"Look, Mayor," Matt said, "this isn't my business. I'm only here—"

"But you're a US deputy marshal!" Hopper reasoned.

Matt looked down, removed the badge from his shirt, and dropped it into his pocket.

"Not here," he said. "Here I'm just Matt Wheeler, a grieving husband who wants to finally put his wife to rest. I—I can't help you, Mayor."

The mayor stared at him, licked his lips, then allowed his shoulders to slump. "I understand," he said, finally. "I—I had to ask. I won't take any more of your time."

The mayor literally slunk from the room, closing the door gently behind him.

Matt knew that Pete Brown had changed, but that much? To become a bully, a dictator, and a killer with a badge? Was that something Matt could ignore? It was something he *had* to ignore, because he was here for Jason Pardee, not for Pete Brown. This wasn't his town. It was the place where he could finally put his wife's soul to rest, but maybe give himself some kind of peace.

He didn't know how this was going to end. Would Pardee allow himself to be taken? Would he make Matt kill him, or would he kill Matt? And if Matt did kill him, how would he explain that to Judge Parker?

Or did Judge Parker, a very smart man, already know how this was all going to end?

CHAPTER FORTY-SEVEN

Matt had supper not far from his hotel on Front Street. He sat in the window so he could watch the activity on the snow-covered street. Afterward, he grabbed a chair in front of his hotel, then just sat and watched. When Pardee came back, he'd ride right in, hiding from nobody. After all, he had left Matt the message that he would be back.

Matt spent the next three days watching the street, sitting in front of the hotel, eating his meals in the same café at the same window, watching. He even found himself watching the cold mist that came from his mouth.

On day four, while he was seated in front of the hotel in the afternoon, a man came up to him. He was tall, wearing black except for a white collar. He had black hair but looked like he hadn't started shaving yet.

"Mind if I sit?" he asked.

"Help yourself. Plenty of chairs."

There were three or four other wooden chairs, and the stranger grabbed one, sat down, and got comfortable, although he looked cold.

"I heard the mayor came to see you," he said.

"That was four days ago," Matt said. "Who are you, by the way?"

"I'm Father Ray," the man said. "I'm the priest here in Fairview."

"You have a church?" Matt asked.

"Yes," the priest said, "at the north end of town."

"Wow," Matt said. "There was no church when I lived here."

"That was a while ago."

"Yes, it was."

"And it's not really a church," Father Ray said. "It's a converted warehouse."

"Ah," Matt said, "I know that building."

"So I have a makeshift altar, but no belfry and no bell. But I hope to have a real church built soon. That's if I'm still alive."

"What do you mean?"

"Well, the mayor, he told you about the sheriff, right?"

"He told me some things."

"Sheriff Brown says he's gonna kill me if I don't leave town."

"Why?"

"He says the town doesn't need a priest."

"When does he want you to leave by?"

"He gave me till the end of the month," Father Ray said. "I got a week left."

"Why'd he give you that long?" Matt asked. "Why not run you out of town by the end of the day?"

"I told him I needed time to get placed elsewhere by the Church."

"But you were lying, right?" Matt asked. "You're kind of young to be a priest."

"Yes," Father Ray said. "I am."

"So you're not really ordained," Matt said, "and you're not getting placed anywhere else by the Church."

Father Ray fell silent, looking worried.

"Look," Matt said, "I'm not concerned with where you got that collar or why you're passing yourself off as a man of God."

"I . . . I just want to do this job," Father Ray said.

"So stay alive, and go somewhere else and do it."

"The mayor says you used to be the sheriff here, and now you're a US deputy marshal."

"I *am* a US deputy marshal," Matt said. "But I'm here just as me. I can't help Mayor Hopper, and I can't help you or anyone else in this town. I'm sorry."

Father Ray shook his head. "I am, too." He stood up, started to walk away.

"Hey," Matt called.

"Yeah?"

"How old are you?"

"I'm twenty-two."

"You could become a real priest, you know," Matt said. "You've got time."

"I'm not even Catholic," Father Ray said, and walked away.

T HE REST OF the day, Matt kept trying to convince himself there was nothing he could do about Pete Brown. The fact was, he was the reason Brown was a lawman. He had put a deputy's badge on him all those years ago, and it had led to this. Could he walk away and leave the town at the mercy of a corrupt lawman?

The answer was, maybe not, but he couldn't consider that until he had dealt with Pardee.

* * *

THE AFTERNOON OF the fifth day, Matt came out from the hotel lobby and sat in his chair. In moments, he was approached by Sheriff Brown.

"You missed him," Brown said, hunching his shoulders against the cold. He was wearing a denim jacket, but it was short, so as not to cover the gun on his hip.

"What?"

"He just rode in."

"That can't be," Matt said. "I was inside for five minutes."

"Well," Brown said, "he's here."

"Where?"

"He sent me to tell you he'll meet you."

"Where?"

"You're not gonna like it."

MATT WALKED TO Fairview's boot hill, saw Jason Pardee standing at the top of it. After all the years that had gone by, he still recognized Pardee from that day. He got that cold feeling in the pit of his stomach, but his face grew hot as his heartbeat quickened.

"Sheriff," Pardee said. "Oh, it's Deputy now, right? Deputy Marshal?"

"That's right."

Pardee looked down. "This is your wife's grave," he said, pointing. "She was a lovely lady."

"You killed her."

"Well," Pardee said, "she was in the way, and I'm afraid I may have overreacted." He smiled. "I was younger then. We both were. But now you're sort of an old codger, ain'tcha? 'Bout ten years older than me?"

"Come on down from there, Pardee," Matt said. "Let's get this over with."

Matt looked around. The kid Layne had told him Pardee had at least five men. By this time, he could have increased that number.

"Where are your men?" he asked.

"On their way," Pardee said. "I thought we'd take the bank while we were here—again. But first, I wanted to settle with you."

"You want to settle with me?"

"You've been doggin' my trail ever since they let you out of Yuma Prison," Pardee said. "I'm tired of feelin' your breath on the back of my neck. So why don't you come on up here so's we can finish this?"

Matt still wasn't sure there weren't some other men around. And he wasn't anxious to have his showdown with Pardee right on Angie's grave site, although he did want her to see Pardee finally pay for what he had done.

The cemetery was actually on a steep hill, so there could have been more men on the other side. But this was what Matt had been waiting for, so there was no point in waiting any longer.

He started up the white-covered slope, snow crunching beneath his boots; he passed other headstones as he went.

"Attaboy!" Pardee said. "Come on up."

Pardee took a few steps back so that he disappeared from view. That was when Matt knew that when he got to the top, to Angie's grave, he'd be facing at least five men.

He kept going, anyway.

CHAPTER FORTY-EIGHT

AS MATT REACHED the top, he saw Angie's grave site for the first time. There was a wooden cross to mark the place.

Just beyond the site, Jason Pardee stood with a big grin on his face, flanked by two men on each side. Apparently, Pardee had only four with him, but it was still five guns against one. *I'll be coming to join you, Angie,* Matt thought, *any second now.*

"Go ahead," Pardee said, "sling that hogleg from your belt, and let's have at it."

"Five to one," Matt said. "That's your idea of getting this done?"

"I'm no fool, Deputy," Pardee said. "Even when you were sheriff here, I knew about your background with Judge Parker's court. That's why we shot first and didn't ask any questions."

"It's not going to be five against one," a voice said from behind Matt.

"What the hell?" Pardee said.

Matt didn't dare turn to see who was speaking. But when the man came up alongside him, he saw that it was Father Ray.

"It's five against two."

"What are you doing?" Matt asked. From the corner of his eye, he could see the priest had two guns tucked into his belt.

"What I did for five years before I came here," Father Ray said.

"Who the hell are you?" Pardee demanded.

"The local priest," Matt said. "Doing God's work."

"Kill 'im!" Pardee shouted, and backed away as his four men stepped up and grabbed for their guns.

Matt was shocked at the speed with which the young priest produced his twin Colts. He drew his own gun, and the top of boot hill erupted into gunfire.

Matt kept waiting for a bullet to hit him, but as lead flew past him on either side, the four men succumbed to the shots he and Father Ray were firing. Before long the four men were lying on the ground, and Pardee was gone.

"Pardee!" Matt shouted.

"Go after him," Father Ray said. "I'll check these men."

Matt nodded, ran past the four fallen gunmen and down the other side of the hill.

Pardee had two choices. He could run out of town or right into town. Running into town would afford him more cover, so Matt lit out that way.

When he got to Front Street, he spotted Pardee, who was still running down the snow-covered street. If Pardee was tired of having Matt's breath on the back of his neck, he hadn't experienced anything yet.

The shots on boot hill had been heard in town, and the streets were fairly deserted. The civilians still there began to scatter as they saw one man chasing another, both carrying guns.

Matt considered firing at Pardee, but he was too far away. He had to close the distance if he could before firing. The truth was, he wanted to see Pardee's face when he shot him.

That was the first time he had admitted to himself that his intention was to kill Pardee, not to bring him to justice.

"Pardee!" Matt shouted. "Stop and face me!"

Pardee turned a corner, and when Matt turned the same corner, he realized it was the street the sheriff's office was on. People were still ducking and dodging to get to safety, but Matt no longer saw Pardee ahead of him. He must've ducked in somewhere, and since Pete Brown had already delivered a couple of Pardee's messages, Matt picked the sheriff's office.

As he burst through the door, he saw Pardee and Brown facing each other.

"He's mine, Sheriff!" Matt shouted.

"You're a fool, Wheeler," Pardee said. "You don't even know what this man did."

"Pardee—," Brown started.

"Why do you think he wasn't there the morning of the robbery?" Pardee asked. "Your deputy! He was in on it."

"What?" Matt could see in Brown's face what he was going to do. "No!"

Then Sheriff Brown drew his gun and shot Pardee in the chest twice.

"Damn it, Pete!" Matt yelled. The feeling of great loss he suddenly felt in that moment was exceeded only by the loss of his wife years earlier.

"He's dead," Brown said, holstering his gun. "Isn't that what you wanted?"

"I wanted to do it myself!" Matt snarled. "I promised Angie."

"Well," Brown said, "it's done. That means it's time for you to go."

"Go?"

"Leave town, Matt," Brown said. "I told you, there's no room here for you."

Matt stared down at Pardee's body, the two bloody holes in his chest; then he looked at Brown again.

"There's another matter."

"I thought there might be," Brown said. "You didn't believe what he was sayin', did you?"

"I wasn't believing what some others told me about you, Pete, but I think now I am. I think I'm believing everything."

"What've they been tellin' you?"

"That you're a bully. Worse, a killer, and they're all afraid of you."

"I'm the law," Brown said. "They should be afraid of me."

"I don't agree."

"I didn't think you would," Brown said, "but the days of the kind of lawman you were are gone."

"And you're the new, improved version?"

"Actually," Brown said, "yes."

"No," Matt said, "I'm not buying it. You're threatening to kill your mayor, a priest, and who knows how many others? That can't go on. And now I know you were part of what happened to Angie and me. So you can't be allowed to just . . . go on."

"So you're gonna stop me?" Brown said. "And then replace me?"

"Stop you, yes," Matt said. "Replace you, no. I told you, I'm not interested."

"Matt," Brown said, "I don't wanna kill you, but if you don't leave—"

"I'm not leaving," Matt said.

"Then put your gun in your belt, and let's do this the right way," Brown challenged.

Brown put his hand on his holstered gun and was almost nonchalant about drawing it; he was that confident. But Matt, who was already holding his gun down at his side, didn't put it in his belt. He had no intention of giving Brown the opportunity to outdraw him and kill him. He raised his gun quickly and shot Brown in the chest.

The lawman's gun fell from his hand, and he crumpled to the floor with a shocked look on his face.

Matt took three steps and loomed over the fallen man, who looked up at him through pain-filled eyes.

"You didn't—That wasn't . . . fair."

"Life ain't fair, kid," Matt said.

I T WASN'T UNTIL the next day that Matt left his hotel after checking out, and walked to boot hill, leading his horse. He stared up the frozen white slope to where Angie's grave was, then walked up and stopped in front of her marker.

"It's over," he told her. "I didn't get to kill him, but Pardee's dead. So . . . I guess my promise has been kept." He reached out and placed his hand on the cross. "But, honey, I can't stay here. I've got to keep moving. Staying in one place is not for me. So I won't be able to come here and see you again. But just wait for me, and eventually, we'll be together."

He became aware of someone at the base of the hill. It was the young would-be priest, Father Ray. Matt hadn't seen him since the shooting. He patted the marker and proceeded down the hill.

"You got something you want to explain to me?" Matt asked.

"Since I was fifteen years old and killed my first man, I've lived by the gun," the younger man explained. "But I've decided not to do that anymore. I wanted to live a different life, so I ended up coming here."

"And impersonating a priest?"

"I found a man on the trail who was dying. He *was* a priest. After I buried him, I kept his collar."

"Well," Matt said, "Sheriff Brown is gone, so now you can stay."

Father Ray reached up and took off his collar. His face was red from the cold. "I can't wear this anymore."

"So what are you going to do?"

"The mayor has offered me the job of sheriff. It's not *so* different from what I used to do—"

"Yes, it is," Matt said. "As a lawman, you don't have to live by the gun. You live by the badge. Use the gun only when you have to."

"I'll try to keep that in mind."

"So if you're not going to be Father Ray anymore, what's your name?"

"You won't know it. My real name's Ray Teal. I'll probably go back to that since I never built up any kind of reputation."

"That's a good idea."

"What do you plan to do?" Ray asked Matt. "Stay on?"

"No," Matt said, "I can't stay. I have some business in Fort Smith. I need to settle up with Judge Parker. After that . . . who knows?"

They turned and started walking back toward town together.

"Tell me something," Matt said. "If you're that good with a gun, why didn't you just take care of the sheriff yourself?"

"You know what I said about not havin' a reputation?" Ray Teal said. "If I killed a lawman, that would've been the beginning."

"That's true. Hey, can you do something for me?" Matt asked.

"Of course."

"I'd like a better marker for my wife's grave, but I'm leaving town now. Maybe a real headstone."

"I can see to that for you," Ray said. "Just tell me what you want it to say."

Matt thought a moment, then said, "Just . . . 'Angie Wheeler, forever in my heart. I'll see you soon.'"

Ready to find
your next great read?

Let us help.

Visit prh.com/nextread